I0724095

TOUGH COOKIE

A DONNER BAKERY NOVEL

TALIA HUNTER

WWW.SMARTYPANTSROMANCE.COM

COPYRIGHT

This book is a work of fiction. Names, characters, places, rants, facts, contrivances, and incidents are either the product of the author's questionable imagination or are used factitiously. Any resemblance to actual persons, living or dead or undead, events, locales is entirely coincidental if not somewhat disturbing/concerning.

Made in the United States of America

Print Edition
ISBN: 978-1-959097-30-3

CHAPTER 1

CARLA

- Nineteen days to Valentine's Day -

"It's nine o'clock exactly," I said out loud, entering today's information into my computer. "I slept well. Most of my symptoms are green, which makes it a great morning. And my mood is…"

I hesitated with my fingers resting on my keyboard. Time to conduct a quick internal assessment before recording the color of my mood in my software.

My gaze drifted to Freud, who was snoring on the easy chair in the corner. Then to the window where soft winter sunshine was spilling into my office. Outside, my three hilarious hens—Meryl Cheep, Yolko Ono, and Henny Lamarr —were all apparently determined to chase the same bug. Their indignant squawking drifted in to me, making me smile.

My body was pain-free, my mind was clear, and I had enough energy for the productive day I had planned. It was one of those unicorn days of feeling *normal*. Rare, beautiful, and precious.

So the question of my mood was clearly a no-brainer.

I was just about to color today's mood square green when an email notification flashed up. Then I made the mistake of clicking on it.

Mom had sent me a very short note, straight to the point.

Carla,
Have you called Sienna yet?
Love, Mom
XO

Ugh. My cousin, Sienna Diaz, had called me months ago. She'd left a message, and I hadn't called her back. Mom had been bugging me about it ever since, making me feel guilty every time.

And the reminder of my failing wasn't even the worst part of the email. Mom had also attached photos from Sienna's recent trip to Australia with her extremely photogenic family. The pictures filled my screen. In one photo, Sienna was posing with a kangaroo, looking as fabulous as ever. My cousin was living a large, exciting life.

I was happy for her.

But her photos made me acutely aware how small my life had become. My world was contained within the walls of my house. I was the same age as Sienna, but unlike her, I wasn't ever going to see an actual kangaroo. Not unless one hopped up to the window—not exactly a likely occurrence in Green Valley, Tennessee.

And I wasn't going to call Sienna back. Not this week. Not next week. No matter how many times Mom bugged me about it, and seriously, my mother was *never* going to let it go.

Civilization could be ending, and as radioactive mushroom clouds darkened the sky, my mother would wag her finger at me and tell me if the Doomsday clock hadn't quite reached midnight, it meant I still had time to call Sienna.

Sorry, Mom. Not going to happen.

It wasn't that I was jealous of my cousin. Well, not exactly. But when we were kids, we'd talked about all the amazing things we were going to do one day. And while Sienna was a famous movie star who'd more than fulfilled her dreams, *my* amazing feats were still a work in progress.

So I had no intention of returning Sienna's call until after I launched my software. That's when my life would expand again.

"My mood is still good," I said aloud, addressing the statement to Freud. "It's still green. No question."

Freud didn't answer. Firstly, because he was curled in a ball with his tail over his eyes, and secondly because the only thing he ever said was *meow*, and that was only at mealtimes.

"Definitely green," I said more firmly. "It's a unicorn day, which means nothing in the world can possibly get me down."

After all, my day was nicely planned out, with no surprises on the agenda. I was about to do fifty minutes of work on my software, followed by ten minutes of stretching. I'd enjoy a freshly laid egg as my morning snack. Then fifty more minutes of work, ten minutes of tai chi, a short rest, and a nutritiously balanced lunch, before repeating my routine in the afternoon.

Unicorn days could only happen if I stuck to my schedule, and there was a whole lot of relief and comfort in knowing they could happen, that they *were* possible.

I was grateful for the day and ready to make the most of it.

Straightening my back in my office chair, I hit the button to color my mood square green.

And that was when the ceiling of my house caved in.

CHAPTER 2

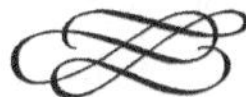

NOAH

*M*y mother was eager for grandbabies the same way zombies were eager for brains.

The fact that her only son was single and childless at the advanced age of thirty-three was a catastrophe Momma was determined to rectify. And judging by the way she kept pushing me toward every eligible woman in town, she seemed to be trying to settle the matter once and for all while I was staying with her in Green Valley.

So, when she asked me to drive out to our old family home to do a repair for the 'pretty young woman' who was renting the place, I tugged my lips to one side and gave her a skeptical look.

"What kind of repair does your tenant need?" I asked. "Is it an urgent and serious case of false pretenses?"

Momma was busy bandaging my forearm, but she huffed out an impatient breath. "Don't be ridiculous, Noah. Carla called to say there was a hole in her ceiling. That's her name, by the way, and Carla's a lovely name, don't you think?"

My mother wasn't renowned for her subtlety. Reluctant to encourage her, I gave a non-committal grunt.

We were at Momma's house, sitting on the couch in her cozy living room. She'd just disinfected the wound in my forearm and taped on gauze before winding the long bandage back around it, a chore she'd been doing every morning since I'd arrived in Green Valley a few days ago.

While she concentrated on the bandage, I studied her face. She had more laugh lines around her eyes and more silver in her curls than when I'd been here last. But her eyes were still as bright as ever and her fingers still deft. She'd retired from her job a few years ago, but my worry that she might get bored or lonely had been for nothing. Among other things, she was on the planning committee for every festival, event, and bake sale in town. If someone needed permission to sneeze, my mother would volunteer to organize the paperwork.

Momma looked both healthy and happy. And I was so glad about that, I couldn't help smiling.

Probably sensing my scrutiny, she flicked her gaze up to mine. A small, questioning crease pinched her brow as she held my eyes for a moment. Then she smiled back at me.

"Shush," she said with a chuckle, though I hadn't said a word. "Let me finish this." Bending her head, she fiddled with the bandage fastener.

Her black cat sidled over, purring as he rubbed his body against our shins. This house was smaller and a lot closer to town than the farmhouse I'd grown up in, but it was a pretty house, surrounded by trees as well as neighbors. This week had been warm enough that it felt like spring might have come early. And so far, my stay in Green Valley had been as relaxing as I'd hoped, only tarnished by my mother's persistent attempts at matchmaking.

There!" she exclaimed after a minute, as though getting the bandage fastened was a significant achievement. "How's that?" She sat back on the couch.

"Perfect. Thanks."

The wound I'd sliced into my arm was healing well. I had to be at a movie set in Arizona in three weeks, but there should barely be a scar by then.

"Good thing it's your left arm, so you shouldn't have any problem fixing the ceiling for Carla." Momma almost managed to make it sound like an offhand comment, though her innocent blinking was too theatrical to be believable.

I let out a deep sigh. "Did your tenant mention what caused a hole to appear?"

"All I know is she's never asked for anything before. Not a single thing in over a year, and she pays her rent on time." More innocent blinking. "Now that she needs help, I'd hate to keep her waiting."

"She lives in the house all alone?" I had to admit, I was a little curious. The farmhouse was a fair distance from its neighbors, and a long way from town, especially when it got cold enough to make the roads treacherous.

"When she leased the place, she said it was just for her, and the poor woman must be real lonely out there. You'll do her repair right away?" It wasn't really a question, and my mother didn't wait for me to answer before dropping her gaze to my sweatshirt. "Change your clothes before you go, Noah. Put on your nice gray jersey."

Like I said, she wasn't about to win any awards for subtlety.

Momma had insisted I accompany her to Friday's jam session at the Community Center, where I'd bumped into at least four different women who each mysteriously believed I was there to see them. And the next day Momma had asked me to deliver an envelope to Patty at Genie's Country Western Bar that turned out to contain two movie tickets, with Patty's name written on one and mine on the other.

Good thing Patty had seen the funny side.

I'd explained to my mother why I didn't want to date anyone from Green Valley, using the excuse that I wouldn't be here for long. But she was so determined to marry me off, I was now resigned to having to humor her.

Mostly.

Rounding my eyes, I feigned surprise. "You're saying I need to dress up to fix a ceiling? Is that a new law? Could Sheriff James book me on an illegal lapse in style?"

Her gaze didn't waver. "And you should tidy your beard."

"Should I add cologne to my toolbox? Will I need to pack a bouquet of flowers? You think the ceiling would appreciate me bringing it a box of chocolates before I start work on it, or should I just talk sweetly to it?"

"Noah Samuel Malone, are you questioning me?" Her voice stayed firm, but she was fighting a smile.

"I wouldn't dare." Standing up, I ruffled her curls. "Don't worry, Momma. I always change into my best clothes before doing any kind of messy building work. It's standard practice."

"Stop that." Laughing, she swatted at my hand. "Go and get changed, and I'll package up some cookies so you can take them to Carla."

"You baked those cookies for me," I protested. "Don't give them away."

Momma had worked as a professional baker most of her life, and there was nothing I liked more than baked goods. I'd been born with a sweet tooth. Sugar ran through my veins.

"Hush now. There are plenty more cookies where those came from. And while you're visiting Carla, think about some other ways you can be neighborly. Valentine's Day is coming up, and you don't want that poor woman to have to spend the evening alone now, do you?" Brushing off my protests about that being a step too far, she got up and bustled into the kitchen.

My mother might be a small woman—barely over five-feet tall—but she was at least ten feet of stubborn, and there was no sense in arguing with her. So I tidied my beard, changed into my gray jersey, and took the jar of cookies without complaint, already planning to eat a few while I drove to the house I'd grown up in.

Matchmaking aside, I was looking forward to visiting the farmhouse. It was a single-story wooden house on fertile land, with the mountains at its back. It was so lovely there, I'd once imagined I'd be happy to stay forever.

But when I was twenty-one, I'd picked up a handyman job helping out on the Sienna Diaz movie that was being shot at Cades Cove, and the night of the wrap party, my best friend had died in a car crash. I'd wanted to get out of town, away from any reminders of what had happened, and twelve years later, I could count on one hand the number of times I'd been back.

These days I traveled to movie sets all over the country. I earned a large paycheck by doing stunts. I fell from tall heights, took punches, and let people set me on fire, but vehicles were my specialty. My latest stunt was nicknamed 'The Bridge Bang' because I'd be flung out of an exploding car.

Pulling my truck up in front of our old farmhouse, the first thing I noticed was how enormous the old oak tree behind the house had grown, and how far its branches stretched over the roof. I made a mental note to trim it back.

The house was even prettier than I remembered, mostly because someone had placed potted herbs along the porch rail to soak up the winter sunshine. My mother had said she hadn't sent anyone over to check on things since her tenant had moved in, yet the place looked well maintained. The vegetable beds had been covered with cold frames, and the plants inside seemed to be thriving. And chickens were scratching around in the large run I built for Momma years ago.

Who was the mysterious tenant who grew her own food and never asked for anything?

Maybe she was on the run, or in witness protection. She could have stolen a bunch of money before holing herself up in the isolated house and was living in constant fear of being found by the feds. Though in all honesty, that *was* the plot of the last movie I'd worked on.

Still, when I mounted the steps to the porch with the jar of cookies under my arm—to my credit, it was still more than half full—and knocked on the front door, I was ready for just about anything.

Anything, that was, except what actually happened.

CHAPTER 3

NOAH

When the door swung open and I saw the woman in the doorway, my jaw loosened. Momma had called her pretty, and though it was a true statement, it didn't do her justice.

The woman's face shape was delicate, but her eyes, cheekbones, and lips were generous, like she'd managed to swipe a little more than her fair share. Her eyes were a rich brown. She had dark, wavy hair that fell past her shoulders and was tucked neatly behind her ears. She was wearing thick, fuzzy socks, sweatpants, and what looked like several layers of warm tops. Despite the layers, her bombshell curves were obvious.

I was struck speechless. But it wasn't just her beauty that made words dry up. It was the way she was looking at me.

Her gaze traveled up from my boots, over my jeans, and cut a slow path across the jersey I'd worn to keep my mother happy. It brushed over the jar of cookies on its way, and grazed my freshly trimmed beard. Her gaze stopped short of reaching my eyes, however. It jerked back to the cookies. And all the while, a frown creased her brow.

She didn't look happy to see me. The opposite, in fact.

"You're Mrs. Malone's son?" She didn't sound friendly. It was as though I'd annoyed her by turning up.

I blinked at her, confused. In all honesty, I was used to an entirely different reaction from most women I encountered.

There had to be an explanation for her frown, but I couldn't think what it might be.

Unless… maybe she wasn't annoyed, but feeling vulnerable and wary. Which, now I thought about it, would be understandable. She was on her own and had opened her door to find a six-foot-two stranger on her welcome mat. It was enough to make anyone cautious. Even when the stranger held cookies and was wearing a jersey that made him laughably overdressed for working on household repairs.

"That's right," I said. Then I offered her the polite-but-distant smile I used with strange women. At least, that was the smile I tried to offer, though it felt slightly stunned and possibly wider than I'd intended. "I'm Noah Malone," I added, stepping closer. I transferred the cookie jar to my left arm so I could offer my hand.

Her frown deepened and she made no immediate move, so for a moment I just stood there with my hand outstretched.

"Carla," she said finally. Though her tone was grudging, I liked the way she pronounced her name in the Spanish way—with a long 'a' and a rolling 'rrr'—despite not having spoken with a Spanish accent.

She slid her warm, small hand into mine with obvious reluctance, as though touching me was the very last thing she wanted to do. But as our skin touched and I caught her very feminine scent, my body reacted to her in an entirely disconcerting way, blood rushing where I didn't want it to go.

Which made no sense.

None.

There was no reason for me to get all hot-and-bothered below the belt buckle when the woman clearly wasn't impressed with me.

Only, come to think of it, maybe that was *why* I felt attracted to her.

The worst moments of my life had happened because I'd given a woman the wrong idea about the level of my romantic interest in them. The first time had been the worst, when a friend's girlfriend thought I had feelings for her. But more recently, one of the women on my stunt crew had come on strongly enough to make working together awkward. So as a rule, I tried not to act too friendly for fear of giving the wrong impression.

But when a gorgeous woman seemed to show an instant aversion to me, I couldn't help but be intrigued.

She gave my hand a quick squeeze before dropping it, and I regained enough of my senses to hold out the cookies.

"My mother sent these for you. They're chocolate chip."

She shook her head. "Oh. No. No, thank you. Come in and see what needs to be done." Instead of taking the jar from me, she turned her back and headed down the hallway.

I blinked at her retreating form, intrigued as to what kind of monster would refuse a jar of cookies. Then I wiped my boots on the welcome mat before following her inside. The door to my old bedroom at the front of the house was open. Glancing into it, I saw a large bed neatly made with a floral bedspread and matching pillows. A chubby black-and-white cat was fast asleep on its back in the center of the bed, its legs spreadeagled to display its fluffy white belly. On the dresser against the wall, some small bottles had been laid out in a neat row.

Catching another whiff of Carla's feminine scent as I passed, I figured it was the bedroom she'd chosen to sleep in. There were two other rooms she could have picked, but my old bedroom had a window that looked over the vegetable garden, and it caught the morning sun.

A little farther down the hall was my momma's old bedroom, which now held a desk with the biggest computer monitor I'd ever seen. Fixed to the wall were several giant whiteboards, all of them covered with notes, numbers, and diagrams in neat, tiny writing. The sight was instantly impressive, even if I had no idea what the indecipherable notes could be about. If this were a movie set, it could be an inspirational true story of a reclusive genius who'd managed to calculate our route to another galaxy before losing the last remnants of her sanity.

I was still trying to make sense of the whiteboards when Carla made an impatient noise from the end of the hallway.

"This way." She still wore a frown.

And sure, I was snooping. Though with the door being wide open, I couldn't have avoided seeing her interstellar voyage calculations. I had a burning desire to ask her about them, but as I had the strong impression she wasn't in a chatty mood, I decided to keep my questions to myself, at least for now.

She walked into the living room, clearly expecting me to follow. But I ducked briefly into the kitchen so I could leave the cookies on the counter before I joined her.

Once I reached the living room, the problem with her ceiling was obvious. The problem being that she no longer had a ceiling in one corner of the room, just a jagged hole. Part of a tree branch was hanging through the hole, and I caught a glimpse of sky.

I let out a low whistle.

"The branch hit the roof this morning." She glared upward at the hole, finally switching the focus of her annoyance away from me. "The noise was deafening. I thought the whole house was collapsing."

The end of the branch had punched through the roof shingles and ceiling and was lodged up there. The couches hadn't been damaged, but debris was scattered over a rug. There were leaves, pieces of drywall, dust, and the remnants of some ceiling insulation strewn around. I wouldn't know for sure how badly damaged the roof was until I climbed up to look, but the hole wasn't too big. Good thing it had happened while I was in Green Valley so I could do the repair.

"How long will it take to fix? The cold air is getting in." Her frown dropped to my torso and deepened, as though the nice jersey I'd worn—or maybe my lack of a coat—was something designed to insult her.

I scanned the hole, estimating its size. Then I worked out how much of the ruined ceiling I'd cut away and mentally calculated the materials I'd need.

While I figured it out, I took in the rest of the room. The built-in bookcase that ran along one wall used to be overflowing with novels, an ancient set of encyclopedias and dictionaries, and the ceramic bowls my mother used to collect. Now it contained medical textbooks. Maybe Carla was a doctor. Perhaps she was conducting secret medical experiments.

Corpse reanimation? Or merging a human with a fly?

Okay, so I'd watched an awful lot of movies, as well as working in the industry. But why else would a beautiful woman shut herself away in a remote farmhouse for an entire year? It couldn't be for anything ordinary. I was getting more curious by the minute.

"It won't take long," I said. "Two or three days. Four, at most."

"Four *days*?" She shook her head so vigorously, her long hair came untucked from behind her ears. "Oh no, no, no. Four days is too long."

I wanted to ask why it was too long, and if it meant her stitched-together corpses would decompose before she could bring them to life. But her forehead was still creased, and her eyes were troubled. Something was clearly very wrong.

"If it's the cold, or the noise and dust you're worried about, I could find you somewhere to stay," I offered.

"Can't you speed up the repair?"

I reached up to give my beard a doubtful scratch. If she was suggesting I rush it, I was going to disappoint her. Doing a half-baked job would be asking for leaks to develop. So I had a choice to make. Either flat out argue, or find a sneakier method of getting her to quit making a fuss.

"You offering to help?" I asked, figuring she'd refuse.

She pressed her lips together and dragged in such a slow, deep breath through her nose that her chest swelled with the amount of air she took in. Not that I was looking at her chest.

Okay, sure, I might have glanced quickly down. But in my defense, the woman had some seriously stunning curves. It wouldn't be overstating things to call her chest majestic. Not taking a quick glance of admiration would have been doing her physical beauty a disservice, akin to hiking the Smoky Mountains while wearing a blindfold.

She held her breath for a long moment, then let the air out so slowly, it was like a tire deflating. It seemed like an awful long time to spend on just one breath, but at least some tension seemed to ease out of her body along with the air.

"Fine," she said finally, looking and sounding unhappy about it. "If it'll get things finished faster."

"You'll help with the repair?" It was the last thing I'd expected.

Her eyes sparked and her tone turned sharp. "You don't think I'm capable?"

Though she'd taken the hint of incredulity in my tone the wrong way, I had to admit, Queen Grumpy McCrankypants was sexy when she was indignant. There was something about her defiant tone and the way she thrust up her chin that was all kinds of appealing. I was finding her more and more intriguing, and the fact there was so much punch in her glove only made it easier for me to relax around her.

"Have you fixed anything before?" I asked, just to see if she'd take another swing at me.

Sure enough, her fists went to her hips. "I sometimes fix drinks. Pretty soon I'll fix lunch. And right now, I'm fixing you with a glare. So what do you think?"

I snorted a laugh, but her lips didn't so much as twitch. It might have sounded like a joke, but she *was* actually glaring, and I had a strong feeling it wasn't for comedic effect.

People didn't usually act so prickly toward me. It seemed like my presence wasn't welcome, and I wanted to know why she found me so repellant.

She was mysterious, reclusive, and stunning. Possibly on the run. Probably a genius. Seemingly incapable of cracking a smile, and apparently struck with an instant distaste for yours truly.

Taking all that into account, I was going to have no choice but to accept her offer.

CHAPTER 4

CARLA

I'd steeled myself for some disruption to my schedule, but I hadn't expected to open the door to such a shockingly attractive stranger, or for my body to react to his good looks in such a violent way.

Since the moment I saw him, a comet had been falling down my throat. Not a small comet, either. It was a planet killer. And my gut had generated a tsunami to go with it. My stomach acid was apocalyptic.

It was a scary feeling.

And maybe I wasn't handling it so well, but I couldn't help it. Better to be blunt with him than let my anxiety take over.

"I'll need to get on the roof and cut that branch into smaller pieces," he said in his deep, rumbly voice with its appealing Southern twang. He was studying the branch thoughtfully, absently rubbing his hand over his beard.

"Fine." I didn't know what to do with my hands, so I put them behind my back.

"I have a saw with me, so I can cut the branch up now. The rest will have to wait until tomorrow. I'll come back after I've picked up the supplies I need for the repair."

"Fine," I said again.

The intruder turned from studying the branch and fixed his gaze on my face. Though his long lashes made his eyes beautiful enough to fill my gut with acid, his irises were a deceptively gentle shade of green. Despite the cold weather, he wasn't wearing a jacket, and he smelled as deliciously fresh as if he'd recently showered.

His dark hair was a little unruly, like it had a rebellious streak and wasn't about to take orders from anybody. In contrast, his beard was perfectly trimmed and very short, so it hugged the lower part of his face without hiding how strong his jaw was. I wasn't usually a fan of facial hair, but his beard made his face look *finished*, somehow. As though his jaw wouldn't have been fully dressed without it. And it made his neck look naked in comparison. It was almost erotic how smooth and bare his neck was, disappearing into his jersey like that.

I couldn't decide whether I was more annoyed with him for being so incredibly attractive, or with myself for getting so agitated by a handsome face and sexy voice.

And it didn't help that he was taller than me, putting his neck at eye level. When he swallowed, his Adam's apple bobbed, drawing even more attention to the silky allure of his throat.

Fact was, his naked neck was a shameless tease. It was *trying* to get me flustered.

"I have a chainsaw in my truck," he said. "But it'll make a mess."

"My living room's already a mess. Believe it or not, this wasn't a design choice. I didn't intentionally bring the outdoors in." I waved a hand at the leaves and dirt scattered over what had previously been a perfectly nice rug. It was my landlady's rug, and I could only hope she wouldn't ask me to replace it.

The intruder's lips twitched with amusement, but his brow wrinkled a little as well. The brow wrinkle seemed to hint that he'd thought I was smarter than my response implied.

"This is a different kind of mess," he said. "It'll spray a lot of fine sawdust, which could get into all kinds of tricky places."

"Right." I tried to put my hands in my pockets and managed to rub them awkwardly down my hips three times before I remembered I was wearing sweatpants, not jeans, and they didn't have pockets.

When Mrs. Malone said she'd send her son to fix my damaged roof, she'd told me he was skilled with his hands. I'd been taken aback by the suggestive way she'd said it, as though she was implying something sexual. I'd brayed an inappropriate burst of nervous laughter and felt immediately embarrassed, knowing I must have read something into her tone that hadn't been there. Then I'd thanked her too profusely before hanging up.

Maybe I was used to the unpunctuality of handymen in New York, but it hadn't occurred to me that her son might turn up so quickly. Or that he'd have such a well-dressed face and a come-hither neck.

Dammit, how could I act like a normal human being when my gut was churning? And what was the intruder's name again? I remembered him introducing himself, but I'd been so busy swallowing bile, his name hadn't penetrated my brain.

"Have you got anything that shouldn't get dusty?" He hooked a lazy thumb toward the hallway, in the direction of my office. "Computer?"

I nodded. "I'll cover it up." At least it gave me an excuse to put some space between me and the intruder. My fight-or-flight response was in full swing and instead of 'fight', it was time to try 'flight'.

"Shut the door and put a towel across the bottom until the dust settles," he said. "That'll keep the room clean."

I busied myself dustproofing both my office and bedroom, then clearing the kitchen counter, putting away clean dishes, and making sure all the cupboards were closed. Having something to do helped to calm my nervous system. By the time I'd finished, my stomach acid had settled.

And by then, the intruder was outside. I could hear the heavy tread of his boots on the wooden porch. After forcing a pair of sneakers over my thick socks and pulling on a warm jacket over all the layers I was wearing, I went to see what he was doing. I found him setting up his ladder against the side of the house, his back to me. He had gloves on his hands, a chainsaw at his feet and a pair of earmuffs around his neck. He was clearly immune to the cold, as he'd pushed up the sleeves of his jersey. With his sleeves up, I could see that one of his forearms was bandaged.

My gaze moved to his pick-up truck, parked near the steps that led to my porch. Though it was well past its prime, it had been custom painted with flames running over its hood and along each side. It was a beautiful paint job. The flames were stylized instead of realistic. Bold, golden shapes against a dark red background. Considering the age and probable top speed of the truck, they had to be ironic.

I let out a little snort of amusement. If I were less anxious, it would have been a laugh.

The snort alerted him to my presence, and he turned to face me. "Ready for the noise and dust?" he asked.

I nodded. "You can climb the ladder carrying a chainsaw?"

"Sure, I can manage."

"What about that?" I frowned at the bandage around his forearm.

"My arm's healing," he said in that delicious drawl of his.

"What's wrong with it?"

"The driveshaft came apart in the car I was rolling. I caught a shard of metal."

"You were *rolling* a car? What does that mean?"

He pointed his gloved index fingers together, then rotated them around each other. "Side, roof, tires, side, roof, tires." His grin was too disarming, and he was far too loose with it for my liking. "Happened just the way it sounds. I do stunts for films, and that one didn't go as planned."

A stuntman. Wow. If I had to come up with a profession that was the complete opposite of my life, that would be top of the list.

"Isn't that dangerous?" I asked. Then, with an internal groan, I silently awarded myself the Dumbest Question of All Time award. Of course being a stuntman was dangerous. That was literally the entire point of the job.

This was why my anxiety was completely justified.

Funny thing was, I never used to have any problems talking to people. A few years ago, having a strange man in my house—even one whose naked neck I couldn't seem to stop looking at—wouldn't have caused so much as a bump in my pulse. I never used to worry much about the things I said, or what other people thought of me. Unfortunately, those days were gone.

The intruder lifted one shoulder and dropped it again, his shrug as easy-going as his grin. He seemed so relaxed, he was practically floating. So laid-back, I had a strong urge to shake him. Nobody who'd chosen to sit in a rolling car had any right to look as though he'd never experienced a moment of worry in his life.

And, dammit, what was his *name*?

"When I cut up the branch, it's going to be loud." He bent to pick up his chainsaw. "I'll aim to throw most of the pieces off the roof, but some might fall into the house."

"I'll stand out of the way until you're done." Instead of moving, I narrowed my eyes at him, trying to remember what he'd said when he'd introduced himself. Hadn't his name been something biblical? Was he Elijah? Or did he look more like a Joseph?

Looping his arm through the handle of the chainsaw, he put his other hand on the ladder, ready to climb.

"By the way," I said. "I know someone with the same name as you, but his has an unusual spelling. How do you spell your name?"

He stopped with one hand and one foot on the ladder, swiveling his head to me. "You don't remember my name, do you?"

"Of course I do. I was just—"

"Then what is my name, *Carla*?" He emphasized my name with a little smirk, like he thought he was being hilarious. Which he most certainly wasn't.

"Did you even say it out loud?" I demanded, hands on hips. "Maybe you imagined saying it. Or you mumbled, so I couldn't hear it."

"My name is Noah. N-O-A-H. How does your friend spell it?"

I lifted my chin. "Turns out, he spells it the same as you. J-E-R-K."

The intruder—Noah—laughed as though my rudeness delighted him.

His laughter was so unexpected, and the rolling boom of it was such a nice sound, that I felt my own lips twitch in response. But Noah was turning away. He hoisted the chainsaw and climbed the ladder, his bandaged arm not seeming to trouble him. And when he got to the top and strolled across the roof to the hole, he was seemingly unbothered by how high it was or that he had to duck under the oak tree's branches. Compared to rolling cars, it was probably nothing, though I couldn't look at him without imagining him plummeting to his death.

The chainsaw started up, roaring as it bit into the wood. The sweet smell of sawdust drifted to me on the breeze. Trying to take my mind off Noah's precarious situation, I wandered over to inspect my garden for weeds. Later, I'd harvest some lettuce, purple broccoli, and spinach to have with dinner.

Now I was thinking about food, it was almost twelve thirty, the time I was scheduled to eat my next meal. I pulled up the reminder on my watch and muted the alarm so it wouldn't go off, then went inside.

The roar of the chainsaw was deafening in the kitchen, and I coughed, breathing in fine sawdust. A heavy thump from the living room told me Noah had to be dropping pieces of the branch through the hole. It wasn't the right time to be fixing a meal, no matter what my watch told me. Grabbing an apple and a handful of nuts, I went back outside to eat them.

Not being able to obey my schedule made me nervous. I could only hope Noah would finish up quickly so everything could go back to normal.

Eating my apple slowly, I took the forced break from my routine as an opportunity to practice mindfulness and use some of my breathing techniques. By the time the roar of the chainsaw cut out and Noah climbed back down the ladder, I had my anxiety firmly in hand. From now on, I'd interact with him in a detached way. I could admire his good looks, but I was determined to do it without my stomach acid turning dystopian.

After he packed his saw and ladder back onto his truck, Noah went into the living room. I followed. Most of the dust had settled, and the house smelled strongly of cut wood. Some short logs were laying on my rug, surrounded by leaves, debris, and sawdust. We'd need to carry them out, and the faster everything got done, the better.

"Don't suppose you have an extra pair of work gloves?" I asked.

He was already bending to pick up the logs, and his rear view was so fine, my mouth went dry, and my lungs decided they were running a sprint instead of a marathon. So much for all my breathing exercises.

"I don't," he said, "and you don't need to help with this part."

I swallowed, forcing my gaze to a fixed point above him instead of staring at the pert roundness of his buttocks. "But I already said I would."

He straightened. "Then take these." Pulling his gloves off, he held them out, offering them to me.

"Oh no. I couldn't."

"Please. My hands are tough."

He clearly meant it as a chivalrous gesture, and I knew I should probably just thank him. But my heart was beating too fast again, and when I opened my mouth, I found myself asking, "How do you know my hands are softer than yours? Because I'm a woman?"

He blinked twice, then that easy-going grin of his came back. "My mistake. You must have some heavy-duty callouses from writing all those equations on your whiteboards."

I sealed my lips to stop a retort, grabbing the gloves and pulling them on. They were way too big, and warm inside from his hands. The feeling of sliding my fingers into gloves he'd just been wearing felt weirdly intimate, flustering me even more.

While I flexed my hands inside them, Noah bent to gather the logs back up. "What is it you're working on anyway?" he asked in a conversational drawl. "Something top secret? Experimenting with corpses?"

"*Corpses*?" I frowned. "What are you talking about?"

"If not corpses, then what?"

It wasn't an easy question to answer, and I stared at the gloves for a few moments, preparing to launch into a full explanation and debating where to start.

While I was thinking about it, he strolled closer with his arms full of wood. His jersey was tight in the bicep area, bulges indicating some impressive muscles. And his pushed-up sleeves showed off ropes of muscle in the forearm that wasn't bandaged. He was way too good looking, almost too handsome to be real.

I didn't like it.

Looking at him put me off balance. He tilted my comfortable world sideways, pushing everything off kilter.

The sooner he was gone, and normality returned, the better.

"It's software," I said.

He raised his eyebrows. "Software?" he prompted.

"Software." Pretending I hadn't heard the question in his tone, I crossed to the debris and squatted to gather some of the smaller branches into a pile. When I looked back up, Noah was watching. He caught my eye and smiled. As if he hadn't been gorgeous enough before, his smile softened his green eyes even more, and flashed white, even teeth. A grin that beautiful could spin my world right off its axis.

And now, *that* was even more troubling.

He was a dangerous man with dangerous physical perfection, causing chaos in his wake. How did he expect me to be coherent in his presence, let alone pleasant?

I frowned at him, and he gave me an amused nod as though my response to his smile hadn't disappointed him. Finally—FINALLY—he turned away from me to carry the logs down the hallway. His gait was a stroll, as unhurried as everything else about him. Unlike me, he was clearly very comfortable in his own body. And with a body like that, why wouldn't he be?

"Get a grip, Carla," I muttered aloud, shaking my head. "His presence is a hiccup, nothing more. An unfortunate bug in my program, but one with an easy fix. He'll be gone soon. Problem solved."

After filling my arms with light, twiggy branches, I followed him outside and found he'd added the logs to the woodpile that was under the extended roof of the small garden shed. I put my branches on the pile while he went inside to get more logs.

By my third trip I was getting tired, so I stopped and handed Noah back his gloves. According to my heart rate monitor, my pulse was still within acceptable limits, but I was starting to lose my breath. My energy was a limited resource, and even if it felt like I could keep going, it was a million times better to stop too soon than too late. If I pushed outside of my energy envelope, I'd pay for it later.

Noah shot me a curious look when I gave him the gloves but didn't ask why

I'd quit helping. Good thing he didn't because I wasn't in the mood for explanations.

But standing by the wood pile to rest meant I had the time to calm my system down again. A few deep breaths, and I started to regret how snappy I'd been with him. It wasn't his fault he'd won the genetic lottery, or that my nervous system was on the fritz. Presumably he hadn't asked to be born looking like that, so it wasn't fair to blame him, no matter how disturbing I found it.

Watching him make two more trips to clear the last of the wood from inside, I came to the reluctant conclusion that I needed to make amends for my rudeness. And by the time he'd added the last of the logs to the pile, I was ready to slice myself a piece of humble pie.

When he pulled off the gloves I'd returned to him, indicating that he'd finished, I worked up the courage to approach him.

"We didn't start out on the best foot," I said awkwardly. "It's just that I wasn't expecting you to be…" I stopped. "Would you please let me start again?" I offered him a handshake. "Hello, I'm Carla. Thank you for coming to fix the roof, Noah."

Weirdly, his smile disappeared. A small frown pinched his brow as he took my hand.

Being so close to him—touching him—while gazing into the green of his eyes made my insides go haywire. My heart jolted painfully, and I was suddenly too hot. At least it wasn't a serious medical issue, or my smartwatch would be sounding an alarm.

"You're welcome," he said. But he didn't say it in the slow, everything-is-secretly-amusing-to-me drawl he'd been using up until now. His tone was distantly formal, and his expression was shuttered.

It was as though he didn't want me to be nicer.

Maybe it was because my face had flushed when our hands had touched. Whatever the reason, he suddenly seemed less friendly. He let go of my hand and as he turned away, he kicked at a piece of wood that had been threatening to escape the pile.

"Is this your family home?" I asked, trying to fill the sudden awkwardness.

"It is." He gave the wood a second kick. So strange. What was with his change in demeanor? Could he really have liked it better when I was grumpy?

"Must have been a nice place to grow up," I said.

"It was." He returned his eyes to mine. "Why are you here?"

I blinked. Now he was the one who sounded blunt.

"I told you. Software." Despite my resolve, my voice regained a little of its sharp edge. And sure enough, some of the reserve immediately left his gaze.

"You running from something?" he asked.

"In a way." I folded my arms across my chest. There had been lots of things I'd needed to escape from, but I wasn't prepared to divulge any of them to a virtual stranger.

His face relaxed and his secret amusement seemed to return. "Let me guess. You stole a bunch of money, right? Now you're holed up here with it."

It was such a ridiculous suggestion, I almost lost my frown. "Millions," I said. "I stuffed my mattress with it."

"That's what I figured." Then he asked, "Mind if I offer a word of advice?"

My heart sank. My mother had given me enough advice to last ten lifetimes. Still, I braced myself for whatever well-intentioned words of wisdom he had for me and nodded for him to continue.

He lowered his voice and leaned in. "If your mattress is stuffed with paper, don't smoke in bed."

I made an involuntary sound, puffing out my breath because I was too surprised to laugh.

"I'm serious," he said. "I had a bank-robbing uncle who learned that lesson the hard way. Uncle Sparky never made that mistake again, God rest his soul."

"You're not funny," I told him.

"You're wrong about that; I'm hilarious." He tilted his head. "But there's something else about me that bugs you."

"What?" My anxiety surged.

"I don't mind. I'd even go so far as to say it's a good thing. But what is it?" When I didn't reply right away, too confused by the question, he added, "I'm curious, is all. In case I want to reproduce the effect with others, I'll know how to go about it." He held the gloves in one hand and slapped them lightly against the other. Not in an impatient way, but clearly waiting for me to answer.

"Your questions bug me," I said, swallowing acid.

"That's good to know." He started strolling toward his flame-painted truck, and somehow I found myself trotting next to him like an obedient puppy. "I'll be back tomorrow around lunchtime, after I've picked up the supplies I'll need for the repair. And I'll have more of those pesky questions for you, not that you've given me much in the way of answers." He shot me a sideways look. "Software," he muttered with a laugh. "You're funny too."

I bit my lip, still not sure whether I should be annoyed, flustered, or amused. I was a mix of all three, and that couldn't be good.

For the last year, I'd been working to stabilize my body and mind, and Noah-the-intruder was a destabilizing influence. As soon as he was gone, I needed to regain my calm.

When we reached his truck, he got in while I kept going toward my front door, determined to put his unsettling presence behind me, both literally and metaphorically. I heard his engine start, and his window must have been down because when I reached my open doorway he called after me, and the words were loud and clear.

"See you tomorrow, Chuckles."

My step faltered and I tripped on the threshold, catapulting headfirst into my sanctuary. *Chuckles? What the hell!*

CHAPTER 5

NOAH

- Eighteen days to Valentine's Day -

"**S**he's pretty, isn't she?" said Momma.

"Huh?" I asked. Not my most eloquent response, but my mother's question had taken me by surprise.

It was the next morning, and I was driving Momma to the Donner Bakery. I'd offered to take her into town so she could pick up some groceries while I got some roof-fixing supplies. The bakery wasn't exactly on our way, but seeing as Momma had worked there when I was younger and I'd spent plenty of time there, I was feeling nostalgic. I was also hankering for something sweet, and it had been a long time since I'd had a slice of their legendary banana cake. When I'd suggested making a detour, Momma had been enthusiastic. She wanted to say hello to the staff and see the latest additions to their display cabinet.

"I'm talking about Carla," my mother clarified. "She's pretty, isn't she?"

I let out a groan, knowing exactly where the conversation was headed. "Don't get the wrong idea," I said. "She might be pretty, but she doesn't like me."

"How could Carla not like you?" My mother pinched her brows together, looking so perplexed, I had to laugh.

"One of life's biggest mysteries." I slowed my truck for a sharp corner. "How much do you know about her and what she's doing all alone at the farmhouse?"

"I know Carla's been polite and friendly each time we've spoken, and she seems very nice. What else do you need to know?" Momma folded her hands on her lap as though that settled the matter.

"She's a little odd." I smiled a little, remembering yesterday's interaction. She hadn't seemed to warm to me at all, and I'd liked not having to worry about being too friendly and accidentally giving her the wrong idea. In fact, I was looking forward to going back. Not that I'd tell Momma. A mere inch of encouragement, and she'd be knitting booties and suggesting baby names.

"How is she *odd*?" Momma seemed offended on Carla's behalf.

"It doesn't matter. It won't take long to fix the roof. Two or three days, then she can be as odd as she likes out there on her own."

"But there must be more work to do on the farmhouse, Noah. It hasn't had any attention for a while."

I shot her a sideways look, silently informing her that blatant attempts to convince me to spend time with her 'pretty tenant' weren't going to work. "Carla has everything under control. She's taking good care of the place, and she doesn't want me hanging around any longer than I need to."

Momma huffed. "Even if she doesn't need your help, there are plenty of folks in Green Valley whose houses could use some repair work. I could get you a job."

"I'm not here for long enough," I objected, turning into the Donner Bakery's parking lot. The lot was half full, and I cruised along the line of cars, looking for a spot that was big enough to park my truck.

I'd left my pick-up behind when I'd skipped town, and it was fun driving it again and rediscovering all its quirks. Like the mysterious chassis rattle when I turned left, and remembering how to punch the radio knob in just the right way to switch it on. Though the roads could be treacherous in winter, my old truck had been built right. Even in icy weather, it hugged the road like a lover.

I had six cars stored in a garage in LA that were far more valuable. I even had a brand-new Lamborghini. A movie star I was doubling for had given it to me after he'd insisted on participating in a stunt and almost gotten me killed. The other five cars were beautiful old classics I'd had fun restoring, including intricate custom paint jobs. The Lambo was the only one I hadn't painted yet. Truth was, I'd barely even driven it. I preferred cars with character, warts and all, and I had a special fondness for my old truck. Momma had been sweet to keep it running for me all these years.

"Every time you come to Green Valley, you stay home and hardly see anyone," Momma complained. "It's about time you were more social. Working would keep you busy."

"Last time I was here, my leg was broken. I couldn't exactly go out dancing."

"You're walking just fine now."

I shook my head, not liking this conversation any more than the matchmaking one. The reason I didn't visit Momma more often, or visit old friends, was because I didn't want reminders of my best friend Liam's death. It was what had driven me out of town in the first place, and a dozen years later, I still didn't like thinking about it.

"I came home to spend time with you," I said.

"And it's lovely to see you. But I don't want you cooped up with me all the time. Less than three weeks until Valentine's Day, and if you end up spending the evening with me, I'll never bake for you again."

I rolled my eyes heavenward. As much as I loved her, I didn't love Momma's conviction that she could get her own way by wearing me down.

"Liam's gone," she said abruptly, making me flinch. "And the accident was terrible, but it was a long time ago. I don't know whether you feel sad or guilty, or whether that's all that's kept you away, but I wish you'd—"

"Please stop," I said, wincing. "It's not that. I have a career and a life outside of Green Valley. I can't get involved with someone here when I'm expected back at work soon. You didn't raise me to go around letting people down."

"Stunt work isn't any kind of a real job, Noah." I had my sleeves pushed up to expose my forearms, and she frowned at my bandage. "How many injuries is that now? Did I raise a son without a lick of common sense? Why do you keep hurting yourself?"

"I know you don't like it, but I'm good at what I do, and I'm well paid." I pulled into a parking spot near the bakery's entrance.

"Good at it?" She shook her head. "Please! *Good* would be coming home in one piece."

I switched off the ignition without responding, but Momma wasn't done with me yet. "Move back home," she urged, making no move to get out of the truck. "Get a job here. Marry a nice local woman and start giving me grandbabies like the good Lord intended."

"I'm not ready to settle down. Maybe in a few years—"

"*Years?*" She recoiled in horror. "Oh no, not years! Haven't you dated *anybody* since you left town?"

"Sure, I have." I opened my door, trying to end the conversation. She had no idea about my track record with women and why I'd become so cautious. And it wasn't something I intended to tell her about.

She clamped her hand on my elbow, stopping me from exiting the vehicle. "There are still lovely women in Green Valley, even if some of the best have been snapped up already. Every wedding I go to is a missed opportunity for you to settle down. If you don't act now, there'll be no single women left for you." Her brow was creased with concern, as though we were teetering on the brink of a catastrophic worldwide single-woman shortage.

"I'm not that old," I said.

"You're thirty-three." She used what could only be described as a dire tone, as though *Thirty-Three* was the fifth horseman of the apocalypse. "And more importantly," she continued, "*I'm* not getting any younger. If you wait any longer, I might not get to enjoy my birthright. I busted my biscuits to bring you up, and now you need to return the favor."

"You're not old either," I protested. "Halle Berry is almost your age, and she does most of her own stunts. Fight scenes and car chases, pretty rough stuff. When I worked on her movie, there wasn't a single person on set who wasn't half in love with her."

Momma let out an un-leading-lady-like snort of derision. "Halle *Berry*? Is that even a real name, or did you just make it up?"

"She's very real. Famous, gorgeous, and not even a little bit old."

"Then she must have grandbabies to keep her young."

"Come on, Momma. Let's go and get some cake." I eased her hand off my arm and gave it a gentle squeeze before letting go. "But you'd better let me come around to help you out of the truck. Seeing as you don't have grandbabies yet, you probably shouldn't try to stand without assistance."

She laughed a little as I got out, and I smiled to myself. At least her sense of humor was intact. Unfortunately, so was her stubbornness. It was a sure bet I hadn't heard the last on the subject.

"You sit down, Momma, while I get coffees and cakes," I said as we reached the bakery's front entrance. "Rest your ancient legs before they give out on you."

"Oh, stop!" She smacked my arm but went to get us a table. Though the Donner Bakery was popular, this morning the line wasn't too long. The tables out front were busy with folks enjoying the winter sunshine, but there were plenty that were free.

I'd only just joined the line of people waiting to order when my phone buzzed with a message. It was from Brash, an up-and-coming stunt performer I mentored. Moose, our stunt director, had done the same for me when I'd started in the business. He'd guided me in what I'd needed to know, and pushed me to take classes in tumbling, martial arts, and sword fighting. Now I figured it was my turn to give back.

Brash had only been nineteen when he'd first shown up on set, and he'd begun earning his nickname from his very first day. Now he was twenty-two, and despite all my lectures and warnings, the kid seemed to be getting even more reckless. Worrying about him had made me realize why Moose's hair was so gray and his face so worn. Had I ever been that cocky?

Bracing myself for news of accidents and injuries, I opened his message.

Brash: How's your arm? Moose said if it's not healed in time to do the Bridge Bang, I can do it instead.

What the fuck?

Instead of messaging him back, I dialed his number.

It took several rings for Brash to pick up, and he didn't bother with a greeting. "Talking on the phone is so last-century, Grandpa," he said with a laugh.

"You're not doing the Bridge Bang." I cut straight to the point, speaking as quietly as possible so as not to share my business with everyone else in the line. "Soon as I'm done chewing you out for even *thinking* about it, I'm calling Moose. After I've spoken to him, he won't let you within a hundred feet of that car."

"Chill, dude." The laughter had died from Brash's voice. "I could do the stunt, easy."

"You've never done anything like it. Moose can't put you in that car. I'll make sure he doesn't."

"What makes you so much better than me, Grandpa?" Now Brash sounded pissed.

"What makes me better? How about the fact I've done explosions before, so I know what I'll be in for?"

"I need to do one sometime."

"Yeah, if you start small. If the Bridge Bang goes wrong, it won't be pretty. I'm not watching them pick bits of your corpse out of the river."

Brash had a lot of guts but not enough caution, probably because he hadn't been in a serious accident yet. Stunt performers without caution tended to die young, but Brash had barely glimpsed his own mortality, let alone come face to face with it like I had.

Ask me, I'd rather keep it that way.

"You could die just as easily as me," he said, as though that was a reasonable argument.

"I'll be back on set in time to do the stunt," I growled, losing patience. "So forget about the Bridge Bang and practice for the fight scene. Last time I saw you fall, you messed it up and could have broken your back."

"Fine. Whatever." He hung up without saying goodbye.

I'd pissed him off. Too fucking bad. I stuck my phone back in my pocket with a sour taste in my mouth, picturing Brash badgering Moose to let him behind the wheel of a car loaded with explosives.

Three years ago, I'd been thinking of cutting back on stunt work when the kid had joined the team. Keeping Brash from getting killed had been one of my main jobs ever since. And if I left, who'd look out for him?

"What can I get you?" asked the server, pulling me out of my thoughts.

While I'd been on the phone, I'd made it to the front of the line. I pushed Brash to the back of my mind while I ordered the coffee and cake. Then I headed to the outside tables to find Momma.

As soon as I spotted her, my heart sank. She wasn't alone, but sitting with a pretty, slender woman with light brown, almost blonde hair that was loose around her shoulders, spilling over her thick coat.

Though there were plenty of empty tables, it seemed Momma had decided we should share one. It was a table for two, with an extra chair jammed in so three could sit around it. The woman with Momma had a plate in front of her that held only crumbs, and a half-finished coffee. Momma must have barged in on the poor woman's breakfast.

As I approached, my hands laden with our food and drinks, Momma and the woman both looked up.

"Noah, do you remember Hannah Townsen?" Momma asked.

"Hi, Hannah." I put our coffee and cakes down, giving her a cool nod. Her family's farm wasn't far from ours, and my momma used to visit Hannah's mother sometimes after work and take her leftovers from the bakery.

"Hello, Noah." Hannah seemed a little confused by our intrusion, and about as excited to see me as I was to see her. Had to admit, I was relieved by her apparent disinterest.

"Sit down." Momma motioned to the empty chair next to Hannah and I did as she asked. But the instant my butt hit the chair, Momma jumped to her feet. "Y'all catch up," she ordered. "I'm going to see if Jennifer's working in the kitchen." She strode off, leaving her coffee and cake behind.

Hannah watched my mother leave with her brow furrowed, then turned her confused gaze to me.

I shrugged. "She's on a mission to launch me at every unmarried woman in town. You were just caught in the crossfire."

"Oh." Luckily, Hannah looked amused rather than annoyed. "Mothers."

"*Mothers*," I agreed with feeling. "I'm not looking to date while I'm in town, only she doesn't let up. It's getting embarrassing."

"She told me you were skilled with your hands. I thought it was a strange thing to say."

I winced, then changed the subject. "How's your momma?"

"Good, actually. She got married."

"She did?" I shook my head in disbelief. "Is there some kind of love potion in the Green Valley water supply? Ask me, folks around here have too much romance on their minds." Putting a forkful of banana cake in my mouth, I let out a small groan of pleasure as it melted on my tongue. "Still the best cake in the whole country, though."

"Isn't it a shame about Jennifer's momma?" Hannah said. "They still haven't found her."

I frowned at her, trying to puzzle out this mystifying snippet of information. I could understand why she'd mention Jennifer Sylvester, seeing as Jennifer was Green Valley's banana cake queen, and the baker of the delicious cake that was giving me mouth-gasms. Her mother, Diane Sylvester, owned the bakery. Had she gone missing?

"Jennifer's momma?" I asked with my mouth full.

"You didn't hear what happened?" When I shook my head, she leaned forward, lowering her voice. "Diane shot Jennifer's father, then ran off."

"Excuse me…what?!"

Hannah nodded. "The police are looking for her, but she's disappeared."

I was struck dumb. Poor Jennifer. She spent a lot of time in the bakery when my momma worked there, so I'd gotten to know her. She'd been shy, but nice, and an excellent baker. She'd taught me how to use a piping bag to decorate cakes, and creating wacky cake designs had kept me from getting bored while I waited for momma to finish work. Seeing as how I was usually allowed to eat the cake I'd been practicing on, I had a lot to thank her for.

Though Momma had told me on one of our phone calls that Jennifer had taken over running the bakery, I'd figured her mother had just decided to retire. But the truth was so much worse. And though I talked to Momma on the phone all the time, she'd kept that extra bit of information to herself.

Sitting back again, Hannah pushed her empty coffee cup away. "Anyway, talking about people disappearing, my mother told me you were doing stunt work. She made it sound like every time you visited Green Valley you were at death's door, expecting your momma to nurse you back to health." She looked down at my bandage pointedly.

My mind was still half on what she'd told me about Jennifer. "This is nothing. I caught a shard of metal, that's all."

"Have you worked on any movies that I might have seen?"

I mentioned a couple of the more famous ones, and we talked a little about each one. In between, I sipped my coffee and savored a little more cake, eating slowly to make it last.

After a while, she tilted her head and said, "You left town right after Liam's funeral, right?'

I flinched. Again.

Though I'd left to avoid reminders of him, I hadn't expected the sound of Liam's name to keep making me flinch so many years later.

"That's right." I picked my coffee cup back up to cover my reaction. "Haven't been back much since."

I braced myself, expecting her to ask me about the car crash.

"Have you seen Liam's parents?" she asked instead.

I nodded. "I visited them the first time I came home." I'd dreaded the visit, but they hadn't wanted to know about the crash. When I'd tried to explain the misunderstanding that had led up to it, they'd changed the subject, instead reminiscing about old football games Liam and I had played, and telling stories about Liam's good heart.

"They've both passed now," she said.

"Momma told me."

"And Liam's girlfriend left town a few years ago," she said, surprising me.

"She did?"

Momma hadn't mentioned that either. But then, Momma hadn't liked Lorelei, and wasn't friendly with her family. It was possible she didn't know.

"I heard she moved to New Orleans and got married."

"Huh." I sipped more coffee, taking in the news.

Truth was, it was a huge relief. All this time, I'd fretted about bumping into Liam's girlfriend while I was in Green Valley, worrying about how hard it would be to see her again. The terrible night Liam died, he'd thought we'd betrayed him. What would I even say to her?

Now I knew I wouldn't have to see her, a weight was lifting. I could put her out of my mind and stop looking sideways every time I left the house.

I grinned at Hannah, suddenly glad Momma had forced us to sit together. "Would you like some cake?" I asked, pushing my plate toward her. Giving up some of my delicious cake was the ultimate way to show gratitude, at least in my eyes.

"Thanks, but I'd better go." She smiled as she stood. "Good luck with your momma."

"I'm afraid I'll need it."

Hannah had gone, and I'd finished my cake and most of my coffee by the time Momma came back, carrying a small cardboard box with a transparent lid.

"Where's Hannah?" she asked, sitting down and putting the box in front of her.

"After I popped the question, she had to go and buy a wedding dress. One with an expandable waist in case I made her pregnant already. You were gone a while, so we had time."

Momma narrowed her eyes. "Are you going to see her again?"

"You didn't tell me about Jennifer's momma. Is it true? Did she kill her husband?"

"Of course not." Her narrow-eyed look turned into a frown of displeasure. "Did Hannah tell you that? She should know better."

"But Jennifer lost her daddy?"

"Yes, but Diane had nothing to do with it. She was a fair boss and a nice lady, and I don't want to hear one word against her." Momma set her mouth into a firm line, as though that were that. One thing about my mother, she was a fiercely loyal friend—a quality I admired. She used her stubborn nature for good as well as evil.

"Is Jennifer okay?" I asked.

"As well as she can be, poor thing. The way folks were so busy gossiping and leaping to conclusions, I don't blame her momma for leaving town. But Jennifer's been brave to keep everything running like she has. It was a lot to take on." Pulling her cake toward her, she carved off a large piece with her fork.

"She still makes delicious cake," I said.

Momma nodded, swallowing a mouthful. "And I got these." She slid the box across the table, and I peered through the lid. It was full of cookies with frosted hearts in shades of red and pink.

"Aren't they lovely?" she asked. "The bakery's going to make cookie gift boxes for Valentine's Day, and I got a sample. You can give the box to Hannah or Carla when you ask one of them to accompany you to dinner."

"I'd rather eat them myself."

"They're not for you. If you don't give them away, I'll be forced to present them to someone on your behalf."

I heaved a loud sigh. "I love you, Momma, but I wish you'd stop. If I want a date, I can find my own."

She reached out to pat my hand. "Oh, Noah. If only that were true. If you can't manage to get yourself a date for Valentine's Day, the most romantic day of the year, what else would any good mother do but find one for you?"

CHAPTER 6

CARLA

I prepped for Noah's arrival.

There would be no internal apocalypse this time. I was going to be calm and collected when he arrived, not nervous, agitated, or hostile. I wouldn't even get upset if he called me Chuckles again. And after a meditation session and lots of positive affirmations, I'd almost talked myself into believing I could pull it off.

One of my favorite guided mediation tracks was called *The Heartbeat of the Universe*. As kooky as it sounded, after listening to the mediation guide's soothing voice for just ten minutes, I could almost imagine that I really was attuned to the heartbeat of the universe, with all the go-with-the-flow, Zen-level serenity that the track encouraged.

This morning, instead of ten minutes, I'd listened to it for an hour. So if the universe really did have a pulse, I was its ECG machine.

Aside from the extra-long meditation, I followed my normal morning schedule of working on my software, broken up with shorter periods of stretching, tai chi, a little gardening, and small, perfectly balanced organic meals.

It wasn't long after lunch, as I was trying to concentrate on a complex piece of code, that some loud noises came from the porch, as though someone was depositing something heavy on the wooden boards. Then there was a knock on the door.

I walked slowly down the hallway, giving myself a final pep-talk, and dragged in one last deep, calming breath before opening the door.

"Hi," said Noah.

I'd thought I was ready to face him, but his appearance knocked all the air out of my lungs. He was wearing dark blue jeans and a snug, charcoal-colored sweatshirt with the sleeves pushed up, as though he was too manly to feel the cold. The darkness of his clothing emphasized his masculine silhouette—wide shoulders with muscles to spare, tapering down to a narrow waist and hips. A battered toolbox was on the porch next to him, and his short beard and strong features were the frosting on the man-cake, so to speak.

Confronted with a living embodiment of testosterone, I was acutely aware of how unkempt I was. Not just because I hadn't had a haircut since my arrival in Green Valley, but I'd also lost weight, and all my clothes were baggy. Especially the old clothes I'd put on today. When I'd gotten dressed, I'd chosen my oldest jeans and hoodie so it wouldn't matter if they got ruined while I was helping Noah with whatever he needed me to do. Only I hadn't fully appreciated how self-conscious I'd feel in them.

Yesterday, I'd answered the door in sweatpants, with no less than five warm tops pulled over each other to counteract the cold air seeping in through the hole in my roof. After that fashion faux-pas, I'd decided not to care how I looked today. Now I regretted that decision.

"Hello." I wiped my suddenly sweaty palms on my jeans. "What's your plan for today? Are you going to climb back on the roof?" His ladder was already set up on the porch behind him, along with a pile of roofing shingles. He seemed ready to spring into action.

"I sure am." He spoke in his lazy drawl, and his expression held a hint of a smile, as though life was nothing but a show being played for his amusement. "I'll patch that hole today. Get it weathertight again."

"I don't think I can climb onto the roof," I said. "Is there anything I can do to help from down here?"

He lifted his eyebrows, his gaze moving over me slowly, leaving disconcerting tingles in its wake. "You're still willing to help?"

"The quicker we get this done, the faster you can leave." I bit my lip because it had sounded a lot ruder out loud than it had in my head. "I have a deadline," I explained. "So I need things to go back to normal as quickly as possible."

"A software deadline?"

"That's right."

"You're a programmer?" When I nodded, he asked, "Are you ready to tell me what kind of software you're working on?"

"It would take a long time to explain." I wiped my palms again. Maybe I should invite him in, or offer him a drink, but I just wanted the conversation to be over, and for him to have finished patching the roof already. "I'm creating something new." I said, hoping it would be enough of an explanation.

"Something to do with medical experiments?"

His question surprised me. "In a way. How did you know?" Could he be familiar enough with process flow diagrams to have deciphered the information on my whiteboards?

He flashed me his dazzling smile. "I'll tell you how I know, if you tell me about your software."

Maybe if the sheer beauty of his smile wasn't making my stomach acid bubble like a volcanic mud pool, I would have been more open to the idea. But I didn't want to prolong this torture.

"Or we could just get on with it?" My tone was unintentionally curt.

Dammit, so much for *The Heartbeat of the Universe*. He'd barely been here for five minutes, and already I was becoming more attuned to the universe's irritable bowel instead of its heartbeat.

I'd been a recluse for over a year. Had I lost my ability to interact with people in general? Or was it only because his good looks were so discombobulating they made my social graces disappear?

Noah's smile widened. He bent to his toolbox, took out a pair of work gloves, and offered them to me. "Well then, these are for you."

Feeling even more like a blockage that should be flushed from the universe's nether regions, I plucked them from his grip. They were stiff and clean, and clearly brand new. "They're in my size?" I asked, pulling them on. "You bought them for me?"

"Now, don't take it the wrong way. I'm not implying your gender has soft hands or is in any way inferior. But you'll need them if you're going to handle the shingles."

My cheeks burned at the reminder of how rude I'd been yesterday. And if I kept going like this, today wasn't shaping up to be any better. Even if Noah preferred my grumpiness, that wasn't how I wanted to act.

"Thank you for the gloves." I softened my tone. "I'm ready to help as much as I can. Please tell me what you'd like me to do."

He strolled toward the ladder he'd set up on the porch. "I'll get on the roof. If you're able to pass the shingles up to me, it'll save me going up and down the ladder."

"Are they heavy?"

"Not very. Test one and see."

I lifted one of the shingles he'd left at the bottom of the ladder. It was lighter than it looked, and probably manageable, though I'd need to monitor my heart rate and make sure I didn't overdo it.

"It's okay," I said.

"Great. Then let's give this a trial run. If it doesn't work, I'll carry the shingles up myself." He climbed up the ladder and moved to the lip of the roof, leaning over so far, my anxiety surged.

"Stop!" I lowered the shingle I was still holding. "Get back from the edge!"

"If I'm not on the edge, I won't be able to reach the shingle." He leaned even farther, stretching his arms toward me as though he were about to dive. "How high can you lift it?"

"Shouldn't you wear a harness?" I was too afraid to move, not wanting to tempt him into leaning over any more.

"No need."

"What if you fall?"

"I promise I won't. It's not slippery up here, and this part isn't steep. It's just like being on the ground."

I closed my eyes for a moment, dragging in a breath. "Do you know how many people are killed falling off roofs each year? And how many of those people insisted they were safe before they plummeted to a gory death?"

"No idea." He sounded cheerful. "How many?"

I shook my head. "Would you please just secure yourself somehow?"

"What if I sit down?" He was doing that very thing as he suggested it, sitting on the edge of the roof with his feet dangling over. "Does that make you feel better?"

Though I could still picture him falling, I gave in and lifted the shingle. I pushed it above my head as high as I could reach. Noah hinged at the waist, leaning forward so much it made my heart feel like it was being swallowed by my stomach. Then the shingle grew lighter. Noah pulled it out of my hands and put it on the roof beside him.

"That wasn't so bad, was it?" he said.

I couldn't answer because I was swallowing bile. My palms felt hot and wet inside the new gloves, and I was dizzy, both from looking up and from imagining his corpse splattered on the porch. Actually, there'd probably be *two* corpses, seeing as he'd be likely to land on top of me.

"Think you'll be okay to pass up another?" he asked.

I clenched my teeth to keep from objecting and bent to pick up another shingle. There were only eight. It wouldn't take long. I just had to get this over with.

Noah didn't say anything while I passed the rest of the shingles up to him, thank goodness, as I was concentrating on not getting so dizzy that I fell over, and not letting him see how sick this small job was making me feel.

After I passed the last one up, I asked, "Is that all you need?"

"That's it for now." He sprang to his feet and grabbed a couple of the shingles. "Fitting these over the hole should only take an hour or two. Might be a little noisy, but I'll do my best to finish quickly."

He carried the shingles over the roof, and I averted my gaze. Didn't he care about the danger?

I fled inside, stripping off my gloves and toeing off my sneakers as soon as I was in the door. In the kitchen, I gulped down a glass of water. Then I went to my bedroom and collapsed on the bed next to my sleeping cat. Freud didn't move, unless it was to close his eyes more tightly. I lay on my back and grabbed my headphones from the nightstand. Firing up my anti-anxiety playlist, I screwed my eyes shut to listen.

Although scientific studies had shown mixed results, I'd found listening to binaural beats helped me relax. It wasn't exactly music, more like tones in different frequencies, and over the past year I'd been programming my brain to chill out when I listened. It was usually effective, but this time, I was too uptight. I couldn't focus on my breath when I was so unsettled.

Perhaps I shouldn't be wearing headphones at all, in case I needed to hear a yell of distress, or the sound of Noah's body hitting the ground outside. If he fell, how long would it take an ambulance to get here? Would I have to perform CPR while I waited?

There was a song you were supposed to sing to help keep time while doing chest compressions—what was it again? It was a pop classic, that much I remembered. Was it a Beatles song? ABBA? No wait, was it Queen? The only Queen song I could think of was 'Another One Bites the Dust'… which described what would probably happen to Noah if I attempted CPR.

But maybe I could give him mouth-to-mouth instead of chest compressions?

And if I was now imagining what it might be like to put my lips to his, did that make me a bad person?

Something touched my foot.

I shrieked, jerking backward and ripping my headphones off.

Noah was at the foot of my bed. "Hey," he said. "Sorry to startle you. I called out but got no reply. Didn't expect to find you in bed."

I clutched my chest where my heart was doing its best to hammer its way through my ribcage, and scrambled up so I was propped against the headboard. At least Noah was still breathing, and my dubious CPR skills weren't required.

"I'm not startled," I said breathlessly. "I always scream when I sit up."

He frowned. "You look pale."

"Do I?" I lifted my hands to my cheeks as though I'd be able to feel their color. "That's the light in here washing out my skin tone. You look ghostly yourself."

"Did I push you too hard? Did lifting the shingles wear you out? Was that why you were lying down?" His tone was far less relaxed than before—almost hard—and his frown was deepening. His gaze devoured my face. I'd been freaked by how nonchalant he'd been about his safety, but now, when I wanted him to chill out, he seemed to be cataloging every one of my facial hairs to make sure they hadn't been bent out of shape.

"I'm okay," I said, desperately hoping it was true.

"I don't believe you."

"You don't believe me? Like I have to prove it?"

"Can you prove it?"

I gave a disbelieving laugh. "Are you for real? Why are you in here, anyway?"

His frown eased. His expression was still worried, but maybe he was reassured that I was being rude again. Not that I wanted to be rude, but my brain was starting to catch up with the fact there was a super-hot man in my bedroom. Hopefully my bedsheets didn't smell funky. When had I last washed them? Five days ago? Six? Longer? Thank goodness I'd put my dirty clothes into the laundry basket.

"I need to run an electrical cord to an outlet. Are you sure you're okay?" He asked the last part in a slightly growly way, like he was giving me a warning. The voice he used was crazy sexy, sending shivers of awareness through my body.

No, wait.

Surely a growly tone couldn't be a turn-on for me. Those shivers I was feeling had to be due to something else. A new symptom of my illness, perhaps?

Because after years of working in the sausage factory that was the male-domi-nated tech industry, being growled at by a man had never been on my fantasy list.

Mind you, none of the programmers I used to work with had ever looked like him.

"I was just a little dizzy," I said. "It was nothing."

Instead of reassuring him, that made his worried frown come back. He sank down on the side of the bed next to Freud, his body facing me. "How are you feeling now? Still dizzy?"

"Um." I would have said no, but considering his proximity, and the fact he was now sitting on my bed, I wasn't so sure. If he was making me dizzy, did that count?

"Are you sick?" He leaned forward, his beautiful green eyes roving over my face. I could tell he was considering putting his palm on my forehead to see if I was running a temperature.

"No," I said. "I mean, yes, but..."

I closed my eyes.

Crap.

Now I may as well tell him the truth.

CHAPTER 7

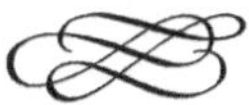

CARLA

"So, you *are* sick?" Noah asked with a frown. "You don't sound sure."

I shifted the pillows behind me so I could lean back more comfortably against the bed's headboard. "It's a long-term thing. I have ME. It stands for myalgic encephalomyelitis."

"What's that?"

"It's also called chronic fatigue syndrome, but I don't like that name. There's a stigma attached."

"I've heard of that. Does it mean you're always tired?"

"It's more than that." I sighed a little, because as understandable as his lack of knowledge was, having to explain was always difficult. "Nobody knows much about it. But it's been linked to brain inflammation, cell damage, and dysfunction of the autonomic nervous system." I'd read dozens of different medical papers, and all the different theories about the illness were so complex, it felt like I was trying to describe quantum physics in two sentences. "The short version is that my body has problems creating energy, and if I use too much, I can crash. It can take days or weeks to recover, and as well as fatigue, I get joint pain, headaches, dizziness, nausea, brain fog… All kinds of fun things."

He looked alarmed. "Did you run out of energy when we were outside?"

"Other things can trigger symptoms as well. Craning my neck makes me lightheaded. Like I said, I got dizzy."

Noah reached out to stroke Freud. My cat cracked one eye open, then closed it again.

"So what does the illness mean?" Noah asked slowly. "In practical terms, I mean. How does it affect you?"

People responded in all kinds of ways to my illness. I'd heard plenty of jokes, been told it was all in my head, that my symptoms were caused by depression, or I was just lazy. I was never sure whether the person I was telling would snicker, or treat me as though I was dying.

Noah did neither of those things. And his was an unusually thoughtful question.

"Getting sick changed everything," I said. "It affects my entire life, all the time." It wasn't until the words were out that I heard how bleak I sounded. I gave myself a mental shake. The last thing I wanted was pity.

"By the way you were strolling over the roof, you're obviously not scared of heights," I said, hoping he'd take the hint and let me change the subject away from my illness.

"Couldn't do my job if I got scared."

"Why *are* you a stuntman? Are you a thrill seeker? Addicted to adrenaline?"

"Nope."

"You're not?"

He leaned over a little more so he could scratch under Freud's chin. Freud adjusted his head to give him better access. My cat's eyes were still tightly closed, but he was purring.

"I don't do it for fun," Noah said.

He didn't seem to want to elaborate, but I tried one more time. "Are you saying you don't like your job?"

He shrugged. "Sometimes."

"You don't sound very sure."

When he didn't answer right away, I wriggled down on my pillows a little to get more comfortable. From my low angle, I could see a small scar on the bottom of Noah's chin, peeking out from under his close-trimmed beard. It was a semi-circle of white skin that stood out against his tan. His naked throat wasn't quite so flawless as I'd first thought, and maybe that should have made it less attractive. Only, nope. It was even sexier than before.

"I specialize in car jobs," he said. "Sometimes, when I'm about to crash a car, I think about getting out and walking away. But then someone else would take over the stunt, and they won't be as good at it as I am."

I blinked at him, because he'd surprised me. I'd half expected him to be flippant or dismissive. Instead, he'd spoken seriously.

"Is that how you got that scar?" I asked. "From a stunt?" I pointed to my chin to indicate the place I was talking about.

He took his hand away from Freud to touch the scar. "You saw that, huh? I thought my beard hid it."

"It does, mostly. Except from down here."

"That scar isn't from my job. It's from a car accident when I was a teenager." He sounded reluctant, as though he didn't want to talk about it, so I didn't press him about it.

"You've had an action-packed life," I mused instead. He probably had lots of scars. All kinds of them, hidden underneath his sweatshirt and jeans. Maybe he had one that climbed the tight ridges of his abs, and another cutting the lean perfection of his thighs. Perhaps he had one on his chest. Hair wouldn't grow over it, so assuming his chest hair was as dark as the hair on his head, the scar would form a smooth track through… *Crap! Stop picturing him naked!*

I cleared my throat. "What do you do for fun when you're not working? Heli-skiing and deep-sea diving?"

"Actually, I like restoring and painting old cars."

"Painting them?" I raised my eyebrows. "Did you paint your truck?"

He gave a reluctant-looking smile. "That was years ago. First one I ever did." Tugging his phone out of his pocket, he pressed a few buttons, then handed it to me. "There's the latest one. I finished it last month." The photo displayed was of a beautiful classic sports car. It was black, with a silver design painted over the hood and down the sides. I blinked at it for a second, then realized it was a pair of angel wings, but stylized, with the feathers wild and three-dimensional, as though they were blowing right off the car.

"It's gorgeous," I breathed.

He grinned, taking his phone back. "Thanks."

"How did you do it?"

"Stencil and spray-paint to start, then an airbrush for the finer details."

"But how did you learn to do it?"

"I like drawing doodles. Painting a car is just doodling in 3-D."

His casual tone, as though it wasn't an impressive talent, made me shake my head at him. "Is there anything you can't do?"

He shrugged. "Always been a jack of all trades."

"Did you ever think about becoming an artist?"

"I'm only good at designs. Not landscapes, or portraits, or the things people want to hang on their walls." He reached out to pet Freud again and I admired his capable-looking fingers. His mother had been right about him being skilled with his hands.

"What do you like about being a programmer?" he asked.

"Solving problems," I said. "Writing software is like figuring out puzzles."

"You must be smart." He said it in an admiring way, and the appreciation in his eyes made my cheeks feel warm.

"My cat's name is Freud. In case you were wondering." It was an abrupt change of subject, but I wanted to divert his focus in case I was blushing.

At least my stomach acid had finally stopped reacting to him. I could hardly believe we were having a normal conversation. Even after his compliment, my insides weren't turning dystopian, and he didn't seem to mind that I wasn't snapping at him. Hopefully that wasn't because he felt sorry for me.

"Does Freud psychoanalyze you?" Noah sounded amused.

"He's my emotional support cat." It was only half a joke. Having Freud meant I didn't feel alone.

"Your what?"

"Petting cats is good for you. A cat's purr is calming for the nervous system."

He gave me a disarming, one-sided smile. "Don't forget about their soft little bellies." He stroked Freud's stomach and Freud promptly rolled farther over to present more of it for his attention. A lot of cats would take Noah's presumption as a signal to attack his hand, but not Freud. He was far too lazy for that kind of nonsense.

"He likes that," I said, unnecessarily.

Noah's hands looked incredibly smooth and unscarred for someone who fixed roofs and painted cars. And he had a confident way of moving that made watching him run his hands through Freud's fur oddly arousing.

"I'd better finish the work on the roof to make it weathertight." He gave Freud's belly a final rub. "It won't take long."

"And you don't need me to help?" I asked.

He shook his head. "I could do with an extra pair of hands when it comes to replacing the ceiling in the living room, that's all. But only if you feel up to it. After that's done, I'll give the ceiling a fresh coat of paint, then I'll be finished and out of your hair."

"Will you paint a design over the ceiling?" A picture flashed through my mind of how great it could look. Giant angel wings stretched across the living room? Or maybe he could do something more suited to a farmhouse.

"Momma wouldn't exactly be thrilled." He stood up. "Mind if I open a window in the living room to run an electrical cord up to the roof? I'll close your door to keep the heat in."

"Go ahead. I'm just going to rest here for a little while, then I'll get up."

He shut my bedroom door behind him, and after a while, I heard the buzz of power tools. I put my headphones back on and closed my eyes. One of the main ways I managed my illness was with pacing, which meant not letting my heart rate or stress levels get too high, and not pushing myself too hard.

Unsurprisingly, I felt a little tired, and after listening to the binaural beats for a while, I dozed off.

I woke to the sound of my phone ringing.

Feeling groggy, I took off my headphones and glanced at the time on my smartwatch to find I'd been asleep a full hour. Then I checked my phone display. Crap. It was my mother calling.

"Hi Mom." I tried to sound like I was awake and cheerful. A difficult task, seeing as my voice was croaky.

"Hello, Carlita." Mom's Spanish accent was still strong despite having lived in the States for almost thirty years. "How are you feeling?"

"I'm fine, thanks."

Mom didn't understand my illness. When my fatigue had gotten so bad I could barely get out of bed, and my fiancé Tomas had ended our engagement, I'd had to move in with my parents for a while. It hadn't gone well. Mom kept trying to convince me to get up, try harder, and push through. It had made my illness worse. Nowadays, I told her I was fine no matter how I was feeling.

"How are you, Mom?" I asked.

"Your father's away on another sales trip," she said, by way of an answer. "And your sisters are trying to kill me."

I grimaced. "That bad?"

"They never listen to their mother. Wasting their lives, both of them."

"They'll be okay. They have time to figure things out."

My sisters were still in their twenties. Josefina had dropped out of art school and gone to a communal living community to 'find herself', which apparently included not having a phone. And Magdalena… well, I loved my youngest sister with all my heart, but I'd never met anyone wilder. Whenever she called, I always half-expected her to ask for bail money.

"Still no call from Josefina; she wants to worry me to death. And Magdalena! That girl is impossible. Carlita, you need to talk to her, okay?"

"Sure, I'll speak to her," I promised. Only it probably wouldn't help. Mags was headstrong and sure of herself, and she'd never exactly clamored for the wise counsel of her older sister.

"Have you called Sienna yet?" Mom asked.

I gritted my teeth. "Not yet."

Mom brought Sienna up every time we talked, and my resolution to be less intimidated by my cousin's success was sometimes set back by Mom's fondness for reading me glowing magazine articles. *Vanity Fair* had called Sienna's latest movie 'uplifting' and 'triumphant', and I could only agree.

"You'd better hurry," Mom said. "She's back from Australia, but she'll only be in town for a few weeks."

Mom was desperate for Sienna and me to rekindle our friendship.

Sienna was actually the reason I'd come to Green Valley, though I hadn't realized it at the time. I'd needed to move away from my family and ex-fiancé so I could focus on trying to get better. When I'd told Mom I wanted to rent a quiet house in the country, she'd found a listing in a remote part of Tennessee. It had looked perfect. I hadn't realized Green Valley was where Sienna lived until after I'd signed the lease.

"Why don't you go and see her?" Mom suggested. "Take her some flowers to say sorry for being so rude and not returning her call. It would do you good to spend time with her."

"I'll think about it," I said, hoping she'd drop the subject.

Mom seemed convinced Sienna could inspire me, and if we became friends again, my cousin's success might rub off on me. Maybe she even believed Sienna could cure me. I wouldn't be surprised.

My watch vibrated and an alert sounded. It was three o'clock. Time for me to eat something. And where was Noah? I couldn't hear any noises. Could he have finished what he was doing and left without waking me?

"Mom, I need to go. I have someone here fixing the roof." I dragged myself out of bed.

"Who's there?" She sounded surprised. Which was understandable, seeing as I'd never had anybody in the house before.

"He's the son of the woman who owns the house."

"You're finally meeting people! That's great, Carlita. You need to make friends. Especially after Tomas..." After mentioning my ex-fiancé's name, she gave a disapproving click of her tongue. She always did that these days, though she'd adored Tomas until we broke up.

"It's not like that. He's just working here for a couple of days." As I left my bedroom, I glanced at the front door, which was wide open. Noah's truck was still parked outside. Maybe he was still on the roof. If he'd fallen off, I'd probably slept through it, and it was too late to attempt resuscitation.

"Carlita, at least think about calling—"

"Sure, Mom," I said because I was too weary to argue. "I'll think about calling Sienna. Talk to you later, okay?"

After saying goodbye and hanging up, I found Noah in the living room. He'd set up his ladder under the hole in the ceiling and was cutting away the torn edges of the damaged drywall. I shoved my phone in my pocket as I walked up to him. "Hey," I said. "You've finished on the roof?" Looking up, I could no longer see sky. And my living room felt warmer, the heat no longer escaping through the hole. Noah had stripped off his sweatshirt and was only wearing a t-shirt. It hugged his muscled chest in a very distracting way.

"The shingles are done." He climbed down from the ladder. "I didn't mean to eavesdrop, but I heard the end of your conversation. Did I hear you say something about Sienna Diaz? You know she lives in Green Valley?"

I rubbed my eyes, wishing I'd thought to wash my face and brush my teeth before emerging from my bedroom. "We're distantly related," I said reluctantly.

"Related? Huh." He nodded as though that somehow made sense. "You look a bit like her."

"I don't! I'm not even Mexican. My mother's Chilean, and that's a whole different country."

He carried his ladder to the side of the room where his toolbox and tools were neatly stacked and set it down before turning to me. "Well, you're both beautiful."

"Um. Thank you." My stomach fluttered and my hand automatically went to my hair to smooth it. My fingers instantly tangled. Uh-oh. Did I have bed hair to go with my unwashed face and furry teeth?

I lowered my hand, wanting to laugh at myself. I was still wearing an oversized hoodie, and there was no way I looked anything but disheveled. Noah was just being nice, complimenting me to make me feel good.

"My mother's obsessed with Sienna," I said. "I can't tell you how many times I've heard how amazing she is. Whenever we talk, Mom raves about Sienna's latest success, or tells me which exotic country she's currently visiting with her gorgeous husband and three adorable sons."

"To be fair, Sienna is amazing." The smile he shot me dared me to smile back, and I couldn't help doing just that.

"And, oh boy, the subject never gets worn out."

He laughed. "So you and Sienna are what? Cousins?"

"Second cousins. Her aunt married my uncle. We were friendly as kids when we both lived in LA, but then my family moved to New York, and I hardly saw her. Last time I bumped into her was at a family wedding, years ago."

It was before I was diagnosed, when I had no idea why I was so tired all the time and was seeing doctor after doctor. I'd dragged myself to the wedding anyway and had made it all the way through the ceremony by pretending I wasn't feeling sick. But at the reception, when I started talking to Sienna, I'd noticed Mom staring at us from across the room. I'd had a weird dizzy spell and been suddenly convinced that Mom wished Sienna was her daughter instead of me. Then I'd broken out into such a bad sweat, I must have looked like I was melting. Sienna had been as nice as always, but I'd panicked.

It was my first real anxiety attack, and it had been scary. I'd fled the wedding, berating myself all the way home. Now, even the thought of seeing Sienna again bought back memories of a racing heart and overwhelming feelings of inadequacy.

With a sigh, I turned toward the kitchen. "Anyway, I need to eat."

"Well, I need to pick up some lumber, so I'll finish cleaning up in here and head off for the day. I'll come back tomorrow."

In the kitchen, I opened the fridge and pulled out the ingredients for a salad. Most of the greens came from my garden, and eggs from my chickens, but I was almost out of the nuts and seeds I needed for extra nutrients and protein. In fact, I was out of a lot of things, so I'd need to go grocery shopping soon. I'd come to Green Valley to improve the symptoms of my illness, and everything I did was designed with that goal in mind, including everything I ate. I'd spent a lot of time coming up with meals that might help.

Noah came into the kitchen while I was mixing a dressing for my salad.

"That looks healthy," he said.

I blinked at him, realizing how impolite I'd been. "Would you like something to eat or drink? I haven't even offered you a glass of water." I looked down at my carefully prepared meal. "Want half my salad? I'll make some more."

He wrinkled his nose. "No offense, but my taste runs more toward sweet foods, or anything that's served with a side order of fries."

"Oh!" I spun to the pantry and pulled out the cookies he'd left in my kitchen on the day he'd arrived. "Eat these. I can't have gluten, sugar, or dairy."

His eyes widened with horror, and he took the jar from me quickly, as though I might throw it away if he didn't get it out of my hands in time. "You just spelled out a tragedy in one sentence. If you can't eat any of those things, what's left?"

I pointed at the salad. "This."

"For every meal?" His brows drew together, and his expression was so shocked, I couldn't help but laugh.

"At least you get to eat the cookies," I said soothingly.

"I guess so." He ran his free hand over his hair, tousling it so it looked unbearably cute, sticking up all over. Then he shook his head and it settled back into being only slightly unruly. The gesture made him seem so boyish and adorable, I was rooted to the spot, struck dumb with admiration.

If there were a male Sienna Diaz, it would be him.

He should be in the movies. And in commercials. He could sell hair products to bald men and, well, just about anything to women. He could probably convince me to buy shares in MySpace.

"Well," he said with a loud huff of breath, clearly still disturbed by the shock of my dietary restrictions. "I'd better go. Tomorrow I'll be back around mid-morning, if that's okay with you?"

I nodded, still speechless.

His striking green eyes landed on me, and he raised his eyebrows as though he could see something odd in my expression. "You okay, Chuckles?"

I nodded again.

Truth was, I wasn't okay at all. Everything I did was designed to regulate my nervous system. I'd carefully calibrated my life to minimize stress. But so far today, I'd let myself get dizzy, skipped my entire morning schedule, slept for an hour, and was late eating lunch. Now I was staring at Noah with my heart beating erratically and a fluttery feeling in my stomach. My chest felt hot, and my cheeks were probably red.

My primary objective was to avoid disturbances to my system.

And Noah was completely and utterly disturbing.

CHAPTER 8

NOAH

- Seventeen days to Valentine's Day -

"*M*omma, what are we really doing back here?" I asked suspiciously, as I parked my truck outside the Donner Bakery. "You haven't arranged to meet Hannah again, have you?"

There was a long line of people snaking from the front door of the bakery. It was a popular place, and this morning was a lot busier than last time we were here. Momma had insisted we needed cake, and that I had to take her to get it.

I sensed a trap. I mean, of course this was some kind of trap. But the sneaky woman had baited it with cake, making me helpless to resist.

"Don't be silly," Momma said. "You're perfectly safe." Worryingly, she gave me an innocent look before getting out of the truck, which only confirmed my worst fears.

"Momma, I swear, if you've arranged another one of your setups, I'm going to—"

"Come on, Noah. Don't dawdle." She was striding away so quickly, she was almost across the parking lot already.

Letting out a groan loud enough that she'd be sure to hear it, I went after her.

Whoever the woman was she had lined up for me, I'd be firm but polite, and try to minimize the embarrassment for both of us.

To my surprise, my mother didn't join the line to be served at the front of the bakery. Instead, she went around to the staff entrance and into the kitchen.

Seeing as the bakery's kitchen was one of my favorite places of all time, it was no hardship to follow her. The smell was delicious. They were clearly baking croissants because the aroma of pastry and butter made my mouth fill with saliva like a drooling Homer Simpson.

The kitchen had changed a little from when I'd hung out in it as a boy. It was busier than it had been back then, with more staff on the floor. And a few of those staff glanced up at us, their eyes curious, clearly wondering what we were doing walking into the busy food preparation area. I was wondering the same thing, but my mother wasn't stopping to explain. She strode over to a short, dark-haired woman who was pulling some cupcakes out of the oven.

"Joy, this is my son, Noah."

Joy's face lit up. "Hi, Noah!" She grabbed hold of my hand with what could only be described as an actual squeal of delight. Her cheeks were covered with freckles, and she wore a smile so wide and bright, it practically glowed. "Am I glad to see you!" she exclaimed.

"Nice to meet you," I said in my most reserved tone, trying to extract my hand from hers.

"When your momma said you were available, I couldn't help getting excited!"

I shot a glare at the woman who seemed determined to embarrass me every chance she got. "My mother said I was *available*?"

"Your momma's been singing your praises. She told me you were skilled with your hands."

"I wish she'd stop saying that," I ground out through gritted teeth.

Joy didn't seem to notice my discomfort because the wattage of her smile didn't dim. "And when Jenn heard, she was every bit as enthusiastic about you as I am."

"Jenn? You mean Jennifer Sylvester?"

"Come on." Joy grabbed my arm and tugged me toward the office at the back of the kitchen. "Let's see if Jenn's free right now. I think she wants you even more than I do."

"Wait." I planted my feet and pulled my arm free from her grip. Whatever she meant by saying that Jennifer wanted me, I sure didn't like the sound of it. "Joy, I don't—"

"There's Blithe Tanner too," Momma said, interrupting my protest. "Noah, do you know Blithe? Goodness, Joy, there are a *lot* of attractive women working here. Are you putting a secret ingredient into your pastries?"

"That's enough, now." I used a firm tone, letting her know I didn't find the situation amusing.

"But Noah, Valentine's Day is right around the corner." Momma's eyes had a determined gleam. "Come to think of it, I don't think it's even marked off on your calendar, seeing as how you're single and don't have a date yet. But it's in a little over two weeks. Isn't that right, Joy?"

"Seventeen days," Joy agreed. She glanced around as another woman came out of an office in the back. "Oh, there she is now. Jennifer! Look who's here!"

"I'll wait outside." My mother turned to hurry away. "Noah, come and find me once y'all are done in here."

I could have explained things to Joy and stomped out as well, but I was too busy blinking at Jennifer Sylvester, who bore little resemblance to the girl I remembered from when we were teenagers. Jennifer used to have blonde hair that was always styled so she looked like she was ready to step onto a TV set, and she'd worn bright yellow dresses. Back then, she'd been quiet and watchful. Easy to overlook, despite her clothing.

Now she was a cool-looking brunette in jeans and a t-shirt.

"Hello, Noah. It's nice to see you again." Jennifer spoke in a self-assured tone that was as new as her appearance.

Well, it was no wonder she'd changed. With her father dead and her mother having run off, the poor woman must have been through hell. Somehow, she'd survived it. Good for her. Had to hand it to her, that must have taken guts.

"Nice to see you too," I said. "But there's clearly been a misunderstanding. I don't know what my mother's been telling you, but this time she's gone too far."

Jennifer's face fell. "You're not available?"

"Absolutely not. Momma may be fixated on getting me married, but I don't want to date anyone, and I'm certainly not looking for a…"

I trailed off because their eyes had gone wide. Joy snorted, then clapped a hand over her mouth. She exchanged an amused look with Jennifer, who was pressing her lips together, clearly struggling not to laugh.

"That's not what you're saying," I said flatly, silently wishing curses onto my wickedly conniving mother.

Jennifer pointed to one of the tables, where a young woman was using a piping bag to decorate a tray of cookies, putting heart shapes onto each one. "For Valentine's Day, we've been experimenting with a new range of decorated cookies, boxed up with a nice ribbon. But we put some on sale for the first time yesterday, and they were even more popular than we'd expected."

Joy spoke up, her eyes still sparkling with suppressed laughter. "Folks loved them, and we had nowhere near enough. It takes time to decorate the cookies, and we're already busy. We'd like to do Valentine's cupcakes as well, but that would push us over the edge."

"We need someone to help with decorating cupcakes and cookies until Valentine's Day, and I thought of how you used to decorate cakes while you waited for your momma to finish work. Do you remember?"

I nodded. "You taught me how."

Jennifer flashed me a smile. "Your momma said you'd be in town until the seventeenth and were looking for something to do. I hoped to offer you a job."

I scratched my beard thoughtfully. As unexpected as it was, standing in the kitchen with the smells of heaven around me, her offer was surprisingly tempting. I'd always loved this place. Being back was triggering fond memories.

"Only, I don't know as I'd have the time," I said slowly, thinking aloud. "See, I'm tied up with fixing the roof at our old farmhouse."

"Oh." Jennifer sighed, her shoulders slumping a little. "Well, that's a real shame. If you change your mind, we could really use you."

Joy looked just as disappointed. "Shoot," she muttered. "Who else can we find at such short notice?"

I looked from her to Jennifer and back again. In addition to them, there were three other women busy making baked goods. When Momma had walked in, she must have seen a cornucopia of potential mothers for her future grandbabies.

"Momma didn't just offer my services to be kind," I explained. "She's been trying to set me up with single women."

"I'm not single," Jennifer said with a smile. "I'm married." She held up her hand to show me a sparkling diamond ring.

"You are?" I rocked back on my heels. "Congratulations. Who's the lucky guy?"

"I'm Jennifer Winston now. I'm married to Cletus."

"Cletus Winston?" The surprise in my voice was probably rude. But I'd never spoken to Cletus, and the only thing I remembered about him was that he had a reputation for being strange.

She gave me a smile. "He's over there, repairing one of our mixers."

I turned and saw a man in coveralls with a wild beard working on one of the industrial mixers at the back of the bakery. He nodded at me, his blue eyes sharp. Though I had no idea how I hadn't seen him before now, I had the feeling he'd been listening in on every word we said.

I nodded politely back to him. If Jennifer had married him, I must have misjudged him. Momma would have said it served me right for listening to small-town gossip.

As I was turning toward Jennifer, I glanced at Joy. She was gazing at Cletus with such an openly wistful look, I had a realization. No matter what Momma was hoping for, I didn't need to worry about Joy. If she was busy pining for Cletus, she wouldn't be pestering me for a date anytime soon.

In fact, Momma may have made a serious tactical error by offering my services here. None of the other women in the kitchen had so much as glanced in my direction. If they had no romantic interest in me, I had nothing to worry about.

"Now that I think on it, fixing the farmhouse roof shouldn't take longer than one more day," I said. "Guess I could start helping out around here after that."

I had to smile at the way Jennifer's face lit up. My new job probably wouldn't quell Momma's obsession with my love-life for long, but it might buy me a little peace in the meantime. And, married or not, Jennifer had clearly had more than her share of misfortune. If I could make her life a little easier, why wouldn't I?

CHAPTER 9

CARLA

I wasn't just anxious. I was anxious about being anxious.

I was worried my anxiety would cause a crash, and my worry about it made it more likely to happen. In programming, that was called an infinite loop. In real life, it was called being seriously messed up.

So I sat in my car outside the Piggly Wiggly, jiggling my car keys and procrastinating about getting out of my car and going inside the store for a lot longer than a normal person would.

Wait. No. Scratch all that. I had to control my thoughts in order to break the loop. I couldn't afford to let myself think that way.

I wasn't messed up. I was a normal person. Hell, a *lot* of people suffered from anxiety. Probably most people did, at some time in their lives. And honestly, with everything I'd been through, it'd be strange if I *wasn't* anxious. Thinking of it that way, any well-adjusted weirdo who didn't have anxiety would be the one with issues, not me.

With a deep breath, I forced myself out of the car. I'd arrived at the Piggly Wiggly early, just after opening, which should be a relatively quiet time, yet the place still seemed full enough to kick up my heart rate.

Since my arrival in Green Valley, the only time I left the house was to go grocery shopping, and that was only once a month. From the day Noah's mother had handed me the keys, some brief interactions at the checkout had been my only social interactions with strangers.

Inside the Piggly Wiggly, soft music was playing. It was a song from the '80s I might have sung along to if I was at home. Fruit and vegetables were arranged near the door in tempting stands. I grabbed a cart, wrapped my damp hands firmly around its handle, and pushed it determinedly into the first aisle.

A teenager was stacking shelves. A young mother was pushing a stroller while she filled her shopping basket. A middle-aged woman was on tiptoe, grabbing something from a high shelf. Two bored-looking teens trailed after a man who had to be their father, their eyes fixed to their phone screens.

All seemed to be preoccupied with what they were doing. I didn't catch any of them so much as glancing at me, let alone staring, no matter what my churning stomach and dry mouth were telling me.

Moving quickly, I headed for the gluten-free aisle, not giving the candy and snack food parts of the store so much as a glance. Well, maybe *one* glance.

For the first few months after quitting sugar, my cravings had made me so grumpy, I'd even yelled at myself. But I'd adjusted, and my symptoms had improved. Whether my strict diet was responsible for the improvement or whether it was some other part of my lifestyle change that had helped, I had no idea. But I wasn't about to risk a relapse by re-introducing forbidden foods. Sure, I missed gummy bears and Cheetos, but if it meant my brain worked and I didn't have to spend my days in bed, I was willing to munch on chickpeas instead.

I'd just thrown a month's worth of lentils into my cart, when a tall, scruffy-looking man in a cowboy hat came around the corner of the aisle. He stopped in front of me, his gaze dipping to my hips before rising back to my face.

"Hey," he drawled, his voice a little slurred. "Well, hello there."

Oh, great. Cowboy Casanova was the last thing I needed.

Giving him a brief nod before fixing my gaze to the shelves, I tried to push my cart past him. Only I couldn't. My cart wouldn't move.

Startled, I glanced back at the man to find he was holding my cart in place. Then I caught the scent of cigarettes and alcohol. Maybe he'd been out drinking all night. Judging from his bleary gaze and slow blinks, he was probably less than sober.

"Lentils, huh?" Cowboy Casanova nodded at the food in my cart. "You're not one of them vegans, are you?" He pronounced it vaay-gaans, his slow drawl making the word extra long.

"Nope." I tried to back my cart up, but he was gripping it too tightly. And the only store employee I could see was a teenager who was smaller than me.

"Then why are you eating that tasteless shit?" Grabbing a packet of bacon-

and-cheese-flavored snacks from the shelf with his free hand, the man waved it under my nose. "Try this instead." He dropped it into my cart. "Thank me later."

I stared at the snacks sitting on top of the food I'd so carefully chosen, and for a moment, the injustice of it robbed me of speech. The snacks represented everything I'd stripped out of my diet. Sugar. Gluten. Sulfites. Preservatives. Parabens. Every additive that had even the smallest chance of causing inflammation or affecting my nervous system.

One thing about my new diet, my hair and nails were thick and healthy. My skin glowed, and I was slimmer than I'd been when I was eighteen. I looked like I could run a daily marathon, though I could barely climb a flight of stairs.

Cowboy Casanova's hair was lank and his skin greasy. He probably lived on candy bars and cheap whisky, while barely getting sick a day in his life. He could be falling-down drunk with a full beer in one hand and a cigarette in the other, and he'd still be able to run rings around me.

"Name's Timothy King." He leered at me. "That's right, I'm a King. You're talking to royalty, and you didn't even know it, baby."

I swallowed, realizing I was letting him hassle me without doing anything to stop it. What was wrong with me? Instead of letting my anxiety get the better of me, I should be getting angry.

Pulling myself together, I reached for my inner rage. "I'm not your baby," I snapped. "Please let go of my cart."

He blinked slowly, then grinned. "You've got a mouth on you. I like that."

"You know what I don't like? Being told what to eat by a stranger."

"Hey now, I'm not a stranger! I told you my name, now you tell me yours. It's only fair."

"My first name is *Let Go*. My last name is *Of My Cart*."

He laughed, which wasn't the reaction I'd been hoping for. I opened my mouth to tell him he was being a *royal* pain in my ass but was interrupted by the roar of motorcycles pulling up outside.

Cowboy Casanova glanced toward the entrance. "Sounds like we got company." He didn't look entirely happy about it.

As the motorcycle engines shut off, I gave him my meanest glare. "Let go of my cart, right the hell now."

"Baby, you need my help. That food you're buying? Ain't nobody can live off that."

"Leave me alone!"

Though I spat the words at him like poisoned darts, he didn't loosen his hold on my cart.

Three big, intimidating gang members wearing matching, patched leather jackets swaggered into the store. They seemed to be in the middle of a loud conversation. One of them—a long-haired, colorfully tattooed man—made what sounded like a rude remark. I didn't catch what he said, but the other two laughed in such a roaring, thigh-slapping, look-at-me type of way, it must have been something disgusting.

Worse, one of the men locked eyes with Cowboy Casanova, and then his gaze went to me while his grin grew wide and feral. It was the smile of a predator. A wolf that's seen an injured rabbit. He was older than Casanova, and wider, with a thick neck and large fists. Fresh grazes reddened his knuckles.

As he strode closer, my heart sank so low, it did a swan dive into the pool of stomach acid that was rising in my gut.

"Hey, Sledgehammer," Casanova called to the man. "How's it hanging?"

"Better by the minute." Sledgehammer called back, still smirking at me. "What have you found here, hiding in the aisles? You keeping that pretty little thing for yourself, or are you going to share her with your brothers?"

Oh, hell to the no!

I had to end this. *Now.*

CHAPTER 10

CARLA

Releasing my cart, I ducked past Casanova. He grabbed for me too late; I was already dodging into the next aisle as fast as my heavy legs could carry me. From there, I went for the door. A woman stared at me wide-eyed from behind the checkout, but I didn't stop to apologize for leaving behind a full cart of groceries, I just burst outside as though the scary bikers were chasing me. Which they might have been. I didn't look back to check.

I jogged for my car faster than I'd moved in years, dove into the driver's seat, and roared away, accelerating out of the parking lot and in the direction of home. I was gasping, fighting to breathe, and I had a sharp pain across my chest.

Worst of all, I was terrified my nervous system would react by crashing. If I ended up back in bed, unable to work for weeks or even months… "No, no, no!" I panted. "That's not going to happen. It won't. I'm okay. I won't crash. I'm fine."

I was shaking, and even after I reached the highway, it took a long time before I could convince myself I was safe. I checked my rearview mirror a dozen times to make sure no motorcycles were following me, and turned down a few side streets, just in case.

The farmhouse was a fair way from town, so I could put a big distance between me and the bikers. And it gave me time to control my emotions and try to calm down. By the time I got close, my heart monitor had stopped warning of my imminent demise, and my chest had loosened to the point where I was once again enjoying the sensation of being able to fill my lungs with air.

"You're okay," I told myself sternly. "Tiny mishap, but you're totally, absolutely fine. Nothing to get worked up about. No big deal."

I was a terrible liar.

Everything was ruined. How could I ever set foot in the Piggly Wiggly again? From now on, I'd have to live solely on what I produced. I'd fade away to nothing. Either that, or I'd have to find somewhere else to get my groceries. The thought only made me more anxious, and even as the shaking slowed and my nervous system calmed, an all-too-familiar heaviness was dragging down my limbs.

All I wanted was to retreat to my bedroom and rest. But when I pulled into my driveway, Noah's truck was already parked, so I had to pull in beside it. He was sitting in the sun on the stairs that led up to my front door, seemingly in no hurry to get to work.

"Noah freaking Malone," I groaned aloud. "Why do you have to be here to see me like this?"

Just *looking* at Noah made my pulse speed up. He was the last thing I needed right now. I should lie down, meditate, and regain my equilibrium, something that would be all but impossible with him around.

Noah was an equilibrium unbalancer. He was a shot of adrenaline. How could I moderate my heart rate when he could spike it so easily?

"Are you okay?" he asked as I got out of my car and walked toward him. His sexy Southern drawl held an edge of concern, though sprawled on the wooden steps with the sun highlighting his gorgeous face, he looked ready for a photo shoot.

I stopped in front of him. He was too much. Too hot. Too nice. I couldn't deal with this. With *him*.

"Yeah, Malone," I said curtly. "I'm dandy."

"Hey." He got up and caught my arm. "What is it?"

I tried to pull out of his grip, and to my horror, hot tears sprung up behind my eyes, trying to force their way out. Who was this weak, pitiful woman? A few years ago, I wouldn't have thought twice about dropping into the Piggly Wiggly. I would have elbowed creeps and Casanovas out of the way, laughed at thugs on motorcycles, and sauntered out with a cart full of whatever food I felt like eating. Once I'd been a powerhouse. I'd worked twenty hours a day, taken back-to-back meetings with the most influential investors in the business, and been convinced I was headed for the top.

My damn illness hadn't just stolen my energy and sapped my strength, it had taken my identity, stripping me of *everything* I used to be. Now all I could think of was how terrified I was of a relapse. How my stomach churned, my head hurt, and my limbs ached with fatigue. How much worse would it get? Would I even be able to get out of bed tomorrow? Had I just blown a year's worth of recovery?

"Nothing," I said, yanking free. "It's stupid." Hating myself, I marched to my front door, and searched my jacket pocket for my key. Noah didn't deserve to be treated like this, but I had to choose anger over fear. If I let fear win, it would swallow me whole.

I was fumbling with the key, dragging it out of my pocket with one hand while I swiped furiously at my eyes with the other, when he stepped up beside me.

"You want to talk about it?" he asked.

"Do I look like I want to talk about it?"

Dammit, why the hell couldn't my clumsy fingers fit my key into the lock?

"Then you must need a hug."

What?

The suggestion—made so easily as to seem almost normal—made more tears break through against my will.

I didn't want to stop my forward momentum to tell him he couldn't go around hugging people. I needed to get away from him so I could lie down.

But how long had it been since anyone had touched me?

Not since I'd been in Green Valley, for sure. And sometimes at night, I rolled onto my side with my eyes closed, imagining there was someone lying behind me, spooning me. I pretended a man's arm was draped over me, his breath warm against my neck.

I hadn't yet reached the point where I'd lie on my hand until it went numb so it would feel like a stranger's hand when I touched myself, but believe me, I wasn't far off.

"I barely know you." My voice wavered a little, and I lifted my chin, hating the vulnerability I heard and the fact those damn tears wouldn't stay behind my eyes where they belonged. "Who offers to hug someone who's practically a stranger? What, you think you're going to move in on me, is that it? You're making a sleazy pass?"

I finally managed to get the door open and stepped inside.

"Wrong." His voice was suddenly hard, like I'd finally managed to piss him off. "You've got it backward, Chuckles. I wasn't going to hug you for free. I was about to tell you how much I charge."

"You charge? For hugs?" My voice rose incredulously, and despite not wanting him to see how close I was to losing it, I spun to face him.

His expression wasn't just serious, it was angry. His brows were drawn together, and his mouth was tight. "It's five bucks for two minutes. Or I'll squeeze your arm for a dollar. That's a special I've got, but it's only for a limited time, so you'd better get it quick. The offer's expiring fast."

I shook my head, the threat of tears receding a little, like a tide reluctant to go out. "You'll squeeze my arm for a dollar?" He was so ridiculous, I had a sudden urge to laugh. Only I couldn't let myself do that. Laughter could too easily turn into sobbing.

He stepped into the hallway with me, closing the door behind us. Leaning his upper arm against the wall, he tilted his chin down, glowering at me. And dammit, even his *glowering* was hot.

"I'll squeeze your upper arm, forearm, or hand," he said. "Your choice. Same price for any location. But like I said, you'd better hurry. Special price is only valid for another minute, and an offer this cheap won't be available again anytime soon."

"Fine." I thrust my arm out, wanting to know if he'd actually squeeze it, or if he was just messing around.

He eyed my warm puffer jacket. "You won't feel anything over that."

Stripping off his own jacket, he hung it on one of the hooks beside the door before walking into the kitchen. I hung mine next to his and pulled off my thick hoodie for good measure. That left me in only a short-sleeved shirt, but I'd left the heat pump on, so the house was cozy.

When I went into the kitchen, he was standing next to the counter, waiting for me.

"Upper arm?" he asked.

"Whatever."

He wrapped his hand around my upper arm, on my bare skin below the sleeve of my shirt, and for some reason, I couldn't help jumping. It was weird how intense it felt to be touched after so long. His hand felt big, and his palm was warm.

At least his touch was distracting me, driving away my anger and frustration over my failed trip to the store.

But Noah was watching me too closely, his gaze too observant. I turned my head away, breathing out, trying to control my heart. Maybe the anger was receding, but my fear was still there. It was always there.

Noah tightened his grip on my arm, squeezing a little. "Nice bicep, Chuckles." His tone had lost its hard edge, and his frown had smoothed away. "I didn't know you worked out."

"Yeah," I managed to say with a hoarse voice. "I'm a badass, so don't mess with me."

I swallowed hard as he slid his hand down an inch, then back up. My voice had disappeared to a place deep in my throat where I couldn't quite get it out. Whenever I hugged myself, I knew how much pressure I was applying, how it would feel, what I was doing. But now, with Noah, I didn't know how he might move his hand. And though my heart was doing its normal tap dance, for once it didn't feel entirely bad.

"More pressure?" he asked. Without waiting for an answer, he squeezed a little harder and his up-and-down motions got longer, so he was rubbing from my upper arm to my elbow.

As much as I loved looking at him, I had to close my eyes as the sensation of being touched filled my senses. I was willing my muscles to relax and my heart to slow, but with my eyes closed, I became more aware of everything. Not just every nuance of his touch, like the way his pinkie had less pressure than his index finger, or the firm flat of his thumb. But also the fragrant scent of the potted herbs on the window sill, the faint aroma still lingering from the omelet I'd had for breakfast, and the low, barely-audible humming coming from the fridge and heat pump.

Mostly, though, I became acutely aware of the desperate longings I'd been suppressing all this time.

Touch was a vital part of good health, both mental and physical. After all the research I'd done, I knew that better than anyone. A human touch had the power to reduce cortisol, decrease pain, improve wellbeing. I'd tried to simulate the sensation, but it was only now I realized how inadequate those simulations had been.

Noah cleared his throat. "While we're talking about special deals, I'm willing to throw in a squeeze for your other arm at the same time, for just fifty cents more." As I opened my eyes, he lifted his left hand, palm up, as though offering it to me. "That's not even close to full price, and it's not something I'd usually discount, but my left hand's right here, and I hate to see resources wasted. May as well get something for it than let it slack off doing nothing."

His eyes were so green, they drew me into them. Like a hypnotist's eyes, they were mesmerizing. I was relieved his expression was still serious. He didn't look like he was mocking me or judging me. The slightest flicker of pity and I was ready to pull away. But he seemed like he was concentrating on what he was doing. As though rubbing my arm was a complicated procedure taking all his focus, and he was determined to do the best job possible.

"Okay." For some reason, I whispered my agreement. Maybe I wasn't sure I wanted him to hear it.

"Two arms for a buck fifty, then." His tone was brisk. "Hope you appreciate what a great deal you're getting." He lifted his left hand toward my arm but stopped just an inch away from touching me. "Wait. You don't have anything sharp you're planning to poke me with, do you? If you're prickly, I'll have to charge extra. I don't need any more injuries."

I gave a reluctant half-smile despite myself. "Nothing sharp."

His other hand settled on my arm. Now we were facing each other directly, although there was at least a foot between us. He rubbed both my upper arms gently, the motion soothing.

Noah smelled better than anyone who was here to repair a roof had any right to smell. He smelled like a pile of freshly folded laundry, only better. If that scent came from the detergent he used to wash his clothes, I had to find out what it was. I felt like a cat discovering cat nip. I wanted to rub my face against him, like how Freud sometimes rubbed against mine.

As self-conscious as I felt, I closed my eyes again to savor his aroma. From now on, whenever I lay alone at night imagining someone was with me, that's what I'd think of. At least Noah's smell would stay with me, if nothing else.

"Okay?" he asked, his tone gentle.

I flicked my eyes back open. "So if I take the hug, that's six fifty total?" My voice came out gruff. "Don't rip me off, Malone."

"Six dollars and fifty cents. I won't even add tax. Can't say fairer than that."

"Fine." I lifted my chin, daring him to laugh at me. "Then let's get this over with."

His arms slid around me. Holding me, he seemed even bigger than before. I felt wrapped up in his arms, completely surrounded by him. He pulled me against his chest, squeezing me tightly. I put my arms around his waist and pressed my cheek against the soft cotton of his shirt. Twisting my fingers into the back of his shirt, I clung to him. The cozy warmth of the house was nothing compared to the heat radiating from his body.

Like a switch flipping on, those damn tears I'd been holding in all sprang free at once. I tried to cry silently, without moving my body or wiping my eyes, or getting tears on his shirt. But my nose was running, and when his arms tightened even more, and he let out a soothing humming sound that made his chest vibrate, I figured he must know I was crying.

The strength drained from my weary legs, as though it was leaking out with my tears. I was conscious of his cheek against my hair. Of the firmness of his chest. Of his big arms pulling me in, holding me tight against him. He felt so good, I never wanted to move. So amazingly, wonderfully good, I'd be happy to stay in his arms forever.

But even as I wished it, I realized I'd let so much of my weight go, Noah was actually holding me up.

This was ludicrous. I'd collapsed into the arms of someone I barely knew. He might be sweet and kind, but he was still practically a stranger. And no matter how good-hearted Noah was, he had to think even less of me now than when I'd been snapping at him.

He felt sorry for me. That's why he was hugging me.

Ugh.

I was being weak.

I *hated* being weak.

Most of the time I couldn't help it. My own damn body kept failing me, not allowing me to be strong. That didn't mean I was willing to act so pitiful.

Sniffing back the last of my tears, I strengthened my legs to support my own weight. He loosened his grip, allowing me to pull back. There was a wet patch on the front of his shirt. My cheeks heated, and I turned my face down. I had to be red-eyed, puffy, and snotty.

"You want to tell me what happened?" he asked, his voice gentle.

I shook my head and moved toward the hallway, heading for my bedroom.

"Allergies." My voice sounded raw and hoarse. "Pollen in the air; it makes my nose run. Um, thanks for the… well, thanks. But I don't need anything else."

He cleared his throat. "If you don't have the six fifty in cash, I'll take some help unloading the drywall from the back of my truck."

I stopped, glancing back at him in surprise.

Though I must have looked terrible, he didn't flinch at the sight of my face. He just raised his eyebrows at me. His gaze was sharply assessing, as though he was conducting a visual check of my condition. "What do you say, Chuckles? A little help? Won't take long."

I went to the front door and cracked it open to look at his truck. He'd backed it up to the bottom of the porch steps. There was only one sheet of drywall on it, and three lengths of lumber. He could easily handle it by himself, and my fatigue made my limbs feel double the weight they normally did. Even the thought of dragging my butt to his truck and hefting wood around made me feel sick, and any more physical activity would make a serious crash more likely.

But even though he was clearly joking about the six fifty, I did still owe him *something* for the hug. And if I helped him, maybe we could forget about how I'd fallen apart, and he wouldn't think of me as quite so weak as I must seem.

Maybe that was even the reason he was asking me. Honestly, I wouldn't put it past him. Helping him might give me some dignity back, and maybe he'd realized that before I did.

Dragging in a steadying breath, I swiped a hand over my face to check I didn't have any obvious snot or tears clinging to me. "Carrying wood sounds like it'd be worth more than six fifty," I said, trying to sound like a tough business-woman even though my nose was still running, and I was trying not to sniff.

"Nope. It's worth six fifty exactly. You still have those gloves handy?"

I nodded.

"Then grab 'em, and come out to the truck." He grabbed his jacket as he went past me, back outside.

I took the time to blow my nose and splash some water on my face first, then fetched the gloves from my bedroom, giving my bed a longing look on the way. Freud was waiting for me there, and my heavy limbs ached to curl up with him.

When I pulled my jacket on and went outside, Noah was dropping the tailgate down for easy access to the wood.

"We'll just carry the drywall in," he said, taking one end of it. "I'll leave the rest out here so I can cut it to size before taking it inside."

I grabbed the other end of the drywall. It was big, but not too heavy, thank goodness. Despite how feeble I felt, we managed to get it off the truck and maneuver it inside. We carried it down the hallway and through the kitchen, carefully easing it around the sticking-out part of the counter.

When we finally leaned it against the wall of the living room, Noah made a show of dusting off his hands. "Guess we're even now."

"Lucky, because I never have any cash." I was breathless and tired, but amazingly, I found myself giving him a small smile. If making me feel less awkward about my breakdown had been his goal, it had worked. Focusing on getting the drywall inside undamaged had helped me push everything else out of my head, and my emotions were back under control. But my bones still ached, and I had an urgent and pressing need to be horizontal.

"You don't need any more help?" I asked.

"I believe I can handle it from here."

"Then I'm going to my room."

"You need anything?" His frown of concern was so sweet, my heart squeezed, and I realized I was longing—actually *longing*—for another hug.

I straightened my back and shook my head. "Thank you, but I'm okay."

Lying on my bed was a huge relief, especially because I could draw Freud close for a cuddle. But when I closed my eyes, I couldn't help replaying what had happened in the Piggly Wiggly.

How could I ever go back there? What if I ran into those bikers again? Even facing the staff would be an ordeal, seeing as I'd abandoned a full cart in one of the aisles.

But if I didn't go back, I wouldn't have any food. Now I was stuck in bed, unable to feed myself, and the worst part of the whole thing was my burning desire for Noah to put his arms around me again.

What the hell was I going to do?

I had no answers. The only thing I could do was pull the pillow over my face so I could let out a muffled scream.

CHAPTER 11

NOAH

I worked in the living room for the rest of the day. First, I finished cutting away the damaged part of the ceiling, making the hole into a neat square. Then I put up some new support beams, and finally, I screwed the replacement drywall into place. It was difficult doing all that on my own, especially holding up the drywall so I could attach it. The pressure made the wound on my forearm throb.

I could have knocked on Carla's door to ask for help, but I didn't want to disturb her if she was sleeping. Instead, I fashioned some bracing and managed to wedge the drywall so it stayed up long enough for me to secure it.

Whatever had happened to upset Carla that morning, it had clearly been bad. I'd had to force myself not to push her for answers, to coax her into talking about what it was that had made her cry. But if she wanted to talk about it, she'd do it of her own accord. She was fierce. Not just New York fierce, but *survivor* fierce.

It was obvious she'd been through a lot. When I'd googled chronic fatigue syndrome, I'd been overwhelmed with information. But one word had leapt out at me.

Incurable.

And when I'd read about some bad cases, I'd been so horrified, I'd had to stop scrolling and walk around for a while. There were people lying in dark, silent rooms because they couldn't stand any light or sound. People who couldn't feed themselves. Some had lost the ability to talk. The suicide rate was appalling.

That sucked so badly it made *me* want to start reading Carla's medical textbooks. No wonder she had them. She'd probably spent a lot of time searching for help.

I'd always had physical jobs. Stunt work, building a movie set, decorating cookies, restoring cars. I couldn't imagine what I'd do if my body stopped working the way I needed it to.

I'd just finished applying the joint compound to the drywall when I looked down to see Carla standing next to my ladder, inspecting my work on the ceiling.

"How does a stuntman know how to do that?" she asked.

She'd changed into a top with a scooped neck, and from above, the view was... Let's just say I had to force myself to descend before she noticed I was staring. From the ground, she was no less appealing. Her curves took my breath away. Her skin was golden brown and beautiful, and looked temptingly smooth.

After a few moments, I realized she was looking quizzically at me. I cleared my throat. Her eyes no longer looked puffy, and she'd fastened her hair back into a ponytail so it didn't hide her lovely face.

"What was your question again?" I asked, my mind blank.

"Shouldn't a stuntman only know how to fall through a roof, not fix one? How'd you learn to do that?"

"I looked it up on YouTube."

"Really?" She sounded surprised.

I grinned. "Not really."

She wrinkled her nose, but her eyes sparkled with amusement. "I already said you weren't funny."

"And you're still wrong about that. But to answer your question, it was just Momma and me when I was growing up, so I learned to fix things around the house. After I left school, I helped out at the local construction company for a while and learned a lot there."

She looked up. "Well, you did a great job."

"How are you feeling?"

"Better. Thank you."

"You've been sleeping?"

She nodded. "Freud was lying on me. He doesn't show his bossy side to strangers, but he's secretly a tyrant. He pins me down and then acts so cute, I can't disturb him by getting up."

"An alpha in the bedroom."

"You know the type?"

"I *am* the type."

She gave me a sideways look. "Well, there's some cat food in the kitchen. Help yourself if you're hungry."

I laughed. She had a quick wit, and it was refreshing not to be taken seriously. The last time I'd indulged in such easy banter with a woman was before Liam died, but with Carla it felt... well, *'safe'* wasn't the right word. *'Good'* would be a better one. No warning bells were going off in my head. Carla was trying not to grin back at me, but her eyes were glinting with humor.

"All that's left is to paint the ceiling," I said as I folded my ladder and put it in the corner of the room with my toolbox. "I'll come back tomorrow for that. Shouldn't take long."

"Noah." She hesitated, and when I glanced over, I saw she'd started fiddling with her fingers, twisting them together. "I have a favor to ask."

"A favor?" That had to be why she was fidgeting. She hadn't asked my momma for a single thing in over a year, so I figured she was fiercely independent. Seemed she'd rather twist her own fingers off than ask for something. And that fact alone made me want to say yes, before I'd even heard what she wanted.

"If I give you the money, would you be willing to get my groceries?" she asked in a rush. "There are some things I need, and in New York I'd just put in an order and the bags would be on my doorstep in an hour. Can you believe I can't get anyone to deliver to me here? They won't go just a few miles past their regular delivery area."

I frowned a little, trying to figure out why she was asking. Something had happened this morning to upset her, and I'd contained my burning desire to know more. But if someone in town had hurt her, I wanted to know who it was so I could make sure they'd never do it again.

"How have you been getting your groceries up until now?" I asked.

"I've been driving into town. But I don't want to do that anymore." Her cheeks were flushing as though it was something she was embarrassed to admit. "Wait." She went back into her bedroom and returned with a piece of paper. "Here."

It was a long list of groceries written out in the same precise handwriting I'd seen on her whiteboards. Every item on the list was identified with the brand name she wanted, as well as the packet size, so there'd be no room for mistakes.

I ran my gaze down the list, taking it all in. It was a long list, the kind you'd make if you were preparing to be snowed in. If I got everything on her list, she wouldn't need to shop again for a long time. Which was probably the point.

"Why are you giving me this?" I asked.

"I told you, because they won't deliver—"

"No, why don't you want to go yourself? Did something happen this morning?"

"Nothing I want to talk about." She tilted her chin up, her gaze direct.

I clenched my jaw, reluctantly accepting the fact she might never be willing to tell me who'd hurt her. "I'd like to help you. Only it might turn into a big deal."

She blinked. "Why?"

"This is a small town. And even though I've been gone a long time, I still know a lot of people, including being acquainted with the cashiers at the Piggly Wiggly. So if I were to walk in there and buy…" I glanced down at the list. "If I buy tampons, somebody will call my momma to gossip about it, and she'll assume…" I stopped short as I realized what I was saying.

Hot damn. I'd been slow to realize it, but this was the perfect plan.

My frown turned into a smile.

"When she hears about this, Momma will think we're a couple," I said in a rush. "Which means she'll stop pushing me at women. No more set-ups. And she'll think she's got what she wants, which will make her happy." I let out a laugh. "This is perfect, Sweet Carla. Not only will I pick up your tampons, but I'll throw in a jumbo-sized box of condoms too. Leave no room for doubt."

Carla's eyes widened and she shook her head. "I don't want to fool your mother." She held out her hand for her list. "Forget it. I changed my mind."

"No take-backs." I waved the list triumphantly out of her reach. "You're going to get every last thing you want. And not just two boxes of tampons, either. I'll pick you up a dozen."

"No *take-backs*? What are you, twelve?"

"I'll make sure I go to the Piggly Wiggly at their busiest time so plenty of people see me buying your groceries."

"Your mother can't be that bad?"

"My mother is the sweetest woman alive. She's also the most stubborn, and she won't let up until I'm dating someone from Green Valley. So if I pick up your groceries for you, you're it." Folding the list, I stuffed it into my jeans pocket. "Quid pro quo, Clarice."

"Clarice?"

"It's a quote from *Silence of the Lambs*. Don't tell me you haven't seen it?"

"No on both counts. I haven't seen the movie, and you can forget about your plan because I don't want to pretend we're dating."

"Then I sure hope you're not in urgent need of tampons."

She folded her arms. "Would you stop talking about tampons? I'm not going to pretend to date you, Malone!"

"All I want is one dinner, scheduled for Valentine's Day. That's two days before I'm leaving for Arizona, and I can use it to stop Momma from setting me up with anyone in the meantime. She's fixated on making sure I have a Valentine's date. If I tell her I have one, I'll get some peace."

"But I don't want to go anywhere."

"We don't have to leave the house," I made my tone cajoling. "We could do it right here in your living room. We can eat, maybe watch a movie. It doesn't have to be a big thing. I'll even eat salad."

"Why don't you just go on a real date with someone who actually wants to go?" She raked her gaze up and down my body, her brow furrowed as though she was taking a visual inventory of all my flaws. "There must be *one* other person in Green Valley who'll agree to eat with you?"

"I don't want a real date. This way I can stop my mother's shenanigans without complicating things." I held up my bandaged arm. "I'm only here to recuperate. Last thing I want is for Momma to fool anyone into thinking I might want to get married."

There was no point in telling Carla how careful I'd tried to be since Liam had gotten the wrong idea about me and his girlfriend. Since then, I'd been blunt about letting women know I was only interested in a fling, but not a relationship. But if Momma got to them first, putting all kinds of notions in their heads, it would make things uncomfortable.

Carla was still glowering at me, and I had to hand it to her, she was very good at glowering. Fierce *and* sexy. It was the perfect combination to make me weak at the knees. When I'd hugged her, her impenetrable armor had slipped just a little as she relaxed against me. Knowing she'd let me in had felt almost as good as her incredible curves pressing against me, and I hadn't been in any hurry to let her go.

And the fact she was so reluctant to date me that I had to resort to blackmail? Well, that only made her more perfect.

"How about I pay you to pick up my groceries and we forget about fooling your mother?" she said.

"Dinner and a movie. That's all I want. One date for Valentine's Day, then you never have to see me again. I'm not asking for much, and it's the only payment I'll take."

"I have a schedule. I always eat at six thirty, and I'm in bed by eight."

As I wasn't entirely foolhardy, I resisted the urge to crack a joke about being okay with us going to bed together at eight. "We can eat in front of the movie," I said instead. "What do you say, Chuckles? Why not help each other out?" I stuck out my hand, coaxing her to shake on it.

She frowned at my hand. When she drew in one of those long breaths as though she was getting stressed, I instantly felt guilty. Maybe my suggestion had upset her and would make her illness worse. My brilliant idea might have been the worst thing I could have done.

I was about to tell her to forget it, that I'd pick up her groceries without forcing an unwanted date on her, when she puffed her breath out.

"You have to promise to stop calling me *Chuckles*," she said. "And I won't watch *Silence of the Lambs*. No horror movies. I'll only watch something light."

"Agreed." I looked down at my outstretched hand.

"Fine." She slid her hand into mine and gave it the briefest of squeezes before letting go.

Yes! I wanted to fist pump but kept my face impassive. "Then the movie's your choice, Sweet Carla."

She stared at me for a long moment, and I just *knew* she was trying to come up with a movie I wouldn't like.

"*Bridget Jones's Diary*," she said finally.

"Great choice. I was hoping you'd pick one I haven't seen yet." I headed for the door, figuring I'd better quit while I was ahead. "See you tomorrow, and make sure you clear enough space in your cupboards for all the tampons I'll bring you."

CHAPTER 12

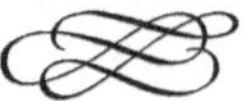

CARLA

- Sixteen days to Valentine's Day -

The video call connected, and Magdalena appeared on the big computer screen in my office.

My sister looked as pretty as always. Her features were more delicate than mine, her face more heart shaped. Her long hair framed her rosy cheeks in gentle waves. Somehow it always looked perfect, as though it styled itself. Her eyes were bright, and her innocent smile was deceptive.

If girls were supposed to be sugar and spice and all things nice, Magdalena had changed the recipe. She was trouble and strife and all things that made our mother switch to speaking Spanish so she could use more descriptive words to complain about her. An imp with the face of an angel. I couldn't help but love her.

"Hello, brat," I said with a smile.

She grinned back at me. "Hey, nerd."

"I was talking to Mom the other day, and she said you're going to be the death of her. Her words, not mine."

"What?" My sister widened her eyes. "I'm not bad, I'm misunderstood."

"What did you do this time?"

"Nothing. Mom has unreasonably high expectations of me. And that's your fault, for setting the bar too high."

I gave an exaggerated sigh, and my sister grinned. "How's your boring place in the country?" she asked, shifting around on her couch to get more comfortable. She had her phone propped up on the coffee table a short distance from her so I could see her whole body. Her knees were pulled up and she was hugging them, her bare feet on the couch cushions. She was wearing black leggings and an oversized t-shirt. I could see part of what looked like a band name on her shirt, though it wasn't one I'd heard of. Her toenails were painted black.

"It's perfect," I said. "Nice and boring. How's the big, bad city?"

"The same as always." She shrugged. "Maybe I should visit you. See some nature. I hear it's nice."

That turned my smile into an alarmed frown. "What's wrong, Mags?"

She wrinkled her nose, then waved a dismissive hand. "Nothing. Forget it. It's probably a terrible idea. Being stuck in the city can't be as bad as talking to cows, or whatever you do all day. Are there really no men there, or are you just too nerdy to meet any?"

I studied her, still frowning. Something had to be wrong for her to even consider leaving New York for a quiet place like Green Valley, but she clearly didn't want to tell me what it was. Maybe she was just missing our other sister, seeing as Josefina had gone off-grid for a while. Hopefully it wasn't something more serious.

If Mags didn't want to open up to me, it was my fault. All those years I'd spent working long hours, I'd often gone months without speaking to her. I'd let her drift away. The one good thing about getting sick had been reassessing my priorities and making sure we spoke regularly. Reconnecting with both my sisters was important to me.

So maybe I needed to open up to her first, and then she might feel comfortable sharing her problems with me.

"Speaking about what I do all day, I've got a problem," I said.

"Oh yeah? Are the cows starting to talk back?"

"My software's almost ready." I grabbed one of the pens from my desk to fiddle with. "I'm about to move into the beta-testing stage."

She frowned. "That's good though, isn't it?"

"Very good. More than a year of hard work, and I'm finally close to releasing it." I clicked the pen rapidly a few times. "Only, I went to the grocery store, and something happened that freaked me out. Now I'm not sure if I can go back there."

"You can't go to the store?"

"Or even into town. I'm anxious about the whole idea of ever leaving my house again. And that makes me feel like my world's getting smaller. What if my anxiety stops me from releasing my software?"

"Would it?"

"I can't release it without talking to investors, employing more programmers, all kinds of things. My old business partner has offered me an office so I can put a small team together. But I'm losing hope that I'll ever be well enough to do it."

Speaking my fears aloud made my chest feel tight. I didn't like being vulnerable and I hated being weak.

She tilted her head, considering my problem. "Well, if there's something you're good at, it's coming up with ways to fix things. You have to get over your anxiety. So how are you going to fix it?"

"I don't know. I could try more medication, I guess."

"I saw a movie the other day," she said. "It was kind of lame, but the main guy reminded me of you."

I blinked. "Why?"

"He had a problem. Like, he was stuck on the moon or something. And he said he was going to science the shit out of it. That made me think of you. When you have a problem, you usually math it, or program it, or whatever nerdy stuff you get off on." She waggled her fingers at me. "You know. Spreadsheets. Your favorite thing."

"Spreadsheets," I repeated slowly, a glimmer of an idea popping into my head. "You mean I should draw up an anxiety-reducing framework using a series of calibrated, accumulative outings in order to reduce my sensitivity to stress and increase my confidence?"

"That's what I said, isn't it?" She rolled her eyes. "Only try not to get too excited about it. I know how that stuff makes you spontaneously orgasm."

I grinned, wishing I could reach right through the screen to hug my sister. "You're so smart, Mags."

"I know."

"So what did you do to torment Mom this time?"

My sister shrugged. "I just like watching the smoke curl out of her ears when she's mad. Anyway, now I've done all the hard work and come up with your plan, what exactly are you going to do about it?"

"I'm thinking about asking someone to help me. He's been doing some work on the roof and—"

"*Wait.*" My sister sat up straight, dropping her feet to the floor and leaning toward the camera. "You met a guy? You mean, there are actual *men* in Tennessee? And you've been wasting all this time talking about your problems! Who is he? He doesn't play the banjo, does he? Or wrestle bears? Have you had sex yet?"

"No! Noah's just… a friend. Like I was trying to tell you, he's been fixing a hole in my ceiling."

She leaned even closer, letting her face fill the screen and exaggerating her excitement. "He's been filling your hole? Finally, you're getting some action!"

I groaned and laughed at the same time. "Stop. Please."

"His name's Noah, huh? Does he have a big ark?" She waggled her eyebrows suggestively.

"Let's get back to you visiting me," I said. "You know that if you need to get away, or to talk, I'm here for you? You can stay as long as you like."

She sat back. "Why would I want to go to the backend of nowhere? And anyway, I can't sit around talking to you all day, I've got things to do. I'll give you one more minute to tell me something about Noah. And make it juicy, okay? Don't waste any more of my time."

I scrunched my face. "He's going to turn up any moment to finish off the ceiling repair. I should go and formalize the plan so I can present it to him once he's done. I'll need to talk him into it."

"You're not even going to tell me what he looks like naked, are you?" She shook her head in disgust. "Fine. Go. See if I care."

"But if you ever want to talk—"

"Whatever," said my sister. "Go have sex." She disconnected the call.

By the time Noah arrived, I'd started working on a spreadsheet.

He was as cheerful as ever, hauling in bags of groceries like they were hunting trophies, and making me laugh with his clowning around. I helped bring the bags in, though I took it slow, only carrying one bag at a time, while he juggled four or five each trip and moved several times as fast.

When all the bags were out of his truck and crowding my counters and kitchen table, I started putting the groceries away. Noah helped, often asking me where to put things.

"You should have seen how folks were staring when I pushed two full carts up to the register," he said as he stacked cans in a cupboard. "My mother will have heard all about it by now."

"She might just think you were doing me a favor as a friend."

"Until I tell her we have a date for Valentine's Day."

I grimaced, making room on a shelf for packets of dried beans. "And you're sure you want to lie to her?"

"It'll make her happy."

"Only to be disappointed later."

"It'll give her hope. And everyone needs hope." As he turned to grab more cans, I was emptying the contents of the final bag. He flashed his gorgeous grin at me, and I felt myself melt. I couldn't argue with that smile. And besides, he was right about needing hope. I'd come to see it as the most essential part of my life.

"That looks like all the groceries." He took the last can out of my hand and put it in the cupboard with the rest. "Now I'll bring in the paint for the ceiling. I'll aim to be finished working here by this afternoon."

"Then I'll make us lunch. We can eat once you're done." He started to say something polite, to tell me I didn't need to, but I cut him off. "I insist."

He gave me another knee-weakening smile. "I accept."

As he went out to his truck to collect his materials, I sagged against the counter for a moment to let my knees regain their strength. Then I started assembling the ingredients for a feast.

Two hours later, Noah was finished with the ceiling, and I went into the living room to admire his handiwork.

"I'm impressed," I told him. "I can't even see where the hole was." As soon as the words were out of my mouth, I thought of my sister laughing about him filling my hole and felt myself blush.

"That's the idea," he said, giving me a quizzical look.

I fanned my burning cheeks. "Cooking lunch made my face hot," I lied. "Anyway, come and eat." I covered my embarrassment by leading the way into the kitchen. Our plates were on the kitchen island, piled up with food.

"Looks great," Noah said, sitting on one of the stools. "What is it?"

"My own version of Chilean empanadas, only I used buckwheat flour to make the pastry. And the salad is from my garden." I picked up one of the empanadas with my hands, nodding for him to do the same.

He took a bite. "Mmm," he said with his mouth full. Then he swallowed.

"That's good. Does it have raisins in it?" Lifting the empanada, he studied the beef filling.

I nodded. "And olives, and there's a hard-boiled egg in the middle."

"Wouldn't have thought those things would be so good together."

"I haven't eaten these for ages," I said, savoring the taste.

"Really? They're delicious. I'd have them every day."

"They take too long to make. When it's just me, I can't be bothered."

"You made these especially for me? I must be growing on you, huh?"

"Don't let it swell your head." I gave him a mock eye roll. "Oh, wait. Too late."

He grinned. "Anyway, how was your morning? Ready to tell me about your mysterious software?"

After hanging up from Mags, I'd spent some time working on my presentation. I was planning to hit him with it after lunch.

"Lately, I've been adding security measures to my software so it can't be hacked," I told him. "The core features are mostly done, so now I'm focusing on all the fiddly things that'll keep it stable and working the way it should."

"Is your software something people will want to hack?" He raised his eyebrows. "That makes me even more curious."

"Not really, but hackers try to get into everything. That's the nature of the internet." I picked up my glass of water to take a sip.

"I once did some stunts for a movie about a kid who accidentally hacked into the Pentagon."

A little water went down the wrong way. I coughed and thumped my hand against my chest. "A kid *accidentally* hacked into one of most secure buildings in the world?" I spluttered.

"I didn't say it was a good movie."

"I can't watch movies about hackers. They usually get too many things wrong."

"What kind of movies do you like, then? Not horror movies, and nothing with hackers? What's left?"

I thought about it for a moment, trying to remember what I'd seen lately. "Honestly, for years I was too busy working to watch movies. Now I've lost my taste for anything scary or violent or sad. I only like movies that make me laugh."

"*Bridget Jones*," he said with a nod, not sounding in the least bit judgmental.

"What about you?" I asked. "Favorite movie?"

He widened his eyes, acting shocked. "Do you have any idea how many movies I've seen or done stunts for? I can't pick just one."

"Well, which was the first movie you thought of when I asked?" When he still hesitated, I added, "Just tell me one. I won't ask you to chisel it into a stone tablet."

"One did flash through my mind. It's called *Life is Beautiful*. Have you seen it?"

"No, but I like the name. Sounds like my type of picture. Did you work on it?"

He shook his head. "It's an Italian movie, quite old. It's about a man trying to keep his son alive in a Nazi concentration camp."

"Oh no!" I recoiled in horror, putting down what was left of my empanada and wiping my hands on my napkin. "That sounds terrible."

"It kind of is," he agreed with a shrug. "It starts off with the main character—Guido—wooing his wife. They have a son, and they're blissfully happy. Then they get sent to Auschwitz and go through hell."

"What exactly do you like about it?" I asked.

"Guido convinces his little boy that life in the concentration camp is only a game. Terrible things happen, but he keeps pretending war is fun. He makes it into a competition to keep them alive. The movie's sad, but it's hopeful. Tragic, but hilarious. It's harrowing and beautiful at the same time."

"Wow." I blinked at him, touched by his description. "Harrowing and beautiful. Sounds like real life."

He nodded, his expression serious. "I laughed and I cried. And I mean proper crying, not just a tear or two. Then I was laughing again, even though it was horrifying. The worst things you can imagine were happening, but Guido managed to make them funny."

I wanted to reach out and hold his hand. My heart had melted into goo, and my ovaries weren't far behind. How many guys would admit a movie made them cry like that?

"The way you describe it makes me want to see it," I said.

He shook his head. "Good try, but you already promised we could watch *Bridget Jones's Diary*. You can't dangle something so tempting in front of me, then change your mind."

He said it in such a deadpan way, it took me a moment to register the twinkle in his eye.

"You'll like *Bridget Jones*, even if it's not so harrowing," I said. "Though in one scene, she gets caught wearing a pair of enormous high-waisted panties. That'll probably make us both sob."

He grinned, finishing his salad and putting his knife and fork together on his empty plate. "Can't wait. And lunch was delicious. I don't usually eat so much green stuff, but now I feel healthy. Like Popeye after he's chugged some spinach." Leaning back on his stool, he flexed one arm. "My bicep looks bigger now, right?"

While working on the ceiling, he'd stripped down to a t-shirt, and his short sleeve strained around the top bulge of his bicep. The rest of his bicep was on full, erotic display. Smooth skin and impressive muscle. Yum.

My throat went dry. Other parts of me… didn't.

"Um," I rasped. "I'm not sure if it's any bigger. Let me get my microscope."

His grin widened, as though I hadn't disappointed him. "You can cook for me anytime, Chuckles."

"Well, I had an ulterior motive." I was able to clear my throat and sound a little more normal now that he'd stopped flexing his muscles. "I have another favor to ask you."

"You need help with something?"

"Yes, but it'll take some explaining." I forced my limbs into action. "Will you come to my office so I can show you?"

He raised his eyebrows and got up. "I'm intrigued."

I led him into my office and pulled a chair around to the far side of my desk, moving my laptop so he could see the screen. "Please sit down." I motioned to the chair.

"What about you?"

"I'll grab the other chair."

He still looked disinclined to sit, so I gave him a little push, urging him into the seat. It would help with my nerves if he wasn't so big and tall, taking up so much room with all his masculine energy and ridiculous muscles. And I didn't want the tempting smoothness of his neck at eye level where it could distract me.

Problem was, even sitting, my office still seemed full of masculine energy and muscles. Noah didn't sit in the chair so much as lounge in it, one leg straight and the other bent, his knee carelessly splayed. He rested both elbows on the chair's armrests and let his gaze linger on my whiteboards.

"Your office is like the set of a movie about Stephen Hawking," he said. "Or that movie about the genius code breaker. What was it called again?"

He was clearly trying to figure out what I was working on, and it had the potential to distract him from my presentation, the same way his body taking possession of the chair was distracting me.

"First I'll tell you about my software," I said. "It's an app that's designed to crowd-source information about illnesses like mine."

"Crowdsourcing?" he interrupted. "That's when you get a lot of people doing something?"

I nodded. "You've noticed I wear a smartwatch and a smart ring?"

He looked at the silver band I wore on my middle finger. "Is that what that is?"

"The ring tracks my blood oxygen, glucose, stress levels, blood pressure, all kinds of things. My watch monitors my heart rate and sleeping patterns. The data gets uploaded into the app I've written."

"So you get a record of your health over time?"

"Exactly. Also, I can use the app to record my daily status, the food I'm eating, medications, and symptoms. Having a record makes it easier to try different treatments and see if anything helps." I opened the app on my laptop so he could see what it looked like. "The software uses all the data to analyze trends. Let's say I decided to lower the dose of one of my meds and it improved my sleep pattern, the app would let me know. If a thousand people are using the app, and the same pattern happens for some of them, it can show that. So when the next person is wondering whether they should lower their dose, they can see forty percent of people slept better. But they can also see sixty-five percent had increased brain fog. Negative effects get flagged to make the risks more visible."

He frowned at the screen. "Isn't that what your doctor does?"

"This isn't meant to replace doctors, but it's hard to find a doctor who knows much about ME. So there are millions of people out there trying anything and everything to improve their symptoms. Medications, dietary changes, acupuncture, glucose injections, nerve stimulation, fecal transplants, alternative therapies, you name it."

"Fecal transplants?"

I shrugged. "When nobody can give you answers, you get desperate. And if someone on one of the forums says a treatment worked for them, everyone tries it. A couple of years ago, people were ingesting hookworm larvae."

"Hookworm...what?"

"It's not a recognized treatment, so not much information was available. You can buy the larvae online, but nobody seemed sure how many parasites they should take, or what side effects were likely."

He screwed up his face. "People ate *parasites*? On purpose?"

I waved a hand to bring his focus back to my app. "A centralized database would collect real-world data. You could get the skinny before swallowing the worms." It was a feeble attempt at a joke, and he didn't do more than blink at me. "Anyway, I know my software will help people, and I'm not looking to make a profit. I just need it to exist. If I can't cure anyone, at least I can give them data to help them make sensible decisions."

"Okay." Thankfully, he dropped the grossed-out look. "It sounds like a great idea. I mean, really impressive. But how do you want me to help?"

"I've put together a presentation to explain that part." I leaned closer to the laptop so I could pull it up.

"You…?" He blinked rapidly. "A presentation? What, with slides?"

He sounded like he thought I'd gone overboard, but I was too busy getting it set up to respond. Besides, there was no such thing as being *too* prepared.

"Is there a handout?" His lips were twitching like he was trying not to laugh.

"Shush. I'm starting." I leaned back a little so he could see the screen. "This is a sample of my daily log," I explained, pointing to a chart that was covered in different colors. "Here's where I record my physical symptoms. Fatigue. Nausea. Pain. Dizziness. Brain fog." I clicked the arrow key to move to the next slide. "This is from a year ago. See how the colors were mainly reds? Red is bad. But this slide shows how as time progressed, the colors shifted to mainly oranges, yellows, and even a few greens. Green is the best color. It means no significant symptoms. And, I mean, there are dips, but you can see the overall trend, can't you?"

He nodded, leaning forward to peer more closely at the screen. "You've been getting better. That day was all green." He pointed.

"A unicorn day. Those are the best." I clicked to the next slide. "This is the same sample, only with an extra column to show my anxiety." I clicked again to display the difference from a year ago versus now. "This column is the inverse of the others. The color trend runs the opposite way."

He frowned. "Your other symptoms have gotten better, but your anxiety has gotten worse."

"Exactly. Because I've shut myself away."

"And that's what you need my help with?" His gaze went to my face. His eyes were very green—the best color—and they seemed more alive than most. I'd never believed you could tell how smart someone was by looking into their eyes, but his held an extra spark that made them hard to look away from. Maybe he'd gained some extra awareness as a result of having such a dangerous job. Maybe it was a stuntman superpower. I couldn't tell, as I didn't have any other stuntmen to compare him to.

I nodded wordlessly, too absorbed in his gaze to speak. But when he raised his eyebrows, prompting me to continue, I pulled myself back together.

"I have an office waiting for me in New York," I said, clearing my throat. "I need to set my business up as a non-profit, talk to investors, and employ more programmers. And to be able to do any of that, I need to start easing myself back into the world." I clicked to the next slide in the presentation. It showed a simple graph, with a series of locations on the Y axis, and days of the week on the X axis. "I'd like to start with small, non-challenging activities, and slowly progress to harder challenges."

He leaned forward even more, squinting at the small font. "Those are things you want to do? *Town visit. Entrance into casual eatery. Seated in dining area. Interaction with a server. Talk to a stranger...* What exactly are you suggesting?"

"I'm saying that instead of having a single dinner at my place, I want us to commit to a longer, more public arrangement. One that will satisfy your mother and help me control my anxiety."

He brought his gorgeous eyes back to mine, his surprise clear. "You want me to take you out?"

"Exactly. Once you agree in principle, we can firm up the schedule."

He stared at me without speaking for a moment. I'd expected him to be enthusiastic about diverting his mother's attention for a longer period, but his expression had turned wary, and he seemed to be mulling over a response. Probably coming up with a way to refuse my request without hurting my feelings.

"We won't really be dating," I clarified. "It'll be a short series of outings so I can get used to being around people again."

"But why do you even need me?" He motioned to the screen. "You can do this on your own."

I shook my head. For someone who rolled cars for a living, it must be unimaginable that I might be too cowardly to walk into a coffee shop. But at least if he was with me, I wouldn't be able to cut and run.

"It could make my symptoms worse if I had a bad experience while I was out. Like if I ran into... the wrong people." I shifted in my chair. "I don't want to risk it."

His brows knitted together. "Is that what happened while you were out yesterday? You ran into the wrong people?"

I should have known he'd guess. I'd been right about that spark in his eyes.

With a sigh, I nodded. "There was an incident with some bikers. I was targeted because I looked weak. But if I'd had someone with me, they might have thought twice."

His jaw tightened and a flash of anger crossed his face. If it had been directed at me, it would have been scary. But he was angry with the bikers, and a small, secret thrill ran down my spine at having caused such a look.

Ugh.

How corny to be aroused by a display of male protectiveness. Sometimes human biology was so primitive it was embarrassing.

"Anyway," I said quickly. "As I said, these dates won't be real. All I want is someone by my side so I don't have to worry about being hassled."

His jaw was still hard, and his eyes held an assessing look. While he studied my face, I wasn't sure if he was evaluating whether he could turn me down, or if he was still upset about the bikers.

"You're sure you won't want anything more from me?" he asked. "If we start going places together, you won't start having feelings?"

I wasn't sure whether he was joking, so I gave a small laugh just in case. "Of course not. I mean, we couldn't be more different, could we?"

Tomas hadn't been able to handle my illness, and compared to Noah, he'd been a dull homebody. Noah was wild and full of life. He had at least ten times more energy than Tomas. The idea Noah and I could ever be suited was ludicrous. Besides, I couldn't risk falling for anyone when I'd put so much work into stabilizing my fragile nervous system. Protecting myself from anything that could upset that balance was vital. Better to be alone than bedridden.

"I want us to be clear." Noah shifted his weight, leaning on the other elbow to angle his body toward me. "I'm all for having fun. Fun is my favorite pastime, and fun with a beautiful woman is even better. But I'm not looking for anything more."

The *beautiful woman* part caused another of those secret shivers to run down my spine. He thought I was beautiful?

Instead of letting out the smile that had formed inside me at the idea, I forced my mind back to more important matters. "You won't have to worry about that," I assured him. "I was engaged once. He broke it off because of my illness. I can't go through anything like that again."

Noah frowned. "Are you telling me you were engaged, and your fiancé left because you got sick?"

"We both agreed we should end it. It was getting too hard to stay together."

"Why was it hard?"

I hadn't intended to talk about my failed engagement. But now we *were* talking about it, it was probably a good thing. At least it would make things clear.

"By the time Tomas left, I hadn't gone anywhere for months," I said. "Not to lunch or dinner, not to see friends, or to a movie. Nothing."

"But you were *engaged*." Noah's frown hadn't eased. "Committed. What, did he think the wedding vows should be, 'In sickness and in health, except if you don't feel well enough to go to a restaurant, in which case I'm out of here?'"

"Tomas was working all day while I lay in bed. My fatigue was worse back then. I couldn't cook a meal or do much around the house."

Noah shook his head as though he still didn't understand.

"Anyway," I said. "The point is, even though it was a mutual decision to end the relationship, it was still painful, and I'm not doing it again."

Saying 'it was painful' was wildly understating what I'd gone through. I'd still been grieving for my former life. Losing Tomas as well had been a devastating double blow. But at the same time, I couldn't blame him for leaving. My illness had been holding him back.

"It was selfish of him to give up on you." Noah's frown was so deep, it made him look different. More severe. Still blindingly handsome, but in a darker way.

"Don't look so upset," I said. "I only wanted you to understand why I can't date anyone for real. You're cute, but I can't have that kind of relationship—"

"Cute?" He blinked at the word. But at least his frown was easing.

"You don't like the word cute?" I asked. "It's a compliment."

"It'd be a compliment if I were a puppy."

"What description would you prefer? Alluring? Enchanting? Beguiling?"

"*Enchanting* works for me. Let's run with that." His good humor was back. It was amazing how effortlessly it returned. What would it be like to always be so lighthearted?

"Okay, Mr. Enchanting. Will you help me?"

He nodded. "If you're sure you'll be able to resist falling for me, even considering how *cute* I am, then I'm in."

CHAPTER 13

NOAH

- Fourteen days to Valentine's Day -

"Your momma was right, Noah," said Joy in an impressed tone. "You're skilled with your hands."

I glanced up from piping a heart shape onto a cupcake and grimaced. "I can't believe she keeps saying that."

"She told every woman in the bakery." Joy placed another full tray of cupcakes on the counter.

"Yesterday, I told Momma I was officially dating Carla," I confided. "Momma immediately called her and insisted she come for lunch this week. She probably wants to measure her for a wedding dress and slip her some fertility drugs."

"You're dating someone?" Joy beamed at me. "Congratulations!" She seemed genuinely delighted, as though the happiness of everyone around her was her main concern. It was my first morning working at the bakery, and from the moment she'd arrived, Joy had been living up to her name.

She planted both elbows on the counter next to the cupcakes and made a show of leaning in to hear more. "So… who's Carla? How'd you meet her? Tell me everything."

"I can't talk while I decorate these cakes. It takes concentration." I kept my gaze on my work, keeping even pressure on the piping bag to make sure every heart shape was perfect.

"You don't want to tell me?"

"You want these to be broken hearts instead of whole ones?" I nodded down at the cupcakes. Truth was, I was proud of how professional they looked, especially considering it had been several years since I'd last decorated a cake. Tomorrow, I might get creative and start adding a few flourishes. Making up my own Valentine-themed decorations would be fun.

"Okay," she said. "Then just tell me one thing and I'll leave you alone."

"Joy…"

"Just one thing. Then I'll stop bugging you, I promise."

I sighed. "Okay, I'll tell you one thing. What do you want to know?"

"How much do you like her?"

I jerked my gaze to her and accidentally turned the heart I'd just piped into a penis. "Shit!"

"Scale of one to ten."

Eleven, I thought, putting the piping bag down and picking up a palette knife to perform a cupcake castration. Then I hesitated. All this time, I'd been wary of giving any woman the wrong idea. Did I like Carla so much because it was so much easier not to have to worry about that?

But no, it was more than that. The presentation she'd given me had knocked me out. Not just how impressive her software was, but the reasons she needed me had triggered every one of my protective instincts. Admittedly, those instincts had been finely honed after my daddy died and I'd helped Momma pick up the pieces and carry on. Still, Carla had blindsided me, and I wasn't sure what to think about it.

"It's too early to tell," I said. "We haven't even had our first date yet."

"You're officially dating, but you haven't had a date yet?" Joy's brow creased.

"Yup."

"Where are you taking her?"

"The Piggly Wiggly."

She looked even more confused. "Not really?"

"I'll do two interlocking hearts on this one," I said. "It'll hide the amputation scar."

"You're not going to tell me, are you?"

"Joy, I can't talk and shape non-phallic hearts at the same time."

She shot me an annoyed look, but at least she let me work.

* * *

When Carla opened her door that afternoon, her hair was tied back in a ponytail, and she wore a blue top that showed off her sensational curves. Her jeans looked a little too loose, but she had a belt to hold them up. I could tell she was nervous by the worried furrow on her brow, and the way she ran her palms over her jeans as though wiping off perspiration.

She stood back to let me come in, and when I stepped past her, she said, "You smell like fresh baking."

"I came straight from the bakery. Probably should have stopped at home to take another shower."

"No!" She almost shouted the word, then flushed, seemingly embarrassed by her own enthusiasm. "I mean, you smell nice."

I managed to keep a straight face, but only just. "Sorry about Momma inviting you to lunch," I said. "Once she gets an idea in her head, she can't be talked out of it."

She grimaced. "Your mother's so sweet, I couldn't say no. But fooling her to her face wasn't part of our deal. Like I said, I don't want to lie to her."

"Don't think of it as lying. Think of it as making her happy."

"Well, I've added the lunch to my spreadsheet." She sounded resigned. "I'll give you an updated copy of our outings. Do you prefer a digital format, or a printout?"

"A printout." I tried not to smile. It obviously helped her to have a formal plan. And it might even stop her from chickening out of our dates, which was important, seeing as we really were about to go to the Piggly Wiggly. After agreeing to her scheme, I'd talked her into making our first date a shopping trip. She needed to overcome her fear so that when I left town, she'd be able to buy her groceries.

"I'll get it." She went into her office and emerged with a piece of paper, which she handed to me.

31 Jan: Buy something from the Piggly Wiggly.

   2 Feb: Go to a casual eatery at a quiet time. Sit in the dining area.

4 Feb: Lunch at Mrs. Malone's house.
6 Feb: Stroll down the main street. Ask a stranger for directions.
8 Feb: Attend a public event. (Cinema, concert, play, etc).
10 Feb: Initiate a conversation with a stranger.
12 Feb: Go to a busy bar or restaurant for dinner.
14 Feb: Movie night – Bridget Jones's Diary

"I shuffled things around to add the extra lunch," she said. "If any of those dates aren't okay—"

"They're fine. The day we have lunch with Momma, I'll finish early at the bakery. Everything else we can do after work."

"If my symptoms dip below orange in the next two weeks, we may have to skip one or more of those tasks. Hopefully they won't." She was pulling on a jacket as she spoke, then added a scarf for good measure. Grabbing her phone off the hall table, she gave me a determined smile. "Are you ready for our first date?"

"That's all you're taking with you?" I folded the schedule and stuffed it into my pocket. "Just your phone?"

"What else do I need?"

"Nothing." I offered her my arm. "Don't worry, I'll look after you."

"Who says I need looking after?" But she slid her hand around my elbow with a relieved look that did something strange to my chest, making it feel like it was both expanding and contracting at the same time.

Once we were in my truck heading for town, Carla kept rubbing her palms up and down the tops of her thighs as though she was nervous, so I attempted to keep her mind off where we were going.

"When I told Momma we were dating, she sang an entire chorus of that 'Hallelujah' song," I said.

"She did?"

"Okay, that's a small exaggeration," I admitted. "But she smiled a lot."

"Why is she so set on you dating someone?"

"She wants grandbabies. And once Momma's got her mind set on something, there's never been anyone more stubborn."

Carla nodded. She glanced out the side window, then nibbled on one of her fingernails for a moment, before scrunching both hands into fists. Then she reached for the radio knob. Turning it did nothing. My truck was quirky that way.

"You want to listen to something?" I asked. "There's a way to hit it that makes it work."

She shook her head. "It's okay. Just fidgeting."

"When I was twelve, Momma thought I should learn to play the banjo," I said. "I went along with it at first, thinking it might be fun. So she bought me a banjo and paid a friend's nineteen-year-old son to teach me. Every Tuesday after school, I was supposed to go to Pete Hodge's house for a banjo lesson."

"Did you learn how to play?" Carla turned curious brown eyes to me.

I shook my head. "Turned out that learning the banjo was less fun than it sounded. I convinced Pete that if he kept Momma's money and didn't rat me out, he could go to his girlfriend's place while I went to the skate park. I learned all kinds of flips and slides and tricks. But what I didn't learn was the banjo."

"Did your mother find out?"

"Not for a whole year."

"Was she angry?"

"Furious. Pete sure did end up regretting that he went along with my plan." I let out a low whistle, shaking my head to convey the magnitude of Pete's remorse. "As for me, she decided to teach me a lesson I'd never forget."

"What did she do?"

"Momma signed me up to play the banjo at the Friday night jam session at the Community Center." I gave her a look that underscored how horrifying that was. "Green Valley is well known for its jam sessions. Everyone goes along, and the standard is high. They even have famous people perform there."

Her lips twitched. "Then you had to apologize?"

"Oh, you have no idea how much I apologized. But Momma wouldn't let me out of it. She said I had to perform anyway."

"Did you play?"

"I kept begging her to let me off the hook. I played the banjo for her to demonstrate how bad I was. I had no idea where to put my fingers on the strings or how to do anything but randomly strum and pluck."

She winched. "That sounds terrible."

"The worst sound you can imagine."

"Your mother didn't relent?"

I shook my head. "My banjo solo was the most embarrassing three minutes of my life. Only it wasn't just me, but the entire town who had to suffer through it. Momma was so set on teaching me a lesson, she was willing to punish everyone."

Carla finally gave me a smile, flashing me her tiny, cute dimples. They were more the suggestion of dimples than the real thing. As though she'd started to get dimples and changed her mind before they could be properly pressed in.

"That's how stubborn my Momma is," I said. "And if she'd been in charge of going up the mountain to bring down the ten commandments, she would have slipped in a few of her own. Instead of *Thou shalt not kill*, it would have been *Thou shalt give thy momma grandbabies*."

Carla smile widened. Her dimples didn't get any deeper, they only got cuter. Causing them to appear could be a highly addictive goal.

"When are you going to start having babies?" she asked.

"Not anytime near as soon as she'd like."

"You're not worried about breaking your poor mother's heart?"

"She has plenty of friends with grandbabies. She can volunteer to babysit them instead."

Carla nodded. She was silent for a minute, gazing out of the window as I drove. Then she asked, "Is driving like this boring for you? Going slowly on all four wheels?"

"It's not boring. It's normal."

"What's it like when you do a stunt? Do you get scared?"

I shook my head. "I used up all my fear when I was younger. Whatever it is that makes people scared, I ran out of it."

"But you could die."

"It's a possibility."

"Why do you do it?"

I shrugged.

"You don't know why you keep risking your life?" She'd started rubbing her palms up and down her thighs again, as though she couldn't be still. She was going to wear holes in her jeans.

"I've been mentoring a kid," I said. "His name's Brash, and he's always pushing himself past his limit, doing things he hasn't trained for. First time doing a high fall, he jumped sixty feet. No easing into it, practicing with lower jumps first. He went straight up to the top of the ladder."

"Fearless?"

"Completely. In my line of work, that's mostly a good thing. He'll go a long way, *if* he doesn't kill himself first. And you may not believe this, but I'm the sensible one who holds him back." I shot her a rueful look. "Get this, he calls me Grandpa."

She laughed. "You're right, I don't believe it."

"Maybe I'm not as brave as you think."

"Braver than me. I don't need to be in a rolling car to have a pounding heart and sweaty hands." She lifted her palms to show me.

"It was bad luck you ran into trouble at the Piggly Wiggly last time," I said, trying to soothe her. "You'll be safe this time, so don't be nervous."

"If anxiety could be cured with logic, life would be so much easier. But sometimes I'm not even worried about anything when my gut starts churning. My body decides I'm anxious before my brain does."

"Is that part of your illness?" I asked.

She shrugged. "I've seen dozens of doctors, and nobody seems able to tell me anything for sure. The human body's a complicated thing. Everyone's different."

There was silence for a while after that. I was mulling over what she'd told me while she stared out of the side window. I was struck by how she thought her brain worked differently than other people's, and how mine did too, only in the opposite way. It was something I didn't usually talk about, but I found myself wanting to share my experience, so she'd know I had some understanding of what she'd been going through.

"When I was twenty-one, my friend Liam died in a car crash," I said abruptly, when we were almost at the Piggly Wiggly. "I was in the car with him when it happened. And afterward, it was like I couldn't feel anything. My whole system was numb."

"I'm sorry." She turned to face me, and I was struck by how pale she looked. While I'd been mulling over my reaction to Liam's death, she'd clearly been fretting about where we were going.

I shouldn't have let the silence go on like that. I'd been focusing on entirely the wrong thing.

"That was when I started doing stunts." I carried on with my story. "I think I was trying to scare myself. To force myself to start feeling things again."

"How did you get the job?"

"There was a movie being shot in Cades Cove." I paused for a moment, considering whether to tell her it was the first movie Sienna Diaz had shot in these parts, and decided against mentioning her cousin. "I got some work on the set as a handyman, and I happened to make friends with the stunt team. After

Liam died, I told the stunt coordinator I wanted to get away from Green Valley, and he offered to train me and give me some work in LA. I'd always been a good driver, and I'd won my share of dirt races at The Canyon—that's a racetrack an hour or so out of town—so I didn't think too hard about it."

"You said you don't get afraid when you do stunts. So if you were trying to feel fear again, it didn't work?"

Turning my truck into the Piggly Wiggly's parking lot, I offered her a rueful smile. "Not completely. But after I broke some bones, some of the numb feeling wore off."

Her lovely eyes widened. If I'd made a mistake letting her sit in silence before, at least I was managing to distract her now.

"How many bones have you broken?" she asked.

"Guess."

"Four."

"Not even close."

"Really? A lot more than four? How many?"

Instead of answering, I pulled into a parking spot. "Here we are."

She dragged in one of those long breaths that seemed to take forever. "Well. Here goes."

Inside the Piggly Wiggly, the store was brightly lit and half-full of shoppers. I hesitated inside the front doors when I spotted Karen Smith selecting cheese from the refrigerated section. When I'd lived in Green Valley, she'd been one of the town's biggest gossips. Carla's spreadsheet had listed 'talking to a stranger' as a challenge she didn't want to face until later, so hopefully Karen wouldn't feel the urge to say hello.

Carla stopped next to me, scanning the store and chewing on her lip. Probably checking for bikers.

"I didn't see any motorbikes outside," I said, reaching over to grab a basket. "Come on, let's buy something."

She nodded. "I could get more herbs."

"Back of the store."

She took the basket from me and went to find them, while I made sure Karen Smith was still distracted by cheese. I was just about to follow Carla when I heard a female voice. "Noah? Is that you?"

Turning, I saw an attractive woman approaching from the direction of the registers. She was tall and lean, wearing a pink coat over jeans, with a white handbag slung over her shoulder. Though I hadn't seen Mandy in well over a decade, I recognized her right away. She'd had a crush on me in high school and had made no secret of it. Her enthusiasm had made me uncomfortable. My friends had called me foolish for keeping her at arm's length when she'd been so eager for more. But at that age, I hadn't only been interested in girls, but also painting, and sports, and cars, and a dozen other things. Mandy had only seemed interested in… well, me.

"Noah, that is you!" she exclaimed.

"Hi, Mandy." I looked down the aisles for Carla, but she'd disappeared.

"I was hoping I'd see you." Mandy tucked her long, blonde hair behind one ear, stepping close enough to intrude into my personal space. She'd always been a close talker. And a toucher. As I remembered that fact, she reached out one hand and rested it on my sleeve.

Unfortunately, a quick glance down confirmed that none of the rings she was wearing looked like an engagement or wedding ring.

"Your momma called to tell me you were in town, and we had a strange conversation," Mandy said. "We were talking about how you'd been away for too long, and then she said you were skilled with your hands."

I groaned. "She didn't."

"Your momma mentioned you don't have plans for Valentine's Day. And neither do I." Mandy's hopeful smile brought back memories of dodging around corners at high school whenever I saw her coming.

"I've met someone," I said. "We're dating."

Carla came into view near the end of one of the aisles. She kept her back to us, but by the way she was intently studying a rack of candy, I was pretty sure she was listening to our conversation. Hopefully it wasn't making her more anxious.

"You haven't! Not really?" A car horn honked from outside and Mandy glanced toward the parking lot, pulling a face. "That's my brother honking. He's so impatient!"

"You should go before he breaks the horn."

She screwed up her nose, giving my arm a squeeze. "I guess so. I wanted to hear all about what you've been up to. And how's your arm healing? Your momma said you'd cut yourself, but the wound wasn't too deep this time."

"It's fine."

"When did you meet someone? It can't be serious, seeing as I only spoke to your momma a few days ago."

The horn sounded again.

"It sounds like your brother needs you." I stepped back, extracting my arm from her grip.

"Will you call me, Noah?" she asked. "We need to catch up properly. I stopped into the bakery, but I guess you must work out back in the kitchen?"

The next blast on the horn was so loud, it saved me from having to answer. Mandy opened her handbag, rustled around for a moment, then tugged out a pen and paper. She scribbled something down, then held it out to me.

Her brother must have decided to lean on the horn, because a continuous blaring came from the parking lot. Cursing, Mandy shot a glare toward the door, then stuffed the paper into my hand. "Here's my number," she half-shouted over the sound. "Call me, okay?"

"Take care, Mandy." I stuffed the paper into my pocket unread, then turned and walked to where Carla was standing. The blare from the horn cut off. Glancing back around, I was glad to see that Mandy had gone.

"Who was that?" Carla asked. "Other than one of the most beautiful women I've ever seen?" Her cheeks were flushed and her hands tight around the handle of her basket, but her chin was lifted. She wore a look of determination, like she was refusing to let her nerves get the better of her.

"Mandy's an old school friend," I said.

I was tempted to tell Carla that if she wanted to see a gorgeous woman, all she needed was a mirror. She was shorter and curvier than Mandy, and dark haired while Mandy was blonde. Carla also had a quick, sharp wit, and a master's degree in sarcasm. She wasn't afraid to speak her mind.

The two women were opposites, but I didn't need to think about which one I preferred. There was no contest.

"Was she ever your girlfriend?" Carla asked.

"Never. That was the first time I've seen her in years."

"She wanted you to ask her out for Valentine's Day."

"I don't want to date anyone, remember?"

"But she's stunning."

"Jealous?" I lifted a suggestive eyebrow, enjoying the idea.

"What, because a supermodel tried to dry hump you in the produce department?" She made a 'pfft' noise. "Can't tell you the number of times I've been propositioned in the grocery store by some gorgeous Idris Elba lookalike."

Idris Elba?

I looked nothing like him. If he was her ideal man, I was way out of luck.

Not that it should matter.

But looking down at her flushed cheeks and plump lips, I had a sudden urge to back her against the shelves and make her forget about Idris Elba.

"She's interested in you," Carla said. "That's obvious."

"I'm irresistible. It's a curse." I narrowed my eyes at her. "By the way, you were supposed to come over to us and act like my girlfriend. That was our agreement."

"Talking to a stranger isn't today's challenge. Besides, I wasn't sure you'd want me to."

I started to reply, but a roar came from outside.

Motorcycles approaching.

Carla's eyes went wide. For a moment we both stood frozen, listening to the roar. My heart beat faster. The local motorcycle gang were bad news, and Carla already looked panicky. If the bikes stopped outside, she might cut and run.

I strained my ears, listening to the sound. The bikes weren't slowing or turning. They had to be going past.

"It's okay. They're not coming in here," I said.

She took a step back, her breaths shallow and fast, and when she flicked her gaze past me, I was afraid she might sprint for the door. Putting my arms around her, I pulled her in for a hug, basket and all.

"Don't freak out," I murmured in her ear. "Listen, can you hear them disappearing? They're going somewhere else."

Sure enough, the roar was starting to fade.

She sucked in a deeper breath. Her muscles were tight, and she seemed on edge, like she could just as easily run toward the door as stay. The basket she was holding bumped against my leg.

"Shake it off," I murmured. "What do you say, Chuckles? You still with me?"

When I called her Chuckles, some of the tension left her body and she sagged a little. "It was never this bad," she ground out, her voice low and hard. "I hate this. My chest hurts and I can't breathe properly. A few years ago, a trip to the store would have been nothing. I did it all the time."

"You're still a badass," I told her.

"Yeah, I'm tough. You can let me go now."

"You're not going to take off, are you?"

"I want to," she admitted. "But if I run away now, it'll be even harder to come back, and I refuse to let this place get the better of me. Not again."

I let her go and she stepped back. The flush had gone from her cheeks. Now she looked pale.

"Okay?" I asked.

"Not really, but I will be. I need a minute to calm my heart down." She pressed her hand against her chest. "Stupid thing is racing like it's trying to kill me."

"Then let's buy tampons."

"What?"

"You must need more tampons. We'll get them in all the sizes."

She frowned. "You already bought more than enough."

"Maxi-pads, then. No, wait. Condoms! You need lots of condoms. Ribbed, flavored, glow-in-the-dark. Let's see what they have."

"Seriously, what's wrong with you?" A little color returned to her cheeks as her frown deepened. "Are you a grown man or a schoolboy?"

"Condoms are over there." I spotted them on one of the top shelves and dragged her over so I could grab the biggest box they had.

"You can't possibly be that immature."

"Can you see the size on the box, Chuckles? Are they extra-large? I'd better go and ask the cashier, just to be sure." I wagged my eyebrows. "Don't want to buy them if they're too small."

"You're not funny."

"How do you keep getting that so wrong? It couldn't be clearer that I'm hilarious."

"You're so unfunny, you should give lessons." She closed her eyes for a moment as she let out a breath. When she opened them again, her lips twitched up into a small, reluctant smile. "Thank you," she said, her eyes clear and beautiful.

I shrugged, smiling back, and my chest did that strange contraction and expansion thing again. "Anytime, Chuckles."

CHAPTER 14

CARLA

- Twelve days to Valentine's Day -

Two days later, our second outing was scheduled, and Noah came by after he'd finished in the bakery to pick me up.

I'd specified that I wanted to go to a casual eatery at a quiet time. I was having a good day with most of my symptoms either green or light orange, and Noah seemed to have an uncanny way of sensing what I needed, so I left the choice of venue up to him.

He took me to a local place called Daisy's Nut House. It looked like a regular diner, only there was a view of the mountains through the back window and fresh, homemade donuts displayed at the front counter. It smelled so good, my mouth started watering the instant we walked in.

It was way past lunchtime, and the place was mostly empty with just a few tables taken and one couple sitting at the counter. My stomach was performing its usual tricks, but just like at the Piggly Wiggly, I was a lot less anxious with Noah beside me. He seemed to have a soothing effect on some parts of my body, and a stimulating effect on others. I managed to partially distract myself from anxious feelings by trying to come up with a medical test to measure the Noah effect on my various limbs and organs.

When the waitress came up to us, Noah put his arm around me, jolting me out of my medical musings and putting my system into an acute state of situational awareness.

"Hi there," he said to the waitress. "We'll take that booth, please." He motioned to a booth in the back that was somewhat isolated, giving an impression of safety. Then he looked at me. "That okay with you, sugar? Nice and private, so no one can see us." He dropped me a wink.

I had an overwhelming urge to let out a nervous bray of laughter. Having his arm around me and being the recipient of a wink was strange enough, but when he called me *sugar*, it made me feel like I had too many arms and legs. I was an octopus of awkwardness.

Clamping my lips together, I nodded. And when we slid into the booth, I hissed, "Were you flirting with me in front of the waitress?"

"Sure was. Who knows how many women Momma's spoken to? The more folks who think we're dating, the better."

I let out a huff, trying not to let him see how flustered I was. "It was weird."

His lips hitched up. "Well, I'm not used to doing it. I don't flirt, as a rule."

"Good thing, too. You should keep it that way."

His eyes sparked as though I'd issued a challenge and he leaned in, his voice low and sexy. "You must be used to being flirted with, sugar? You can't tell me men don't fall at your feet. The first time I laid eyes on you, I thought I'd never seen a woman so beautiful."

The breath left my lungs and my chest contracted. My ears felt hot, and a tingling sensation spread through my body.

Damn, he was good.

"Until you opened your mouth," he drawled with a smirk. "Then I was too busy running for cover to think much of anything."

I let out a laugh, hoping I wasn't blushing. "Well, you deserved a little attitude, seeing as you were so sure of yourself."

"I'm still sure of myself, and you're still giving me attitude."

"You like it."

He smiled back at me, his eyes warm. "I have to admit, I do. And I can't promise I won't subject you to any more flirting when we're in public. But after a little practice, I'll get better at it."

With *practice*? Oh no, practice was the last thing he needed. Not when he was already hot enough when he flirted to make me rethink this entire arrangement.

Thankfully, he dropped his gaze to his menu, so I had a chance to pull myself together. I stared at my menu too, but couldn't concentrate enough to read it. Not until the tingles went away.

"Why don't you flirt with other women?" I asked eventually.

He looked up at me. "Like I said, I don't want anyone to get the wrong idea."

"But I'm safe?"

"You've promised not to fall for me. It'll be difficult for you to stop yourself, but I'm sure you can do it if you really set your mind to it."

"Oh, I know I can stop myself." I pretended to roll my eyes and tried not to smile.

A few more blinks, and I was able to force my attention away from Noah's hotness long enough to focus on the menu. It was a big menu, with a large selection of pancakes and burgers.

"You hungry?" asked Noah.

"I already had lunch, but I'm due for a snack in..." I checked the time on my watch. "Well, not for an hour, but that's okay. No big deal if I have it early."

His lips tugged to the side as though he found my schedule amusing. "Remind me, what foods can't you eat? You're gluten free, right?"

"Unfortunately, I can't eat any of the things that smell so good. I'd love a donut, but I'll just have to enjoy the aroma." Though I kept my tone light, Noah's smile turned into a worried frown.

"There must be something you can order?"

"I'll have a side salad and see if they can add some protein. Egg, or nuts, or meat." Even if the salad dressing was store bought, a few additives probably wouldn't affect me.

"That's it?" His face fell. "What about apple pie? Fruit's healthy, right? And they have the best pie in town."

I shook my head. "My fatigue improves when I keep my blood sugar stable all day, without letting it spike. I eat lots of small meals, limit my carbs, and don't eat refined sugars."

"No carbs? Really?"

"I can have complex carbohydrates, if I have some protein with them." I grimaced, because my diet was so restrictive and boring, it exhausted even me. "Before I got sick, I would have had a donut for sure. But I'm sure they do a great tuna salad."

"Let's not stay here." He put his menu down. "Let's grab a couple of takeout drinks and go for a walk instead."

"But it's on the spreadsheet." I pulled it up on my phone so I could remind him of the schedule. "See? We can't leave."

"It only says we need to sit in the dining area. We're sitting. Let's tick that off and order coffee to go." He cut a sideways glance at me. "Wait. Let me guess. No coffee, either?"

"Coffee's okay. Decaf, with no cream or sugar."

He shook his head and I had to laugh at his expression. Then he called the waitress over to place the order.

"You're not going to get a donut?" I asked when she'd bustled away to get our coffees.

"I can have one anytime."

"Don't hold back on my account."

"I'm not hungry."

I had a feeling he was lying about that. Sure enough, when the waitress gave us our coffees and we got up to leave, he grabbed a bag of mixed nuts from a stand near the counter.

"Where will we go?" I asked as we got back into the car.

"Just down the valley. I know a place we can stop. It's not far."

He drove a short distance down a winding road, then pulled over next to a path that disappeared into the trees. We got out with our drinks and walked along the narrow dirt track. In no time, the road had disappeared behind us, and we could have been in the middle of the forest. Tall trees rose around us. The silence was only broken by birdsong and the breeze rustling the leaves. Out of the sun, it was cold enough to see my breath, but I was wearing my thick puffer jacket, a scarf, and a beanie. Noah had his coat. He also seemed impervious to the cold.

"How far are we walking?" I asked, stepping over a log.

"This is the start of a long hike, but if I remember rightly, just ahead is a good place to sit."

Sure enough, a few minutes later we reached an outcropping of stone. Years ago—maybe centuries ago—the stone had broken, and the resulting boulders had been worn smooth. One large boulder was flat and easy to climb onto. We sat next to each other on the cold rock, and I wrapped my hands around my coffee to keep them warm. The track was bordered by green shrubs, and sunlight filtered through the tall trees to us, delivering some precious heat. Overhead, two birds were calling to each other, but the only other sound was the rustling of leaves.

"It's beautiful." I shifted a little on the rock as the cold seeped through my jeans.

Noah nodded. "Nothing like these mountains anywhere else. Not that I've seen, anyway." He set his coffee cup down on the rock beside him.

"Do you ever think about moving back here for good?" I asked.

"I like it here, but I have bad memories too, so it's easier not to be here. Still, sooner or later I'll probably move back. I'll have to, eventually, to make sure my mother's okay. She's been alone for a few years now, and I hate the thought of something happening to her when I'm not around." He opened the nuts and offered me the bag.

"You don't have any brothers or sisters?" Taking a few nuts, I crunched a cashew.

He shook his head, putting the open bag on the rock between us so we could snack. "Momma wanted lots of kids, but it didn't happen for her, and then my daddy died. She never remarried, and never had any more children. I wish she had. Maybe then she wouldn't put me under so much pressure to give her grandbabies."

"I'm sorry about your dad. How did he die?"

"Car crash."

I frowned. "Wait. Your friend died in a car crash, and so did your dad?"

He nodded.

"And now you roll cars for a living?"

He lifted one shoulder and dropped it again. His casual response said he was aware of the link between what had happened to them and his stunt work. It also said he was reluctant for me to push him on it.

"You never told me how many bones you'd broken," I said.

"You were going to guess."

"Ten?" I aimed high.

"Nope."

"Then how many?"

"Hmm." He lifted his eyes heavenward, as though trying to remember. "Three ribs… no, four ribs. My collarbone, twice, which wasn't fun. These three fingers got twisted in a tow line and had multiple fractures." He wriggled them. "An engine block landed on my foot, breaking two toes and my ankle. I've broken both my—"

"Omigod, stop!" I threw a peanut at his chest. It hit and bounced off.

"Hey!"

"I changed my mind. I don't want to picture your limbs getting mangled. Tell me how you went from stunt work to decorating cupcakes."

Putting his hands on the rock behind him, he leaned back, gazing up into the canopy of the trees. "As a kid, I used to go to the bakery after school to wait for Momma to finish work. The bakery owner's daughter taught me to decorate cakes. She's running the place now, and I heard she had some bad things happen to her. So when she asked me to help with the Valentine's cookies, I said yes."

I paused with my coffee cup at my lips. "Wait. That's why you took the job? To help her out?"

"Sure. Why not?"

"That's… generous."

I was trying not to look incredulous, but maybe I failed because he said, "Around here, folks look out for each other."

"I get that. But you're working in the bakery every day. Every. Single. Day. That's a huge favor. I can't imagine doing anyone a favor that big."

"But decorating cupcakes is fun. My favorite things are made of sugar." He had a glint in his eye as he said it, and I couldn't help thinking of the way he'd called me *sugar*.

But dammit, I refused to blush again. I'd never been a blusher. At least not until I met Noah.

I crunched on an almond instead. "Is stunt work your passion?" I asked.

"My passion?" He shook his head. "It's a job."

"Then why not quit and work in the bakery instead? It'd be safer."

"The stunts I've been doing pay well. I only need to do one to earn as much as I would for a month or two in the bakery."

"But the money doesn't matter, does it? Not when it comes to hurting yourself." I met his gaze. "Like, if I gave you a million dollars right now to break your neck, would you do it?"

"Of course not. But I need to stay on the stunt team so I can keep the kid I'm mentoring alive. Knowing him, he'd take the million bucks."

"You're willing to kill yourself in his place?"

He gave another of his ultra-relaxed shrugs, as though nothing could ever bother him. "I've already seen someone die. I don't want to see it again."

"You're too nice. And I didn't even know that was a thing until I met you."

"You're nice yourself. Except for your anti-social habit of throwing nuts."

"I'm not *nice*." I pretended to scowl. "Take that back or risk a cashew in your eye."

"Okay, okay. I'm the only nice one."

"Too nice," I reminded him.

"That's what makes me irresistible." His eyes sparkled as he sipped his coffee.

And though he was joking, he was right. He was easy to talk to and he made me laugh. I liked him a lot. His easy confidence made anything else impossible.

He put his cup back down. "That's enough about me. I want to hear about you. Tell me what you did before you came to Green Valley."

"I was one of the founders of a tech startup," I said. "There were three of us, and we developed some software to help companies track their finances. We worked hard for years, like most people do who start a company. Night and day, high pressure and high stress. Until I got sick and couldn't do my job anymore."

"That's why you came here?"

"First, I sold all my shares in the company to buy myself some time. When I sold out, I made enough money to live off of for a while." I grimaced, hating to tell him the next part. Wanting to stall a little, I drank some of my coffee. Noah waited patiently, and when I couldn't wait any longer, I let out a sigh. "About a month after I sold my entire share of the company, Elon Musk tweeted about our software."

He raised his eyebrows questioningly, clearly not wanting to interrupt.

I sighed again. "Just one tweet made the number of people using the software suddenly skyrocket. Six months later, the company was bought out by a bigger player. If I hadn't sold my shares when I did, I would have made twenty times as much. I would have been a wealthy woman."

"Bad timing," he said. The understatement of the century.

I screwed my face up. "I'm like the fifth Beatle who quit the band to get married. Or like Mark Zuckerberg's roommate, the one who helped him create Facebook before deciding he didn't want to be involved."

He patted my knee. "Money doesn't matter, remember?"

"It does *sometimes*."

"What if I gave you a million dollars right now, but you had to go back to your company and work night and day, high stress and high pressure, for another six months?"

"If you could also give me enough energy to do that, I'd pay *you* a billion dollars."

He raised his eyebrows. "You'd pay a billion for that, huh?" Then he shook his head in apparent disgust. "Knew I undercharged you for that hug."

I grinned.

And considering the subject of our conversation, I didn't expect to grin. I didn't like to tell people about missing out on all that money, and the few people that knew had acted like it was a huge deal. Noah brushed it away like it didn't matter, and weirdly, that made me feel better about the whole thing.

"What about your family?" he asked. "Do they live in New York?"

"Usually. One of my sisters took off to stay at a communal living place and left her phone behind. If she's out of contact for too much longer, one of us will need to go looking for her."

"Are you worried about her?"

"Not yet. It's only been a few weeks. Hopefully she'll resurface soon."

"How many siblings do you have?"

"Two sisters, both younger than me."

"What are they like?"

"Neither of them are anything like me, but they're both great. Josefina's the one who's gone offgrid, and Magdalena…" Even thinking about my youngest sister made me smile. "She's funny and kind, but she drives my mom to distraction. And while I was in math club, she majored in petty crime."

"Now I want to meet her. Does she ever visit you in Green Valley?"

I shook my head. "When I decided to come here, I told my sisters I wanted to concentrate on keeping to a set schedule. Now I think Mags is afraid to come and upset my routine."

"You haven't seen any friends or family for more than a year?" His gaze turned sympathetic. "I can't imagine being alone for that long."

"It wasn't easy, but it's helped. I'm a lot better than I was. I've been able to work on my software, and I'm almost ready to release it. I just need to get an investor on board."

"Haven't you been lonely?" he asked.

Now it was my turn to shrug, seeing as it wasn't a question I was prepared to answer. Not truthfully, anyway. I didn't want his pity.

He leaned closer, lifting his hand toward me. My heart stopped beating as he ran a light finger down my cheek. "I think we should kiss." The suggestion was accompanied by a soft quirk of his lips, and somehow he made it sound completely reasonable instead of utterly outrageous.

"What?" I asked, though I'd heard him clearly. My heart had come back to life, but instead of beating normally, it was bouncing off my ribs, doing its best imitation of a rubber ball. My eyes dropped to his lips, and I swallowed. Ever since he'd hugged me—first in my kitchen, then in the Piggly Wiggly—I'd been dreaming about being back in his arms.

"We're having lunch at Momma's place tomorrow. If we don't convince her we're really dating, she won't let up."

"Are you saying you want to kiss in front of her?" I gave a forced-sounding laugh to hide the fact my body was flushing with heat.

"We should accidentally let her catch us in a kiss." He made air quotes around the word *accidentally*. "That's what it'll take to make sure I'm off the hook."

"Just telling her we're dating won't do it?"

"She's too stubborn for that. Besides, a kiss could be part of your therapy. It'll be good for you."

"My *therapy*?"

He nodded. "We have a clear agreement, and neither of us are going to get confused and start thinking this is a real relationship. So who better to kiss than me?"

I let out another burst of nervous laughter. "Congratulations, I've never heard of a lamer excuse to fool around."

He drew his brows together in supposed puzzlement. "But kissing me makes total sense. If you prefer, I can add it to the spreadsheet as one of your challenges. But it's a better idea to get a practice kiss over and done with now, so we can make sure it looks real when we let Momma catch us."

"Nice try, Malone."

"Don't tell me you're afraid?" His tone was teasing, but also… well, his eyes held a hot intensity that said Noah Malone was deadly serious about kissing me.

And why shouldn't I kiss him?

So long as the boundaries were clear, would it be such a terrible thing to do? My heart clearly thought it was in a mosh pit, but that was just nerves and excitement. It had been a long time since Tomas left, and I'd deliberately pushed romance—and sex—from my mind. But now I was alone in the forest with the most attractive man I'd seen since… well, since birth, and the thought of kissing him was making me squirm in a good way. If he put his arms around me, would I even be able to stop?

"I'm not afraid," I managed to say, though my mouth was bone dry. "I'm waiting for you to tell me how much you charge."

"It's your lucky day, Chuckles. Our practice kiss is free. After that…" He shrugged. "I'll give you my price list when we get that far."

"Isn't that how drug dealers operate?"

He flashed me his beautiful grin. "Exactly."

The first time I'd seen that smile, I'd been afraid it could spin my world off its axis. I'd been right to worry. It was a tractor beam pulling me in. The one thing I should fear most was that it might capture more of me than I could afford to give.

Swallowing, I tried to take control of the situation. "I suppose we could kiss. But anything more than that is off the table." Sex was an issue for me, and Tomas had gotten frustrated when I couldn't orgasm. No matter how tempting it was to think about getting naked with Noah, I wasn't ready to face that embarrassment again.

"Okay." Noah's gaze traced the shape of my lips. "But don't blame me if you change your mind about that after I kiss you."

His voice was laced with some kind of magic. It did that growly thing that shouldn't be a turn-on but still managed to send tremors of anticipation up my spine.

His lips looked lovely. They looked soft, especially in contrast with his beard. Would they be soft? I desperately wanted to know. Even more desperately, I wanted more of the feeling he gave me. More of the shivery, excited feeling that radiated out from low in my belly. When he looked at me that way, my body came alive.

"One kiss," I said. "Then we'll see." Though I was trying to play it cool, the words tumbled out a little too fast.

He moved closer, taking his time. His large hand moved behind my neck, under my hair. It felt solid there, in the best possible way. His other hand moved to my hip. "You ready?" he asked, tilting his head a little.

His eyes grazed hotly over my lips. If just his gaze was enough to intensify my tingles that much, what would his touch do?

The suspense was killing me.

"No," I whispered, ending my torment by pressing my lips to his.

They were even softer than I'd dreamed of. And warm, so warm. When he licked my top lip, I gasped, overcome by the sensation. My body shuddered. I *hungered.* It was all I could do not to climb onto him and straddle him, tearing at his clothes and desperately begging for more. I arched into his kiss, trying not to groan with pleasure.

I'd had nowhere near enough of his kiss when Noah pulled back. His eyes were blazing, a vivid shade of green. But though his eyes were full of fire and heat, the grin he gave me was soft.

"Quick check," he said. "You haven't fallen in love with me yet, have you, Chuckles?"

I shook my head wordlessly, dragging in a breath. My face was so hot, it had to be bright red. I needed to hide myself from his sharp gaze. *Coffee.* That's what I needed. Grabbing my cup, I brought it to my lips. My hand trembled and I could only hope he didn't notice.

"You okay?" he asked.

I nodded again, silently cursing the way he flustered me.

It had only been a kiss, and clearly the strength of my feelings was out of proportion to the event. I was too aroused. Too turned on. Maybe it was a previously undiscovered symptom of my illness, something not documented in the medical studies. Either that, or I was just embarrassingly horny for Noah.

I took a big gulp of cold coffee, pulling myself together.

"I'm fine," I said. "That was fine."

He raised his eyebrows, his smile telling me he didn't believe my casual tone. "Only *fine*?"

"Uh-huh."

"And you'll be ready to do it again at Momma's place?"

"Uh-huh. Shall we go, Malone?"

I pulled myself off the rock to head back the way we'd come. Kissing Noah definitely hadn't been on my spreadsheet. It hadn't been any part of my plan.

But now?

Hell, maybe I needed to add another column.

CHAPTER 15

CARLA

- Ten days to Valentine's Day -

Before heading out the door for lunch with Noah and his mother, I studied myself nervously in the mirror, adjusting my hair and considering changing my outfit for the tenth time. None of my dresses seemed like the right choice for lunch, so I settled for a shirt and slacks underneath a long woolen coat, though I was tempted to wear something sexier.

Not that wearing something sexy for lunch with Noah's mother would be appropriate. And it wouldn't have even crossed my mind if Noah hadn't promised to repeat our sensational kiss at his mother's house.

Now kissing him was all I could think about.

The address Noah had given me turned out to be a cute bungalow in town, close enough to the houses beside it to call out to the neighbors, but with tall trees surrounding it. Smoke drifted lazily from the chimney and the faint aroma of burning wood sweetened the air.

With limited choices, I'd had trouble coming up with a gift for Noah's mom. At the last minute, I'd decided on a box of eggs. Holding the box in one hand, I ran a nervous hand over my hair, then knocked on the front door.

Noah opened it, looking mouthwateringly handsome in jeans and the gray jersey he'd worn on the first day we'd met. That day, his good looks had caused an internal apocalypse. Now the tremors he gave me originated from a lower place and were far more pleasurable. And when his smile made me dizzy, it happened in a good way.

"Come on in, Chuckles. Let me take your coat." He hung it on the coat rack, then took my free hand in his. "You look beautiful. Come and say hi to Momma."

In the kitchen, my smiling landlady was chopping tomatoes. Wiping her hands on her apron, she moved in for a hug. "Welcome, Carla. I'm glad to see you again." She pulled back to beam at me. "Tell me, are you happy with the roof repair?"

She was so warm and friendly, my nervousness eased. "Noah did a great job. And these are for you." I gave her the box of eggs. "I have chickens and I figured now that you live in town, you might like some eggs that have been freshly laid."

"Now, isn't that just the most thoughtful gift." She put the box on the counter so she could open the small, home-made card I'd attached. In it, I'd written:

Breakfast from the farmhouse, from Meryl Cheep, Yolko Ono, and Henny Lamarr.

It took her a moment to read it, and when she looked back up at me, her eyes were a little misty. "I used to love my chickens," she said. "I miss having them around. Are yours laying well?"

"Very well. Even in this cold weather, I'm still getting one or two eggs a day."

"That's a good number."

"And I love watching the chickens fuss about. They're such characters."

"Oh, I know. I used to think it was better than watching television." Noah's mother had a lovely laugh, and I could tell she spent a lot of time laughing by the way her eyes crinkled. She was a beautiful woman, and I could see a lot of Noah in her face. Her eyes were almost as green as his, and her chin was strong.

"Mostly I have store-bought eggs these days," she said. "They're not as tasty as the ones my lovely girls used to lay for me. Thank you for such a thoughtful gift. I can't think of a single thing I'd rather have had." She put a hand on my arm to give it a quick squeeze, then turned to Noah. "Why don't you get Carla settled in the living room while I finish getting lunch ready?"

I offered to help with the lunch preparations, though it was smarter for me not to attempt too much. I didn't want to overexert myself and flake out during lunch, so I was relieved when Mrs. Malone insisted that Noah and I leave her to it.

The living room was warm and cozy, with a fire crackling in the fireplace. There were photos of Noah on a tall bookcase at one end of the living room, and older photos of a man who looked a lot like him. "Your father?" I asked, walking over for a closer look.

"That's him." Noah moved up beside me.

The man in the photos was clean shaven, giving me a hint of how Noah would look without his beard. *Very nice.* He and Noah's mother had made a lovely couple. And Noah's baby photos were too freakin' adorable. The family had great genes, and one day Noah's children would be just as cute.

The thought sent a pang of longing through me, quickly followed by a stronger pang of regret.

It was unlikely I'd ever be able to have children. Not unless they found a cure for my illness, or I was one of the eight percent of ME patients who miraculously recovered. Otherwise, I'd never have enough energy for a baby. On my bad days, I could barely take care of myself.

"You look a little sad." Noah put his hand on my lower back. "What's wrong?"

"Nothing." It wasn't a lie, seeing as the warm, suggestive pressure of his hand instantly made any trace of melancholy vanish. I liked it when he touched me. And we were going to kiss again soon, weren't we? My body tingled with anticipation.

"You were a cute kid." I nodded at the photos. "No. Wait. You were an *enchanting* kid."

He grinned. "I was. Thanks for noticing."

I started to reply but was distracted by movement at the edge of my vision. A black cat was slinking out of the room. "Your mother has a cat?" I asked. His hand was still on my back. I liked his touch so much, my legs felt weak.

Noah nodded. "That's Bandit. When I was growing up, Momma said she didn't like cats. Until Bandit showed up and decided to move in. Now my momma likes him better than she likes me." His eyes grew warm, and he lowered his voice to an intimate murmur. "Cats are funny like that. They're so independent, you don't expect to feel strongly about them. Then one day you realize how important they've become to you." His Southern accent trickled over my senses like warm honey.

"You're very sweet," I said.

His lips curved up. "It's one of my many exceptional qualities."

I gave a laugh that sounded breathless. It *was* breathless, because he was very close, and we were alone, and I wanted him to kiss me again a lot more than I wanted to do something so boring as breathe.

As though he could read my mind, he dipped his head to bring our faces even closer. "Lunch will be ready soon," he murmured.

I nodded. "Your mother might come in to get us. If we weren't kissing, she might get suspicious."

He slid his hand under my hair to gently cradle the back of my neck. "You're right." His heated gaze caressed my lips. "We'd better do all we can to fool her."

He dipped his face closer, and my body quivered with anticipation. I strained up into him as his lips grazed against mine.

A polite, throat-clearing noise came from the door. Noah pulled back, releasing his grip on me. His mother was peeking in, a wide smile lighting up her face.

"Sorry to interrupt." She looked delighted by what she saw. "Lunch is ready."

I wanted to protest. To grab Noah by the front of his jersey and demand he finish kissing me. How could he leave me with only a tiny fraction of the kiss I'd been anticipating? I'd been so close to enjoying another sensational kissing experience, my entire *being* was silently sobbing with disappointment.

But Noah was already stepping away.

"Come into the dining room," he said, taking my hand.

I swallowed hard, sure that my hand was trembling a little against his. Couldn't he sense my frustration?

He led me into a small room off the kitchen, to a table that was already set for our meal, complete with linen tablecloth and napkins. He pulled a chair out for me so I could sit down. When he went to help his mother bring the food to the table, I took a breath and gave myself a pep talk.

So what if we hadn't needed to kiss properly to convince Noah's mother we were really dating? That was fine. It didn't matter. I could brush it off. No problem.

"Here you go," Mrs. Malone said, putting some plates down. "Noah said it would be easiest if we kept things simple. I roasted meat and vegetables, while he made two different salads. I hope that's okay?"

"The food looks wonderful," I said gratefully. "I hope I haven't put you out with my restrictions."

"Not at all. Now, tell me how you like living in the farmhouse. Noah said you were growing vegetables. Your crops survived that snow we had last month?"

She and Noah sat down, and as we ate, I talked about how much I was enjoying the lovely house I was renting from her.

Noah and his mother both told stories about their life there, including telling me about the animals they'd raised in the field behind the house. Noah described riding their neighbor's horses, and the adventures he'd had in the woods with his friends. His childhood in rural Tennessee, seemingly allowed to roam free, had been a world away from my urban upbringing with strict parents. I could see how he'd become a stuntman. It was clear he had a wild streak.

When Bandit came back in, I told Noah and his mother about how when I'd decided to come here on my own, I'd called up an animal shelter and asked to adopt the oldest, sleepiest cat they had. Seeing as I spent so much time resting, I'd figured it would be nice to have company, and even when I was at my sickest, I could manage to feed and care for a cat.

I'd lucked out with Freud, as he was perfectly suited to the assignment. I'd gotten a companion, and he got to live out his senior years in comfort. Adopting him was the best decision I'd ever made.

Noah's mother asked why I needed to rest so much, and I told her a little about my illness. She listened attentively and asked intelligent questions. I could easily see where Noah had inherited his charm. When the conversation turned to other things, I found myself laughing a lot and enjoying myself immensely.

It was lovely—but a little bittersweet—to witness the easy relationship Noah had with his mother. They chimed in on each other's stories and teased each other with obvious affection. And though Noah complained about his mother's determination to set him up with unwanted dates, I envied their closeness.

As much as my mother loved me, I hadn't lived up to her expectations. She'd grown up in poverty, and she was always telling me and my sisters how easy our lives were. She'd given us all the opportunities she'd never had. As the oldest daughter, I'd been expected to set a good example. So I understood her disappointment as she'd watched me leave my job and spend months in bed.

The three of us sat talking for a long time after we'd finished eating, but eventually Mrs. Malone got up. "Y'all stay here," she said. "I'll clear the plates."

Noah immediately jumped to his feet. "Please sit down, Momma. I'll wash up."

"And you have to let me help," I added, getting up and stretching my aching limbs. Maybe if we got some alone time in the kitchen, Noah might finish kissing me.

His mother reached out a hand to stop me from moving away. "Aren't you sweet, Carla. But what kind of host would I be if I let you work? Sit with me a while."

I sat back down a little reluctantly, although it was no hardship getting to watch Noah as he cleared the plates. His rear view as he strolled away with them was particularly pleasant. The man looked mighty fine in his snug jeans.

When he'd vanished into the kitchen, Mrs. Malone turned to me with a smile. "I'm relieved to think Noah might finally settle down."

"Hmm." Picking up my almost-empty glass, I sipped what was left of my water. Noah's mother was such a lovely woman, I hated lying to her.

She leaned in, lowering her voice as though confiding in me. "I've been without him long enough. It's time for him to move back to Green Valley. I'm happy you're giving him a reason to stay."

I tried not to grimace. She'd been nothing but nice to me, and it seemed wrong to repay her kindness this way.

"Noah's wonderful," I said, putting my glass down. "But we haven't known each other very long."

"Oh, but y'all make such a lovely couple. I knew Noah's father was the one for me from the first moment I laid eyes on him. After he introduced himself, I told him I planned to marry him. You should have seen his surprise." She gave me a smile, her eyes soft with fond memories. "We met on Valentine's Day. And sure enough, he proposed two weeks later. We got married the following Valentine's Day. The happiest day of my life."

"He must have been a wonderful man."

"He was. And so is his son."

I nodded my agreement. "Noah's a special person."

"And now he's found someone as special as he is."

Ugh. Could she make this any more difficult? When I swallowed, all I could taste was my own guilt.

"That reminds me," she said. "I hate to mention business, but your lease on the farmhouse is expiring soon, and my lawyer is drawing up a new contract. He suggested it would be for a year, but we could make it longer?"

"I'm sorry, but I may not be able to sign another contract."

Her brow furrowed. "Why not?"

"Well, I'll need to go back to New York soon."

"Why would you do that?" She sounded astonished.

"I came to Green Valley so I could get well enough to write some software. Now my software's almost ready for release, and a friend's offered me an office in the city."

Her expression fell. "But that's no good. New York is too far away. Have you talked about it with Noah?"

I cleared my throat nervously. When I'd agreed to Noah's deal, it hadn't occurred to me that his mother might assume Noah and I would start consulting each other on our plans for the future. She couldn't really think we'd get serious that quickly?

"Um." I toyed with my empty glass. "We haven't discussed it, Mrs. Malone. I mean, we've only just started dating."

Lifting her chin, she gave me a determined look. Too late, I remembered Noah's stories about her legendary stubbornness.

"There's only one thing for it," she said firmly. "We need to figure out a way for you to do your software things from right here in Green Valley. What do you need to go to New York for anyway? I'm sure there's no problem we can't overcome if we put our heads together."

"Oh," I stammered. "But I don't know if that could work."

"We'll make it work." She leaned in. "Noah hasn't shown a bit of interest in Hannah, or Patty, or Joy, or Blithe, or any other woman but you." As she patted my hand, her smile returned. "He's smitten with you. And if y'all stay in Green Valley, everything will be perfect. We can make it happen. I know we can."

"He seemed interested in a woman we ran into," I said in a rush. "She gave him her number." As soon as the words were out, I felt terrible. I was betraying Noah and breaking our agreement. But I had to do something to distract his mother.

"Noah accepted another woman's phone number while he was on a date with you?" Mrs. Malone sounded horrified.

"I can't blame him," I said quickly. "Her name's Mandy, and she's stunning. Tall, blonde, and elegant."

"Mandy Rayner?" Noah's mom made a tsking sound. "She should know better."

"Mandy and Noah might be better suited for each other."

I hated having to admit that.

But there was no logical reason to hate it.

As tempting as it might be to imagine a world where I'd be able to date Noah for real, it wasn't what he wanted. And he had his whole life in front of him to fill with fun, travel, and adventure. Not to mention children, when he decided to have them. I couldn't do any of that.

Even if he'd wanted to date for real, it would have been out of the question. It wouldn't be fair to hold him back. And if I pushed myself to keep up with him, it could make my illness worse. That wouldn't be fair on me.

So, seeing as we were an impossible match, there was no reason to hate the thought of him with another woman.

No reason at all.

Noah's mother looked confused. "Why would you say that? You're the one Noah wants."

"But Noah said he hadn't seen Mandy for years. They've barely even spoken. Maybe if they bumped into each other again…"

I had to stop talking.

It was all too easy to imagine Noah and Mandy together. Noah's mother wanted grandchildren, and Noah and Mandy's offspring would be spectacular. A race of genetically superior superbeings.

They'd make the perfect couple.

And even though I had no right to feel jealous, I felt sick with it.

Mrs. Malone seemed lost for words. She gave me a mystified look.

"Never mind." I forced a laugh. "Please forget I said that. I don't know what I was thinking."

Her frown eased. "Why don't you tell me about the office you need for your work?"

"Um." I had no idea how to dissuade her from finding an office without blurting out the truth about my arrangement with Noah. So I babbled about desks and dimensions until I finally managed to divert her with questions about how cute Noah had been when he was a baby. By that time, Noah was done with the dishes, and it was time to say goodbye.

But all the way home, the all-too-perfect image of Noah and Mandy together was stuck uncomfortably in my mind.

CHAPTER 16

NOAH

- Nine days to Valentine's Day -

The next day, Carla and I didn't have a date planned, but I messaged her to say I was going to drop by after work.

After I finished decorating the Valentine's Day cookies and cupcakes, it was time to have some fun. I mixed up two small batches of cookies and put them all in the oven together. When the timer went off, Jennifer came out of her office to watch me pull them out.

Since going to Daisy's with Carla, I hadn't been able to stop thinking about how hard it must be for her not to be able to indulge in any treats. This morning, I'd explained to the others how Carla ate more protein than carbs and restricted her sugar intake. When I'd explained she was also gluten and dairy free, Jennifer's eyes had gleamed, and Joy had been enthusiastic to help. Together, we'd come up with some options.

"The cookies look good," Jennifer said with an approving smile.

"Good? They look perfect! But the important part is the taste test." I reached for a cookie, but Jennifer touched my arm, making me pause.

"You're not going to let them cool?" she asked.

"Stunt professional, remember? I'm used to living dangerously." I grabbed one. "Ouch!" Breaking off a corner, I blew on it, then chewed. "It's good," I said with my mouth full. "Really good. The dates give it just enough sweetness."

"Something like this might be okay for people on keto diets," Jennifer said.

"And folks with diabetes?" suggested Joy.

"We could add some to our Valentine's offerings," Jennifer mused. "A short-term trial to see whether they sell."

That's what I'd been hoping she'd say. I nodded enthusiastically. "There must be plenty of other people who can't eat too much sugar. Everyone deserves a treat at least once a year. And I bet I can come up with some sugar-free frosting to put some hearts on them. Make them look pretty."

Joy grabbed one. "Hot!" Then she bit it. "Mmm, good. That's really good."

"Leave some for Carla," I said jokingly.

"Is she okay?" asked Joy. Her kind eyes were crinkled with concern. We'd only been working together for a week, but she was one of the most soft-hearted people I'd ever met.

"She's fine," I said. Part of me wanted to ask what they knew about chronic fatigue syndrome. But Carla wouldn't appreciate me telling everyone about her illness.

"You think she'd be willing to come in and talk to me about what she can and can't eat?" Jennifer asked. "If we're going to do a selection for people on different diets, it would be nice to get her perspective."

"I'll ask her." I smiled to myself. "Or maybe I'll just add it to her spread-sheet. Then she'll have to come. She'll have no choice."

* * *

An hour or so later, holding a bag of cookies, I knocked on Carla's door.

When she opened the door, she was wearing jeans and a long-sleeved top. Her hair was loose over her shoulders, and I hadn't realized how much I'd missed her smile until I glimpsed the world's tiniest dimples. The sight made my insides get tighter, making it seem like each breath I took was big enough to fill my entire body with air.

"Hey, Malone." She stepped aside for me to come in. When I took my coat off, her gaze went to my bare forearm. "You took your bandage off?"

"My arm's healed." The scar stood out sharply against my skin, but it'd fade over time, just like the others. "How are you feeling?" I asked.

"I spent the morning working on a tricky part of my app. I thought it might take me a week or two to finish. Longer, if my brain fog was bad. But my brain was working, and I figured out a way to solve it, which means I'm done already."

She sounded so excited about it, I had to smile. "Great news," I said. "What was it?"

"A failsafe, so data can be input from different devices, and it'll sync without overwriting information. Even if, say, a heart monitor is uploading data at the same time as a glucose monitor." She waved a hand. "It might sound easy, but there was some complicated backend technical stuff to work out."

"It doesn't sound easy to me," I said honestly.

There was a spring in her step as she led me down the hallway. "You want to help me celebrate the milestone? I've made a citrus drink and added some fresh mint. I'm going wild."

"Count me in." It was so nice seeing her that lighthearted, I would have agreed to just about anything. And when we reached the kitchen, I handed her the bag I was carrying. "I made cookies. Four of them are pistachio and date. The other four are fig and almond. I've only used nut flours and oats. No gluten or dairy. They're low in carbohydrates and high in protein, and the only sugar comes from the fruit." If Carla couldn't eat the cookies, it wouldn't be for lack of trying on my part.

Her eyes were wide. "You did that for me?" She sounded so incredulous, I could almost imagine this was the first time anyone had ever given her anything.

"Here." I pulled a piece of paper out of my pocket. "I wrote down the ingredients so you can make sure they're safe for you to eat."

She ran her gaze over the paper. "This is… I can't believe you did this." Opening the bag, she peered inside.

I grabbed a plate from the cupboard. "Are you hungry now? You should try one."

I wasn't sure why I was so eager to see her taste a cookie. Okay, okay, that wasn't true. I did know. And it wasn't to report back to Jennifer, even if I was prepared to pretend that was the reason. Truthfully, I just wanted to enjoy watching her eat something really delicious. Not that I was against all that healthy food she ate. Not at all. But there was food that was good for your body, and food that was good for your *soul*, and I was willing to bet she hadn't had much of the latter in a good long while.

She sat on a stool at the counter. Taking a bite, she closed her eyes and chewed slowly. "Oh my God," she said with her mouth full, only talking through the cookie made it sound like "Ohmmgo."

The expression of bliss on her face was everything I could have asked for. As she swallowed the mouthful, I couldn't help but grin.

"It's delicious." She gifted me with another glimpse of dimples. "You really made it?"

"With Jennifer's help. I couldn't have done it without her. That's Jennifer Winston. She runs the bakery."

Carla had been about to take another bite, but she lowered the hand that held the cookie. "Winston? Sienna married a Winston. In fact, Mom has mentioned Jennifer. She's Sienna's sister-in-law."

"That means you and Jennifer are related," I said.

"Only distantly."

"Well, Jennifer said if you were willing to stop in and see her, she'd like to talk through some other ideas."

"Other ideas? Like what?"

"She's considering adding a small keto menu. Would you consider coming into the bakery? We could add the trip to your spreadsheet."

She chewed her lower lip for a moment as though the idea made her nervous. The action made me focus on her lips. They had a very appealing shape. I'd loved the way they'd felt when I'd kissed her.

"Maybe it could replace the task where I initiate a conversation with a stranger," she said. "Well, technically Jennifer *is* a stranger, so it fits the brief."

"She's nice. Everyone who works at the bakery is friendly."

Carla nodded. "I'd like to thank her. It's a good idea."

When she picked up the cookie and took another bite, I realized I was watching her mouth intently and licking my lips. Not because I wanted more cookies, but because I wanted to kiss her again. Like, I *really* wanted to kiss her again.

She let out a little groan as she chewed, and I found myself wanting to groan with her.

"Seriously, these are so good," she said. "I can't believe you made them for me."

"That was fig. Try the pecan one."

After she'd demolished the pecan cookie, and had let out several more erotic, jeans-tightening groans, and complimented my baking a satisfying number of times, she said, "It's weird you're a stuntman, when you're so good at baking and decorating cakes."

"I'm a complicated person."

"You need to be a baker from now on. Give up stunt work."

"So I can make you more cookies?"

"Of course! What, you think that it's that I don't want you to die?" She shook her head. "It's the cookies. Definitely."

I smirked. "You don't want me to die?"

"I'd prefer if you didn't."

"See, you do like me."

She rolled her eyes, a smile lifting her lips. "Don't worry, I won't fall in love with you."

"Keep repeating it to yourself. It'll help."

Instead of laughing, she hesitated. Maybe it was my imagination, but it almost seemed like a cloud crossed her face.

"What about the woman from the Piggly Wiggly?" she asked.

I scratched my beard, confused. "Who?"

"Mandy. She gave you her phone number."

"Oh yeah. What about her?"

"She seems nice." Carla shot me a questioning look that confused me even more. Why was Carla asking about Mandy? At the Piggly Wiggly, I'd teased her about being jealous, but I hadn't thought she really was. She couldn't be, could she?

I was about to ask her when she picked up the last cookie crumb and licked it off her finger. The way her tongue flicked out held me transfixed. Her lips were beautiful. Lush and pillowy. The kind of lips to make a man instantly forget everything but his need to taste them. And watching her lick her finger made me want to watch her lick other things…

"We should kiss," I said.

Her eyes widened. "Us? Or you and Mandy?"

"Definitely us." Whatever her sudden interest in Mandy was about, I wanted to draw her attention back to what mattered.

"But your mother already believes we're dating." Despite her protest, Carla's gaze dropped to my lips and her gaze darkened. It was obvious she liked the idea.

"This time, it wouldn't be for my benefit, but for yours," I said. "Kissing is good therapy. It'll help with aspects of your illness. Anxiety, and such."

She stared at me wordlessly for a moment. Her cheeks were flushed. I leaned casually against the kitchen counter, trying to pretend I wasn't on fire for her. Hoping the desire I felt wasn't shining through my eyes, giving me away.

She dragged in one of those ultra-long breaths she was so good at and let it out again before she answered. "You think kissing could help with my symptoms?" Her tone was so casual, it almost made me smile.

"I'm no doctor," I said. "But it's got to be better than eating parasites."

"Then I suppose it could be worth a try."

"It couldn't hurt." I pushed off the kitchen counter and stepped closer to her.

She swiveled on her stool, turning to face me. Her hair was loose over her shoulders, and I put my hand in it because I wanted to feel it run through my fingers. I carefully brushed it away from her face, savoring the moment. Her face was lifted, her hands gripping her thighs as though she was nervous. Her eyes were large and dark, her lips slightly parted. She was so beautiful, I almost wanted to freeze time so I could be caught in this moment of delicious anticipation forever.

I *almost* wanted to freeze time.

But I wanted to kiss her a whole lot more.

"It's scientific," she whispered.

"What is?"

"This. It's a scientific experiment on the effects of kissing on the symptoms of ME."

"Gotta love science," I said. Then I kissed her.

She tasted like fresh, warm cookies, and she leaned her body against me, opening her lips to me. It had been a while since I'd kissed anyone other than Carla, but I didn't remember it ever making me feel as though I'd been set alight before.

And I wasn't talking about being set on fire as in the stunt sense, where even though I was protected by a thick suit, the heat was still intense, my eyes watered, and I had to breathe through a tube.

No, kissing her made me feel hot from the inside out. Every nerve was ignited as need seared through me. Come to think of it, my desire for her was more like lightning than fire. It hit fast, consuming me, making me instantly hard.

Maybe it was because I liked her so much, or maybe it was that her body also seemed to vibrate. She felt like she was as eager for more than kissing as I was. As though she was undressing me with her mind. And believe me, I wanted to undress her right back. I had resolved to remain a gentleman—to keep one hand on her neck and the other on her back—but as her tongue stroked mine and I lost myself in the sensations of her mouth, I teetered on the edge of control.

I had a choice, to go further or to stop. And we'd only agreed on a kiss.

When I pulled back, her eyelashes fluttered open. Her eyes were deliciously hazy, a warm, liquid brown, and her expression was softer than I'd ever seen it. Her lips looked a little redder than usual, and she looked beautiful enough to make any man fall in love with her.

Could *I* fall in love with her?

I'd spent the last decade being so cautious around women, making sure they knew I wasn't interested in a relationship, that all this time I'd barely considered whether one day I might want that very thing. Until now, I'd never met anyone I wanted to spend all my time with. Someone I thought about when we weren't together, who made me smile and impressed the hell out of me, and who I looked forward to seeing.

Huh. How ironic would it be if I fell for someone who didn't want a relationship?

No, I couldn't fall for Carla, no matter how much I liked her. She'd made it clear she didn't have room for me in her life, and I wasn't about to force myself on her. Besides, I was heading back to the movie set soon. No point in complicating things.

I wouldn't let myself fall for Carla and that was all there was to it.

"I'm leaving now," I told her, clenching my jaw and forcing myself to step backward. There was a serious throbbing situation going on in my jeans. "When does your spreadsheet say our next date will be?"

"Um." Her eyes were still hazy. She was so damn beautiful, the urge to keep kissing her almost overpowered me. "It's tomorrow. A stroll down the main street."

"Then I'll see you tomorrow."

I left quickly, before I did anything I might regret.

CHAPTER 17

CARLA

- Eight days to Valentine's Day -

The next day, I woke up feeling bad. My fatigue had dipped to dark orange on my scale.

Still, I tried to follow my morning routine as much as possible. I fed Freud and the chickens before eating breakfast and taking the combination of vitamins and supplements that I was trialing this month.

My brain was too foggy for work, and my body too weary for even the lightest exercise. After breakfast, I messaged Noah to let him know we'd need to cancel today's scheduled activity. I deleted it from the spreadsheet. And after a failed attempt to meditate, I eventually gave up on doing anything even remotely productive and went back to bed.

Freud fitted himself into my elbow, snuggling up as I curled my arm around him. If it were possible for a room to be good for illness, this room was the best I'd been in. The winter sun poured in through the window, filling the room with golden light. From the bed I could see my vegetables growing inside the cold frames, watch my chickens fussing around, and spot birds swooping from tree to tree. As much as I hated having to stay in bed, this room made it easier.

Around mid-morning, my watch reminded me that I'd been planning to call

Magdalena today. As I didn't want her to know I'd crashed, I messaged her instead.

Carla: Been thinking about you, brat. How's your Saturday?
    Mags: Shopping. Bored. You?
    Carla: It's a nice day in nowheresville. Want to visit? I'll send you the fare.
    Mags: Not that bored, nerd.
    Mags: How's your bearded banjo player?
    Carla: I know you're teasing, but he has a beard and a banjo.
    Mags: GET OUT NOW!
    Carla: Call you next week?
    Mags: I dunno. I don't want to catch redneck. How contagious is it?
    Carla: If you get the urge to wear flannel, seek medical help.
    Mags: Don't even joke.

After messaging my sister, I dozed a little. I ignored my alarm that told me it was time to eat again, although around lunchtime I dragged myself out of bed to heat up some soup. When I went back to bed, Freud was so fast asleep, he didn't seem to notice.

A little after three o'clock that afternoon, there was a knock on the door.

"Carla?" Noah's voice called from outside. "It's me."

"It's unlocked," I called back, struggling up to sitting. I heard the front door open and his footsteps down the wooden hallway. "In here." I pushed an extra pillow under my head.

He appeared in my doorway still stripping off his coat, his brow creased with worry.

"Didn't you get my message?" I asked.

He nodded. "I came to check on you. Is there anything I can do?"

"Nothing. I need to rest until I get over this crash."

He came right in and sat on the edge of the bed. Under his coat, he wore a navy button-down, and it looked great on him, like it had been fitted by a tailor. He smelled wonderful too, the aroma of the bakery clinging to him.

"What caused you to crash?" His frown deepened when I shrugged. "It wasn't kissing, was it?"

I shook my head, gazing at his lips. Even the word 'kissing' sent a shiver of longing into me. Why was I so obsessed with his kisses? Last time hadn't been enough to satisfy me. Kissing him again was all I could think about.

"Are you sure?" he asked.

I managed a smile. "Don't get excited. You're good, but not *that* good."

Relief eased his frown away. "I *am* that good."

Though he was joking, he wasn't wrong. My stomach fluttered when I thought about kissing him, and in my current state, feeling fluttery about anything was a miracle.

"I don't always know what triggers my fatigue," I said. "It usually gets worse if I try to do too much, but sometimes it hits hard for no reason at all."

"How do you know how much you can do?"

"I don't. All I know is that today I'm low in spoons."

"What?"

"Spoons," I repeated. "It's a way to describe how much energy I have."

His brow furrowed again, telling me he'd never heard of spoon theory. "Interesting way to measure energy. What does it mean?"

"Healthy people have lots of spoons. But being sick means I only get a limited number. Every time I get out of bed to do something, it costs me a spoon. If I run out of spoons, it means my energy is gone, and I can forget about doing anything else until tomorrow."

"But why spoons?"

"Look it up on the Internet." I waved a weary hand. "There's a story behind it, but I don't have the energy to explain."

He nodded. "Will you be okay?"

"Hopefully. But it's been a while since I've been this bad."

"Is there anything that can help?"

He was helping just by sitting there, taking my mind off it. He was a lot nicer to look at than my garden, that was for sure. But as much as I wanted to suggest that more kisses might help, I forced myself to shake my head.

"Nothing but time," I said.

"There must be something I can get you. Something to eat or drink? It doesn't feel right to do nothing." He reached out to stroke Freud, who was on my other side. My cat didn't open his eyes but rolled over a little more to offer him his belly.

"No. But thanks," I said, wondering if it would be a bad idea to ask Noah to rub *my* belly.

"Do you have a book to read? Or do you want to move to the couch so you can watch some TV?"

"I'm too tired for that." I tried not to sound sorry for myself but being this low in energy meant my body couldn't manufacture any of the hormones I needed to feel happy. The fatigue sapped me on a cellular level. My brain was starved of dopamine.

He reached for my hand and held it in his. He had strong, capable fingers. His touch was comforting. In fact, everything about him was comforting. He was so full of life and vitality, he glowed with it. It was like he had a direct channel to the source of the world's energy. Maybe that should have made me envious, or resentful, but strangely enough, his presence made me feel more secure. His touch anchored me to life. It gave me hope and made me feel warm.

It might not have been physically possible for me to feel happy without the right chemicals in my brain, but his touch brought me as close as I could get.

"How long will this last?" he asked.

"Ah, the million-dollar question." I tugged my lips to the side. "If only I knew."

"There has to be something I can do for you," he repeated.

"Talk to me for a while," I suggested. Usually when my symptoms were this bad, processing information was exhausting. But the fluttering in my stomach must have stimulated my nervous system because the fog in my brain had lifted a little.

"Okay." He shifted to make himself more comfortable. His leg rested against mine, and he kept hold of my hand. "What do you want to talk about?"

"Why don't you date?" I asked.

He wrinkled his nose. "You really want to know? You'll think it's funny."

"Good. Tell me."

"It's because women fall for me, and I don't like hurting them."

I gave him a smile that was small but real. He really was a miracle worker. "You're telling me you're so irresistible that women just can't help themselves?" I rolled my eyes, though honestly, it wasn't hard to believe. Not at all.

"I'm naturally friendly," he said with a shrug. "And you may not have noticed, but I can get a little protective. Some women have read more into it than I meant them to. I put out vibes that make them think I'm interested without even realizing."

"How many women?"

"It's happened a few times. The first was the worst, and that was here in

Green Valley. The second time was a woman in Virginia who had her sights set on turning one night into something longer. She was so persistent, things got rough. And more recently, a woman on the stunt crew got the wrong idea. I tried to make things clear, but she wouldn't take no for an answer. Finally, she quit, which wasn't what I'd wanted."

"Well, you don't have to worry about me," I told him. "I'm not going to fall in love with you."

"You'll be the first," he said so seriously that it made me laugh a little, despite how laughing made me short of breath.

Yes, I *laughed*. Amazing.

But when I'd finished laughing, I stared down at his hand still wrapped around mine, and realized I was jealous of the women he'd slept with, even if it had ended badly.

Logically, I knew I had no right to be jealous of him and *anyone*. But while my brain couldn't manufacture some of the chemicals I needed, it seemed to be doing just fine at manufacturing inappropriate envy.

"So you never date for real anymore?" I found myself asking. "Does that mean you're celibate?"

"I have been for a while. But I'm not opposed to having a fling, so long as it's clear where things stand." His tone was casual, but his eyes weren't. They held mine, seeming to make his statement into a suggestion.

I tightened my fingers around his. "Is that so?"

"I especially like kissing." His gaze dropped to my mouth and lingered there, tracing the curve of my lips, making my heart speed up.

"Do you enjoy kissing people you're pretending to date?" My voice had gone hoarse, and my throat had gone dry. The fluttering in my stomach had intensified, and a slow, delicious heat was developing as well. I shifted a little higher on the pillows, trying not to wince at the effort of having to drag aching bones upward.

He leaned forward even more, bringing his face close. His voice dropped to a murmur. "I like kissing those people the most."

His lips met mine, the kiss soft and tender. His lips coaxed mine open before he gave me his tongue. I wanted to groan with pleasure. The hot, shivery sensation spread through my body, making my pain fade. His mouth teased me with light pressure, not giving me enough of what I craved.

He was still holding my hand, and I wanted to pull it free so I could drag him closer. But he eased backward too soon, leaving me hungry for more.

With a serious expression, he gazed into my eyes. "You still haven't fallen in love with me, right?"

I let out another small laugh. "Not even close."

The smile that tugged at his lips was slow and warm, softening his face and making it even more gorgeous. "Keep fighting it."

I dragged in more air, trying to pull myself together and sound normal. If I had more energy, I'd kiss him again, only deeper and harder and longer. If my limbs could move freely, I'd grab his beard and use it to hold his face in place while I ravished his beautiful, amazing lips. And if my body didn't feel like it was rusted in place, I'd climb on him and rub myself against him, tearing off all our clothes in the process so I could satisfy the need he'd awakened.

Instead of doing any of those things, I let out a sigh. "I told you, I don't have the energy to fall in love."

"Do you have enough energy for another kiss?"

"That I can do."

This time, his kiss was firmer and deeper, and I strained my face upward into his kiss, greedy for him. He ran a hand into my hair, then lifted the back of my head, supporting it with his palm. What he did with my mouth could only be described as *WOW*. Before that moment, I'd firmly believed I preferred to be in control of every part of my life, including my body. But he controlled the kiss, moving my head the way he wanted and bossing my mouth with his, like he was the one in charge. It should have been everything I hated. Only it was by far the hottest kiss I'd ever experienced.

If I hadn't believed he had a problem with women falling in love with him before, that kiss wiped away any trace of doubt.

When he finally pulled away, I couldn't help gasping.

"You okay?" he asked.

"Uh-huh." Somehow I made a reassuring sound, though parts of me were at war with each other. Exhaustion was battling with desire. My limbs were still lead weights, but my stomach was turning cartwheels.

"I'll stay and cook you dinner," he said in a totally normal voice, as though he hadn't just torn my world apart and put it back together the way he wanted it.

I blinked wordlessly at him. If I could have spoken, I would probably have said he could do anything he wanted, so long as he kissed me like that again.

But my brain had stalled, and it was only when it roared back into life a few moments later that I realized I was driving straight into a danger zone. My nervous system was doing weird and probably dangerous things, and I needed to calm down. Overexerting myself when I was already fatigued meant risking a more serious relapse.

"No," I said hoarsely. "Please don't stay. I need you to leave."

He studied my face a moment, then reached for Freud to pet him. "Is this a real cat? He didn't move a muscle when we kissed, and I've never seen him on four legs."

My thoughts were sluggish, so it took me a moment to register the subject change. "He stands up twice a day. At mealtimes."

"If I stick around, I can feed him," he suggested. "Then I can see the miracle for myself."

I dragged in another deep breath, trying to relax my overactive insides. "You can't stay."

His gaze landed back on me. His eyes were darker than before, and I saw his concern for me as clearly as though he'd drawn a diagram. "You shouldn't be alone."

"I have to be alone." I was proud my voice didn't catch, that I was able to say it without giving any sign of how hard-won the realization had been. Far better to be alone than suffer through another painful breakup that would damage my nervous system even more. For months before Tomas finally moved out, I'd seen the end coming, known it would be inevitable. And the torment of watching our relationship crumble had made my illness so much worse.

The only really scary thing was that even knowing all that, there was still a part of me that didn't want Noah to leave.

"No, you don't," he said, because he had no idea what I'd been through.

"Please don't argue. I don't have the strength for it."

He stood up but didn't walk to the door. His frown hadn't budged. "I'll go if you insist, but I'll come back later to check on you."

"Give me three or four days. I doubt I'll start feeling better before then."

"I'll wait until tomorrow."

I shook my head. "Wednesday."

"*Wednesday*? No way. I'm not waiting that long."

"Malone, I'm serious. Call me Wednesday after work. No earlier."

"Will you swear to me you'll be okay until then? And that you'll call me if you're not?"

I relented a little. "Thank you for being worried. I'll be fine. Really."

As he walked toward the door, I felt a stab of regret and a strong urge to ask him to come back.

Then I told myself not to be silly.

My regret was a warning sign.

The smart thing to do would be to encourage him to get reacquainted with Mandy. If they hit it off, it'd end my longings for what I couldn't have.

Everyone would get what they needed.

He paused at the door and turned back to me. His frown was deeper than ever, and the worry in his eyes made my chest feel several sizes too small.

"Get better, Chuckles," he ordered. "Okay?"

CHAPTER 18

NOAH

- Seven days to Valentine's Day -

On Monday, at the bakery, I added even more swirls and flourishes when I decorated the cupcakes.

I added a *whole lot* of swirls and flourishes. In fact, some of the cupcakes became so thickly covered with swirls and flourishes, there was more frosting than cake. But I was worrying about Carla and keeping my hands busy helped a little. So over the course of the day, they became even more ornate. Joy kept exclaiming over how pretty they were, and apparently the customers liked them. Nobody seemed to mind that I was creating cupcake versions of a Valentine's-themed Taj Mahal.

Carla had survived her whole life without me to look after her. But I still hated the fact there was nothing I could do for her. And I hated the man who'd run out on her after she got sick. Whatever excuses she'd been prepared to accept from him, her ex-fiancé was an asshole. It didn't matter that Carla wasn't mad at him; I was mad enough for the both of us.

If only she'd agreed I could go and see her before Wednesday, or at least call her, I wouldn't feel so edgy. My worry was like having insects gnaw at me, and I kept getting my phone out and having to put it away again. Did she really expect me to wait all that time before making sure she was okay?

I was frowning down at the cakes, topping off another towering creation, when I was interrupted by Jennifer's voice.

"You're very good at that."

I looked up to meet her violet eyes and put the piping bag down so I wouldn't accidentally topple my creation. "Hi Jennifer."

She leaned against the counter. "I know you only agreed to work until Valentine's Day, but you have a permanent job here, if you want it. I'd like you to stay and decorate our birthday and holiday cakes."

I shook my head. "Thanks, but I can't stay. They're expecting me back at a movie set in Arizona."

I'd told Joy and the others I did stunts, but had glossed over the details, not telling them I was one of the few drivers in the business who did the really dangerous car work. I wasn't even sure why I'd kept quiet about it, only that in the warm, comforting atmosphere of the bakery, I couldn't imagine how to explain it to them.

She looked disappointed. "Well, if you change your mind, I'd be glad to welcome you back."

When she'd gone, I picked the piping bag back up and bent back to my work. Not that it felt much like work. I restored cars in my spare time because I needed a creative outlet. Painting them was the best part, and when I got engrossed in a design, time seemed to slip away. Decorating cupcakes wasn't as engrossing, but it was still fun.

"Hey." It was Joy's cheerful voice interrupting me this time.

I looked up with a sigh, making a show of reluctantly putting the piping bag back down, though I didn't mind when Joy stopped to chat. While I frosted cakes, I was a captive audience for her. At first, I'd been a little flummoxed by the way she'd assumed we were instantly friends, telling me all kinds of things about her life. But I was coming to appreciate her. It was a real shame there weren't two Cletus Winstons in the world. Joy deserved to be happy, and I felt bad that she'd fallen for someone she couldn't have.

"Are you due for a break yet?" Joy asked.

I perked up. "You have cake?"

Her ever-present smile widened. "Two of the caramel cakes collapsed in the middle."

"Give me five minutes to finish this tray, then I'll grab the spoons."

We sat in the small break room at the back of the bakery, and I already had a mouthful of delicious caramel cake when Joy said, "You turned Jennifer's offer down, huh?"

I nodded, swallowing. "I have a contract on another job."

"What kind of job?"

"Exploding car."

Her spoon stopped halfway to her mouth. "Really? And what? You're going to be *inside* the car when it blows up?"

I shrugged, taking another bite.

"Why would you do something like that?" she asked.

"The money's good."

"But I don't think you care that much about money," she said, surprising me. "You never even asked how much you'd get paid before taking the job here."

I finished my cake and licked my spoon clean while she watched. Though she still had half her cake left, she seemed more interested in studying my face than in finishing it.

"There's a kid I'm looking after," I said finally. "He's a hotshot. Needs someone to keep him in line, or he'll do things he's not ready for."

"And that's your job?"

"Nobody else is doing it."

She nodded, taking another mouthful of cake. "Nice of you to look out for him, but at some point, he'll need to take care of himself."

"At some point," I agreed.

"You ever think you might be *too* nice?"

"Nope." I stole a heaping spoonful of her cake.

"Hey!" She laughed, fending off my spoon as I tried to go in for another bite. "How's Carla?" she asked. "When am I going to meet her?"

"Hopefully she'll be well enough to come into the bakery this week."

"I can't believe she's been living in Green Valley for a year, and I haven't heard anything about her."

"She doesn't go out much."

"Because of her illness?"

"That's not my story to tell."

"Okay." Joy gave me a smug smile. "I'll wait until she comes in here, then we'll become best friends and I'll learn all her secrets the way I'm learning yours. Isn't that right, bestie?"

"You don't know all my secrets."

"Not yet. But I have plenty more cake."

Damn, she was good.

We'd finished our cakes and were heading back to our counters when my phone rang. "I need to take this," I said, seeing my stunt director's name flash up on the screen.

"Sure, bestie," said Joy. "Tell me all about it later."

I shook my head at her, then walked back into the break room to get some privacy as I answered the call.

"Hey, Moose," I said. "What's up?"

"Noah! How's the arm?"

"Fine." I flexed my hand into a fist, looking down at my scar. It had healed well and wasn't stiff anymore.

"The engineering team have finished work on the bridge, and the shoot's running to schedule. Director wants a few set-ups in the can first, and we'll shoot the Bridge Bang on the twentieth."

I hesitated, thinking about Carla.

But there was no reason to be reluctant to leave her. I wasn't supposed to be getting attached. Besides, she'd said she needed to be on her own and there wasn't anything I could do for her. She'd told me without any doubt or hesitation that I'd only get in the way if I hung around.

"Brash has been on my ass," Moose said when I didn't answer right away. "He thinks he's ready for the big jobs. Do you?"

"Nope. He's not ready."

There were only a few of us in the industry who could get the most cutting-edge stunts done safely. And there was a good reason we earned more than anyone else. The profession had a high mortality rate. Moose once told me he'd broken fifty-six bones. He winced every time he got out of his chair.

Brash was determined to follow in our footsteps, and I couldn't stop him. I could only slow him down, teach him all I knew, and give him a chance to build up to the really dangerous stunts, making sure he knew exactly what he was doing. One day, I'd have to walk away and trust that I'd taught him enough.

Not yet, though. And he couldn't do the Bridge Bang.

"What day are you flying in?" asked Moose.

"The seventeenth."

"Good. Then you'll be ready to work on the twentieth."

"Sure," I said. "I've got a contract, don't I? That means I'll be there."

CHAPTER 19

CARLA

- Four days to Valentine's Day -

"**A**re you ready?" asked Noah, his hand on the door that led to the kitchen of the Donner Bakery.

Before answering, I took a moment to do a quick mental and physical check. My palms were sweaty with nerves. Could I handle the stress of meeting Noah's boss and co-workers?

My fatigue had improved over the past few days, but even very brief stretching and tai chi routines were taking more out of me than they should, and I'd had to shorten my workdays to make sure I was getting enough rest to recover.

Though I'd felt well enough to drive myself to the bakery, I would have preferred to wait another day or two before making the trip to thank Noah's boss for the cookies. But the longer I left it, the more time I'd have to worry about my visit, and the more ungrateful I'd seem.

Besides, I'd been forced to delete two tasks from my spreadsheet. This was a chance to resume my progress. And if I were being completely honest, my willingness to do this had a lot to do with the affectionate way Noah talked about the bakery. His childhood memories sounded so nice, how stressful could visiting the bakery really be? Besides, I liked the idea of being able to picture him at work, decorating cakes.

Not that I thought about him when we weren't together... Well, okay, maybe I did. Maybe I thought about him all the time. So what? It didn't *necessarily* mean I was getting too attached to him, just because it made me feel good to think about what he might be doing and imagine him—

"Chuckles?" His hand was frozen on the door as his eyes darkened with worry at the length of my hesitation. His brow creased and he searched my face, clearly looking for signs of illness.

"Yes. Ready." I brushed my palms over my coat, then nodded firmly, though my heart was pounding, and I was starting to feel a little breathless.

Noah gave my face one more searching look, then pushed open the door. At the same time, he reached for my hand and held it as we went inside.

The first thing to hit me was the aroma of fresh baking, so delicious it made my mouth water. Though Noah had finished work for the day, others clearly hadn't. A man was kneading dough, and a woman was chopping chocolate brownies into squares. The woman was singing to herself, having clearly not noticed us come in. The man nodded at us.

The kitchen was so warm, I would have unbuttoned my coat if I didn't have one hand wrapped inside Noah's. It was bright, with gleaming surfaces. I instantly got why Noah liked working there. Despite being a commercial kitchen, somehow it still managed to have a homey feel. Maybe it was the woman singing to herself, or the clatter of the knife on the tray, or the aroma of... Wait, were those banana cakes in the oven? No wonder the place smelled like heaven.

It really was as nice as Noah had described. The tightness in my chest eased. Maybe I'd been worried about nothing and ticking this task off the spreadsheet would be easy.

"There's Jennifer," Noah said as a woman came out of an office at the back of the kitchen. She was short and pretty, with dark hair and lovely violet eyes.

Noah tugged my hand, drawing me closer, and Jennifer gave me a warm smile. "You must be Carla," she said. "It's a pleasure to meet you."

"Pleasure to meet you too." I made sure my breathing was even, focusing on keeping my system as calm as possible. "And thank you for the cookies. They were delicious."

"Oh, I can't claim all the credit." She gave a musical laugh. "Noah did most of the work. Though I did want to ask how you liked them."

"You have no idea how wonderful it was to have something different to eat," I said with feeling. "Something I didn't make myself."

"I know just what you mean. There's nothing better than having someone to take care of you."

Her words sounded innocent enough, but when I glanced at Noah, he was looking back at me with such warmth in his eyes that I wanted to blush. He was still holding my hand, and I was acutely aware of how good his big, capable hand felt wrapped around mine.

I didn't want his grip to feel so nice. It wouldn't do me any good to get used to it.

"Were the cookies sweet enough for your taste?" asked Jennifer. "We want to offer a selection of low-carb, low-sugar cookies."

"They were perfect. I loved the pistachio ones. Such a nice flavor."

She tilted her head thoughtfully. "Walnut would be nice, too, don't you think?"

"Walnut would be lovely." She was so sweet, I gave her a grateful smile. I felt more comfortable with her than I'd expected.

"I've been thinking about ways to make them crunchier," Jennifer went on. "The thing with almond flour is that it gives them a soft texture."

"I liked the texture. Not crunchy, but firm."

"What about an alternative without nuts? Coconut and orange zest, perhaps." Her gaze went to the ceiling, as she was clearly thinking aloud. "Not sweetened coconut. Maybe a teaspoon of coconut crystals? They're lower on the glycemic index than sugar." She dropped her gaze back to me. "Would they still be okay for your diet with coconut crystals?"

"I don't know what coconut crystals are," I admitted.

"Let me get the packet so you can take a look." As she opened a cupboard to search for what she wanted, I felt my tension drain. Was being here really going to be this easy? I wanted to laugh with relief.

Noah squeezed my hand and gave me a questioning look that turned into a smile. "Told you," he said softly.

"Don't look so smug." I pulled my hand free from his to poke his arm. "Show me the cookies you decorate."

"I'll grab some." He walked away as Jennifer came back with a packet in her hand.

"They're made by heating the sap of the coconut flower," she said. "This is an organic version that's barely processed and..." She broke off, her gaze shifting to the door we'd entered through.

I heard the commotion and turned.

Three young boys were coming into the kitchen, all talking excitedly in loud voices. A large, bearded man was behind them. He looked familiar, and for a moment I wondered where I'd seen him before. Then a woman walked in behind him, and my heart plummeted like a dying bird, dropping into the sea of stomach acid that was starting to bubble.

"Aunty Jenn!" yelled the youngest of the boys, bounding toward Jennifer. "Can I have some cake?"

"Now, Pedro," his father chided. "Have you forgotten your manners?"

"Well, hello. What a lovely surprise." Jennifer's smile grew even larger as the small boy skidded up to her. "As it so happens, I have some freshly baked chocolate cake that absolutely must be eaten." She dropped an affectionate hand on the boy's shoulder as she turned to Noah and me. "Have y'all met Jethro and Sienna, and my three ravenous nephews? This hungry rascal is Pedro."

"Nice to meet you, Pedro," said Noah.

I was frozen, unable to look around or smile at Sienna's son. I certainly couldn't say anything. I was focused on one person only.

My cousin was standing next to her husband, flashing her charismatic smile at me. She looked delighted to see me, but I could only stare at her in horror as I flashed back to the first—and by far the worst—anxiety attack I'd ever had.

Last time I'd seen my cousin, my system had gone into overdrive, my heart pounding so hard it had felt like it was smashing its way free. My panic had caused a serious crash, and my health had taken a long-term dive.

Now my heart was doing the same thing all over again. My lungs emptied themselves and couldn't refill.

There was no air in the bakery.

What if I crashed again this time? What if I lost every one of the painfully slow gains I'd made?

"Hello!" Sienna said brightly. And everyone in the bakery gazed with adoration at her. Because how could they not? My cousin was even more brilliant and beautiful in real life than she was in her movies.

Any moment, she'd start talking to me. What would I say if she asked how I was doing? We'd shared big dreams as kids, but what did I have to talk about now? Only my illness. Or Tomas leaving me. Or how I'd left work and sold my shares at the wrong time.

And I couldn't even fill my lungs, so how could I possibly form words?

My legs trembled and pain lanced through my chest. I was going to vomit. My body was already wet with sweat.

Running out of the Piggly Wiggly had worked for me. If I rapidly exited the bakery, Sienna wouldn't be able to ask about my life, or notice I was gasping instead of breathing.

Yanking my hand from Noah's, I stumbled backward. I skirted the tables to avoid barreling into Sienna, her husband, or children.

"Hi Sienna!" I gasped out as I went. "I'm sorry I can't stick around. I just remembered I have…" I ran out of breath and the words turned into a weirdly strangled sound. My feet were the only things working properly, carrying me toward the door.

"Carla." Noah sounded shocked. "Are you—"

"Fine!" It came out too loud, like a bark. "I'm fine! Sorry, I have this thing. A thing that I need to do."

"Carla?" Sienna's brow was furrowed, her eyes worried.

Her expression made me even more aware of how pitiful my sudden escape must look.

There was no saving the situation now.

I waved a hand in the air as I went. "Sorry. Nice to see you! I have to go." I bolted through the door, hating myself as I went.

Even as the door was closing behind me, I regretted leaving. I was doing it because I was so afraid of what Sienna must think of me, but my disappearing act would make it so much worse. I could imagine everyone in the bakery turning to each other with mystified looks. They'd be too polite to say how weird and rude I was, even if they were all thinking the same thing.

The scene was so clear in my head and so unspeakably awful, it only made me jog faster. Even though exhausting myself made another crash more likely, I moved as fast as my heavy legs could carry me. I burst through the door without stopping, then kept going to the parking lot, to the safety of my car.

As I got into the car and shut the door, I saw Noah coming after me. Hands shaking, I managed to start the ignition before he reached me.

"Carla, wait!" He bent to look at me through the window, his eyes wide with questions.

"I'm sorry." I shifted the car into reverse. "Please tell them I'm sorry."

He said something else, but I was focused on pulling out of the parking spot.

I forced myself not to look back to see if he was still standing there as I drove away.

It felt like a very long drive to get home. My head was pounding, and my limbs were weak and trembling, but the worst part was my self-loathing. What kind of person ran away from their own cousin? How had I sunk so low? I should turn around and drive back. Explain and apologize. It would be the only decent—the only *normal*—thing to do. But I couldn't make myself do it.

I shed a frustrated tear or two on the way home, but by the time I got there, I was almost dry-eyed. Considering what had happened, that seemed like a minor miracle.

I made it into my bedroom on legs that were shakier than ever, and collapsed on my bed with Freud, curling into a ball around him. As I screwed my eyes shut, dragging in fast, shallow breaths, all I could think about were the shocked expressions of everyone in the bakery.

How could I face Noah again?

Rushing out must have embarrassed him. He wouldn't want anything more to do with me after that shameful scene. There'd be no more fake dates. No more laughing together. No more long conversations.

No more kisses.

I'd send him a text message to apologize, but if he didn't reply, I'd have to suck it up. He'd probably tell his mother we broke up. Seeing as he was leaving soon, she might not have time to set him up with anyone else in the meantime.

I rubbed my chest. It was aching worse than ever.

Maybe Noah's mother would set him up with Mandy. It would be for the best. I only hoped Mandy would appreciate how lucky she was.

I was going to cry. Or throw up. Probably both.

My watch was warning me about my heart rate. Somehow, I managed to drag in some deep breaths. Then I forced myself to try to meditate. After a while, the pain in my chest lessened.

"Carla?" Noah's voice called from the porch. He rapped on the front door. "Chuckles, let me in."

I pushed myself up to sitting. "Noah?"

By rights, I should tell him to go away and leave me to my self-induced misery before I embarrassed him any more than I already had. But I got out of bed and made my weak legs carry me to the front door. As I pulled it open, I was already apologizing.

"I'm sorry, Noah. I shouldn't have rushed out like that, but when I saw

Sienna, I got so overwhelmed. I made a fool of myself and made you look bad and—"

"Hush." He put his arms around my shoulders to draw me against him. "It's okay. Are you okay?" His voice was a comforting rumble, and he smelled like the bakery, like chocolate and banana deliciousness.

I dragged in as deep a breath as I could manage, sliding my hands around his waist and pressing my face against his chest.

"I'm… yes," I mumbled into his coat. "But more importantly, are you okay? That was your boss, and the people you work with, and I embarrassed you."

"No, you didn't. I was just worried about you."

"I feel like a weak, pathetic fool. I *hate* being weak."

"You're not weak, and you're not a fool. Nobody thinks you're either of those things."

"Jennifer was being so nice." I let out a groan. "I was so rude and weird."

He drew back a little so he could see my face. "Jennifer's cool. When you go back to the bakery, she won't say a word."

"Go back?" I shook my head. "There's no way. I couldn't."

He stared down at me for a moment, then looked behind him at the front door. It was ajar, and cold air was seeping in. He pulled away from me so he could shut it, and I took a moment to pull myself straighter and tell myself to stop being so pitiful. But I was shaking. My nerves were still jangling, and my gut was churning.

Making a fist, I covered it with my other shaky hand, squeezing it hard. "I need to calm down. I'm still recovering from my last crash, and if my nervous system overworks itself, I'll end up back in bed."

He stripped off his coat and hung it up. "You want a drink or something?"

"Maybe some ice water?"

I followed him into the kitchen and eased onto a stool next to the counter while he poured us both a glass of water. Watching his capable movements, I gave myself a pep talk. There was nothing worse than being weak. I couldn't change what I'd done, but I could start acting like someone with a backbone.

Putting our water glasses on the counter, Noah sat on the stool next to mine. "Now, let's talk about it."

I took a sip before I spoke. "I wasn't expecting Sienna to turn up."

"Neither was I. But what exactly made you freak out?"

"She called me months ago, and I should have called her back. I've been feeling guilty about it." I was hoping that would be enough to satisfy him, but

Noah didn't say anything. I took another sip of water, meeting his gaze. He still didn't say anything, and his expression was weighted with expectation.

Dammit, I *had* to keep talking.

"Okay, so I had a flashback to the last time I saw my cousin," I said in a rush, setting my glass back down. "I told you it was at a family wedding, didn't I? Well, it was before I was diagnosed, and I couldn't find a doctor who could tell me what was wrong with me. The medical tests all said I was fine, even though I was getting sicker. I was trying to keep working, but it wasn't going well. I was struggling."

"Sounds like a rough time."

I nodded. "I was in a bad place, and probably shouldn't have forced myself out of bed to go to the wedding. Tomas…" I hesitated, remembering how my fiancé had gotten angry because I hadn't felt well enough to go to his work function. "Tomas was supposed to go with me, but we had a fight, so he bailed. I was on my own, and seeing Sienna there, with my mother watching us…" I shook my head. "I had my first bad anxiety attack. It wasn't anything Sienna did. It was that I had no idea what I'd say when she asked me how I was doing."

"You couldn't tell her the truth?"

"When we were kids, we talked about all the great things we were going to do. Only she's gone and done them."

His brow furrowed. "You've done great things, too."

I shook my head. "Sienna walks red carpets. Her life is amazing. And I spend most of my time staring at the ceiling above my bed."

"Why are you comparing your life to hers? You're different. Not better or worse."

"Ugh." I dropped my face into my hands and mumbled around them. "But my mother's been in my ear about Sienna for so many years, she's not even my cousin anymore. She's become a symbol of how disappointed Mom is in me."

"You think your mother's disappointed in you because you got sick?" I could hear the frown in his voice. "It wasn't something you could control."

"Sure it's not logical, but try telling that to my sweaty palms." With a grimace, I lifted my face off those still-damp palms. "When I saw Sienna at the wedding, I was overwhelmed. Afterward, I crashed badly, and I kept getting worse. All that was in my head when I saw her this time. So, like a genius, I handled my feelings of inadequacy in a way that made them worse."

"I get why you felt overwhelmed, but you're being too hard on yourself."

"And you're being sweet, but I know how bad it must have looked when I ran out." I sucked in a breath, trying to inject a little steel back into my spine. "I guess I'll have to go back to the bakery to apologize to Jennifer. But how can I explain? She must think I'm such a freak."

He swiveled on his stool to face me more completely, then twisted my stool so I was facing him. Putting his knees on either side of mine, he fixed me with his gorgeous green eyes. Trapped, I couldn't do anything but gaze back at him.

"It doesn't matter what anyone thinks. You've faced more adversity than most, and you're still going." His expression was so serious, he looked stern. "You're fierce, and you're resilient. Far from freakish. I'd even go so far as to call you impressive."

I swallowed a lump in my throat. He was being so nice, he was triggering my urge to cry. But there was no way I'd let tears out. Not going to happen.

"Impressive might be overstating things," I said. "You should know that one time my brain was so foggy, I poured Fraud's cat treats into the soup I was cooking. *And* I almost ate the entire bowl before I realized what the crunchy bits were."

Though I was trying to lighten the mood, he didn't smile.

"You haven't just been surviving your illness. You've been trying everything humanely possible to get better. And what energy you have, you're using to create software to help other people. If you're ever stuck for something to say, talk about that."

His gaze was direct, his eyes warm. When he looked at me like that, I felt like I could do anything.

"I hate telling people about my illness," I admitted. "Because I don't look sick, I worry they assume I'm lazy or weak."

"I didn't think that."

"You're nicer than other people."

"And you're not weak," he fired back. "When you got sick, you could have given up. Instead, you moved across the country to a strange town, all alone, doing everything you could so you could work on your software. It must have been scary moving here by yourself when you didn't know if you might relapse."

It wasn't *not* scary," I admitted. But he was making me out to be a whole lot braver than I deserved. I'd been terrified. I was *still* terrified. But it would have been even scarier staying in my parents' house, feeling like my life was over at thirty, that after missing my one shot at success, I had nothing left to give.

"You were scared but you did it anyway." He took one of my hands in his and rubbed the pad of his thumb across the back of it. A small gesture, but it gave me a huge number of squishy feelings. "Like I said, Chuckles. Impressive."

His gaze didn't drop. The clear green of his eyes took my breath away, but in a good way. He looked at me as though he was only seeing the best of me. It made me want to live up to what he saw.

Why had I been feeling sorry for myself?

I was lucky enough to be sitting here with him. And the way he was looking at me, I should feel sorry for anyone who wasn't me.

"Thank you." I hadn't meant to lower my voice, but the words came out barely louder than a whisper.

He sat back a little. Though he'd only retreated an inch or two, I immediately wished he hadn't. I liked being close to him, trapped between his knees, with his hand wrapped around mine.

"And that's not all." His mouth softened, his expression becoming less serious. "I haven't even told you my favorite thing about you yet." He reached up to my face and I couldn't breathe as he ran the back of his index finger very gently down my cheek. "You have the most adorable dimples in the world," he said softly.

My chest tightened, as though my heart was getting larger and there wasn't enough room for it to expand. I blinked rapidly, strictly forbidding any tears to escape.

"I don't have dimples." I tried to inject a note of sternness into my voice to keep from falling apart.

"You're right, they're more like dimplettes."

Even if he hadn't been utterly gorgeous, Noah would still be the most beautiful person I knew. How was it possible for anyone to be so kind and sweet?

Over the last few years, my opinion of myself had sunk. I'd been thinking of myself as something broken. But when he looked at me like that, with his lovely green eyes so hot and hazy, I felt whole.

More than whole.

I felt invincible.

"You're only saying I have dimples because you're hoping I'll hug you." My voice was suddenly gruff. There was a hole in my chest that could only be filled by his touch. I needed his arms around me again, and I didn't care how shameless I had to be to get it. "Honestly, Malone, if you want a hug so badly that you're prepared to make up non-existent dimples to get one, why not just ask?"

He grinned. "It's my way of asking."

I stood up, almost knocking the stool over in my haste, and then his arms were around me, holding me as tightly as I needed him to hold me. So tightly, he straightened my world, setting it to right. Making it perfect.

I slid my hands around his waist and pressed my cheek against his shirt. He smelled comforting, and delicious, and exciting all at once. I loved how his clothes absorbed the aroma of the bakery, making him smell like the forbidden foods I could only dream of tasting.

He stroked my back, and I felt his lips on my hair as he kissed the top of my head. "Is that better?" he murmured.

I made a 'Mmm' noise to tell him it was perfect. My muscles were relaxing into him and the noise in my head was quietening, my chaotic thoughts softening into mindfulness far more easily than when I'd tried to meditate. Which made total sense. I mean, how could I be anywhere but in the moment, in the *now*, when he felt this good?

One of his hands was making circles on my upper back, massaging me over my shirt. The other was on my lower back, a comforting weight.

I kissed his soft, naked neck, filling myself with his scent. The tremor of my nerves was being replaced with another, far nicer sensation. A heavy wanting that came from low in my body. An arousal that felt like an ache.

"How are you so nice?" I asked, my lips against his skin. "Were you born this sweet?"

"Actually, I was. My mother worked in the bakery and ate cake every single day when she was pregnant."

"That explains it." Angling my face up, I found his lips waiting for me. His short beard was rough against my face, but the roughness only made his lips feel softer. Closing my eyes, I let the sensation of his mouth consume me. Everything else dropped away, leaving just the intense pleasure of his tongue dancing with mine.

My ache of longing intensified as he hardened against me. As good as he felt, I needed to touch him. Instead of clothing, I needed his skin.

Shoving my hands under his shirt, I ran them upward, exploring the muscles of his back, wanting to know every part of him. He let out a low groan. His erection pressed into me, and his kiss became more insistent. I could feel how aroused he was, and all I wanted was to lose myself in him.

"Will you stay the night with me?" I could barely lift my lips from his for long enough to ask.

He drew back from me, wrapping his hands around my upper arms to move me away and look into my face.

"Chuckles." His tone was serious, his eyes dark with hunger. "Are you sure?"

"Totally sure." I needed to press my body back to his, but his hands were still holding my arms, and he wasn't kissing me. Why wasn't he kissing me? Was his hesitation about our agreement, how he was afraid I might fall in love with him?

But then he asked, "Do you have enough spoons?"

"You looked it up?" I didn't wait for him to nod, but said, "I have spoons. Plenty of spoons. We can spoon. If you don't spoon me, I'm going to…" I bit my lip, wanting to scream. "You don't want to do this?"

He was too serious. I couldn't believe he was the daredevil, the one who rolled cars, and *he* was the one being cautious. I was the sensible one, the one who could crash if I got too wired, the one who'd sworn never to have another relationship unless I was miraculously cured, the one with the most to lose. Yet none of that mattered when I ached for him so badly, I felt like I might burst if he refused me.

"Of course I want you." Each word came out slowly. Almost reluctantly. As though he didn't trust himself to speak. His expression was tight. Controlled. But his gaze was intense, and his shoulders were high, as though his muscles had gone rigid. His fingers pressed a little too tightly into my arms.

He had to be feeling the same overwhelming longing for me as I was for him. I just had to convince him not to hold back.

"I'm not going to fall for you, if that's what you're worried about. This is just for tonight." I closed my eyes, hating how desperate I sounded and fighting to get my control back. How could he be so controlled when I was so on edge?

"It's been two years since I so much as kissed anyone else, Malone." I spoke with my eyes closed so I didn't have to see his reaction. "If you don't want to do this, I won't force you. But tell me now so I can go and take a cold shower."

"You have no idea how much I want you." His voice scraped over gravel and broken glass. "I just need to be sure you won't get hurt."

"I won't get hurt." I opened my eyes. "I have enough spoons, and despite what you think, you're not irresistible." Only the last part was a bald-faced lie. "Does that about cover it?" I held up one hand in the universal gesture for making a promise. "I solemnly swear I won't run out of spoons tonight, and I even-more-solemnly swear not to fall in love with you. Is that good enough? Oh, and that giant box of extra-large condoms you insisted on buying happens to be waiting on my nightstand, and we should make sure they're the right size. Not that we can return them, but I'm not sure buying an entire carton of the jumbo ones was—"

Before I'd finished talking, he was kissing me again.

"They're the right size," he growled against my lips.

Then he lifted me, still kissing me, and I wrapped my legs around him, clinging to him as he carried me into the bedroom.

CHAPTER 20

NOAH

his was a dream.

At least, it felt like one. Lately, I'd been spending a considerable amount of time fantasizing about undressing Carla. I'd pictured myself slowly peeling her clothes off, kissing every inch of her incredible body, and driving her mad with passion. I wanted to savor every moment, to gaze into her eyes as she came, to make her feel better than she'd ever felt.

Now the fantasy was coming true, but there was nothing slow about the way her clothes came off.

As soon as we reached the bedroom and her feet touched the floor, she stepped back from me to whip off her top and slacks, yanking them off so eagerly, it made me hope she'd been craving this moment as much as I had.

And holy shit, was her white cotton bra supposed to be that sexy?

I imagined she was wearing it because of its practical nature, but the way it both hid and revealed her magnificent breasts made my blood run even hotter. I'd always been an equal-opportunity breast admirer, and whether they were big or small hadn't mattered to me. But now I felt like a kid who'd been playing on swing sets, and I'd just glimpsed Disneyland.

In her sensible bra and panties, she was even more beautiful than I could have imagined. She looked better—more real, and more authentically *her*, somehow—than if she'd been wearing lacy lingerie. And as much as I wanted to reach for her, to have her in my arms again, she was such a feast for my eyes, I stayed right where I was, imprinting her into my memory.

I must have stayed frozen for a beat too long because Carla stopped and tilted her head, linking her hands in front of her as though she wasn't sure what to do with them.

"It's been a while since I've done anything like this, but if I remember correctly, don't you need to undress as well?" There was amusement in her tone, but a flicker of uncertainty in her eyes.

"You're gorgeous," I said sincerely, staying right where I was. "Do you have any idea how stunning you are?"

She laughed, her expression lightening. "I bet you say that to all the almost-naked women who undress in front of you."

"I told you, you're special." Though she was clearly joking, I didn't want her to get the wrong idea, so I stepped forward and took her hands. "Carla, this isn't something I do often."

"It isn't?"

I shook my head, thinking about how I should remind her that this couldn't lead to anything serious. But I no longer wanted to.

Only minutes ago, I'd been telling her how incredible she was, and I'd meant every word. For years she'd been fighting a daily battle for her strength and independence, yet she kept astonishing me with both. From the first moment she'd glared at me for disrupting her precious work time, to when she'd only consented to receive a hug if she was giving me something in return, she'd been impressing me and making me smile in equal measure.

Her resilience had been so hard-won, what right did I have to remind her of anything? All I wanted was to make love to her the way she deserved.

"I don't do this often either," she said. "And I have to tell you something." She lifted her chin, her expression suddenly serious. "I might not be able to orgasm. And if I can't, that's okay. You don't need to worry about it." She gave me a look that said she wasn't about to apologize for what she obviously believed was a shortcoming.

It took an effort to contain my reaction, but I did it. Even if whoever had made her feel that way deserved to feel the force of my wrath, I wasn't about to let any trace of that emotion show on my face.

"Okay." I lifted a hand to cup her cheek and matched her serious look with one of my own. "No expectations. Let's just enjoy ourselves."

She gave a slight nod. "If I don't orgasm, it doesn't mean I'm not having a good time. It's difficult sometimes, that's all. When my energy levels are low, or if my brain isn't working right."

"Duly noted." My voice was even, but inside I felt anything but. Her illness even affected this part of her life, and someone in her past had clearly made her feel bad about it.

"How are your energy levels now?" I asked.

"Now?" Her smile was so sweet, and at the same time so playful, it cracked my heart wide open. "Right now, I feel good. All systems green. And I hope I'm about to feel even better."

"That's the idea." Pulling her closer to kiss her, I ran my hands down her sides, loving the curve from her waist to her hips. How was such a fiery soul contained in such a beautiful package? Her shape was so feminine, she drove me wild. And as much as I loved the way she looked in that bra, it had to go.

When I unclasped her bra and her breasts fell free, I sucked in a breath of pure appreciation. I dropped my head to them, sucking one nipple into my mouth while I caressed the other.

Welcome to Disneyland.

Her breath deepened, and she let out a small groan of pleasure. I pushed her panties down, and while she kicked them off, she fumbled with the front of my jeans, trying to get my button undone.

I pulled back to help her, but she made a sound of protest when my mouth left her breast.

"Get on the bed," I told her.

"Wait." She turned to scoop up a large, fluffy lump from the bed and I realized it was Freud. Her cat didn't object to being set down on the floor. He yawned as he padded out of the room, probably in search of a quieter place to sleep.

"Now I get to watch you take your clothes off?" she asked, sitting down. Her gaze roved hungrily over my torso as I peeled off my shirt.

After toeing off my shoes, I stripped off my jeans. My erection sprang free with only the thin fabric of my boxer briefs to contain it. My dick was demanding attention, and I fisted myself over the fabric. Her eyes widened, and the lust I saw in her face made my dick throb even harder.

"Come here," she said, and I didn't need to be asked twice. I stripped naked before I joined her on the bed, lying next to her, facing her.

For a moment, we just gazed into each other's eyes, both of us smiling.

"Hi there," she said with a laugh.

"Hi yourself." I grinned back, enjoying the moment of anticipation before I kissed her again. She was magnificent. Her breasts overflowed my hands. Her skin was silky smooth. I stroked down her stomach, exploring between her legs. She was so wet. So warm and tight. So perfect.

"Are you okay?" I whispered, wanting to be sure.

"Very okay."

I stroked her, watching her face as she moaned, checking on the lengths of her panting breaths, adjusting the rhythm of my fingers as her eyelashes fluttered.

"You like it soft?" I murmured.

"That's perfect." She moaned again. "Just like that. Don't stop."

As I worked my fingers between her legs, I sucked on her nipples, letting my beard graze the sensitive underside of her breasts when I saw how she responded. Her nipples hardened even more under the attention of my tongue, and the soft flesh of her breast moved with each of her gasping breaths.

Sliding my finger into her made my dick jerk and strain as it demanded to replace my hand. But judging by the speed of her breaths, the little pants she gave, she was close to climax. Even more than being inside her, I wanted to watch her come.

The hand that had been digging into my shoulder hit the bed beside her, and she scrunched the sheets into her fist. Every exhalation turned into a moan. I kissed down her stomach, careful not to alter the movement of my hand between her legs. When I rasped my beard across the soft flesh of her belly, her cries got louder.

Then she let out a wail, and her body shuddered.

Part of me wished I had my mouth between her legs as she came, wanting to taste her and enjoy the intimacy of it. But at the same time, I relished the sight of her. She was utterly beautiful with her hair spread out, her gorgeous lips parted, her body shaking and jerking, moans of pleasure tearing from her throat. I loved seeing her so uncontrolled, with nothing to worry about but the sensations shuddering through her.

Finally, after her body stilled, she gazed at me with light, hazy eyes and such a happy smile that my heart expanded.

"God," she said in a dazed voice. "That was so good. It was almost too easy. It's not usually that easy for me."

I moved back up her body so I could gently kiss her lips. "No need to call me God. Just Noah will do."

She gave a breathless laugh. "You have a right to be smug. I didn't think I'd come, but it didn't even take long."

I drew back a little to study her face. "What's that?" I asked with a frown, squinting at her. "There's something in there."

"In where? What?" She lifted a lazy hand to her cheek. "You mean there's something on my face?"

"No, there's something waiting to come out of you. I think it's… yes, it is! It's another orgasm."

She gave what could only be called a giggle, and it was the most light-hearted sound—and therefore the best sound—I'd ever heard her make. "Not possible. I'm done."

"You want to bet?"

"It's your turn now, and the condoms are on the nightstand." She directed her gaze down, her eyes dancing. "Good thing you got the extra-large size."

I smirked. "Told you so."

She shifted so she could stroke my erection. My dick was so hard it ached, and her touch made me groan with need. Running my hand over her naked body, I caressed her breasts and stomach. She shivered a little under my touch at first, her skin extra sensitive after her orgasm. But when I turned some gentle attention back to her nipples, her breaths grew faster, and she let out a little moan. She tried to rub my dick harder, but I kept it pressed against her hip, limiting her access.

Slipping my hand between her thighs again, I gently stroked her. The feel of her soft, slippery heat almost made me lose control. But I just pressed my dick harder against her hip and told it to shut up until she was ready. She definitely had another orgasm in her, and I needed it to happen before I let myself go.

Lifting myself onto my free arm, I nuzzled her ear. "Which position is best for you?"

"I can't come from penetration."

"We'll see about that." I pressed my erection more firmly against her hip. Theoretically, this wasn't dirty talk, but try telling that to my dick. It couldn't be more enthusiastic about the topic of conversation. Especially if it was presented with a challenge.

"Well, I guess…" She hesitated. "On top."

"You have enough energy?"

She flashed a wicked smile. "I'll make do."

"Then on top it is." Her choice of position wasn't surprising, knowing how she liked to be in control.

She shifted to grab a condom from the box, and I took it from her and rolled it on. Then I lay back as she straddled me. At first she just sat over me, so she could kiss me, and as desperate as I was to be inside her, kissing her from underneath was pure pleasure. Her hair fell down on either side, forming a private curtain around us. Her breasts hung over me in the perfect position for me to admire their full beauty, and to be able to cradle them in my hands and worship their perfection.

She ground against me, teasing me by sliding back and forth over my dick. And when she finally took me deep inside her, I choked out an exclamation, barely able to keep from coming too soon.

Clenching her thighs, I stilled her. "Give me a second," I ground out. "Don't move." Then I dragged in a breath, getting myself under control again.

She smiled down at me, her hair falling forward, looking so beautiful, she just about stopped my heart. "You okay?" she asked.

I grinned. "Not terrible."

She gave a loud belly laugh that caused delicious tremors in my dick, and I released her thighs so I could stroke the incredible curves of her breasts. She planted both her hands on my chest and rode me, and I rolled my hips upward, driving myself deeply into her. Then I moved one hand to the juncture of her thighs so I could stroke her.

"That feels good," she gasped, putting her hands on my thighs and leaning back to give me better access.

I thrust upward as she drove down, lifting my head to watch myself slide in and out of her. At the same time, I teased her clit with my fingers, using her moans to judge the speed and pressure of my touch. She looked so sexy on top of me, it got harder and harder to hold myself back, so I had to concentrate on making sure she got there first. But by the time she threw her head back and unleashed cries of pure pleasure, coming on my dick in long, hot waves, I couldn't have held back a second longer if the survival of the entire human race had depended on it.

I exploded into her so hard, it felt like my balls turned inside out. And when she finally collapsed on top of me, I barely had the strength to pull her hair off my face and then wrap my arms around her.

We lay there for a long time, her full weight on me, her body as breathless as mine. Neither of us spoke. I wasn't sure I could have formed words if I'd tried. I was wrung out. Spent. But that wasn't the only reason for my silence. Underneath the blissed-out, post-coital feeling that was sending waves of well-being and contentment through me, there was an uneasy feeling deep in my gut.

What we'd just done had been great. But weirdly, the part I was lying there thinking about—smiling about—wasn't the orgasm I'd been so desperate for. It was that moment when she'd looked down at me and let out a belly laugh that had made her breasts jiggle and sent tremors through my dick. I couldn't stop thinking how that laugh had filled me with warmth. How making her laugh had made me feel like the king of the world. And that feeling had been even better than the orgasm.

Despite all the assurances we'd given each other that we were going to have no-strings-attached, means-nothing sex, I felt a tenderness toward her that had me holding her tight. I wanted to kiss her, and keep kissing her, until we had the strength to make love again. And again.

That was a dangerous feeling to have when it so clearly wasn't what Carla wanted.

I made myself loosen my arms and let her go.

Rolling off me slowly, she tucked herself into my side with her head on my chest. She glided her fingers over my stomach in a few lazy circles while I enjoyed the bliss of pure relaxation.

After a while, her finger went up to my shoulder and stopped.

"What's this scar from?" she asked.

I lifted my head to glance down. "That one? I had to drive through a junk yard, crashing through big piles of trash. It almost went perfectly, but a tiny piece of metal punched through the windshield like a little bullet." When she jerked her worried gaze up to mine, I added, "It wasn't nearly as bad as it looks. A tiny wound that somehow turned into a much bigger scar."

"What movie was it for?"

"A thriller called *Jumpstart*. Have you seen it?"

She shook her head.

"Don't bother. It wasn't good."

"But you donated a piece of your flesh to making it." She was running her finger back and forth along my scar. "It changed you forever. Good thing that little bullet didn't hit your eye."

"They paid me a massive bonus." It sounded a little lame, but she didn't say anything else about it, just moved her finger to another faded ridge on my bicep. "And this scar?"

"That one came from an action movie I liked a lot better."

"No matter how good the movie is, I hate the thought of you getting more scars or breaking any more bones." Resting her chin on my chest, she looked up at me sternly. "Promise me? No more accidents?"

I gave a little shrug. Though it felt good that she cared, it wasn't a promise I could make. "I do everything I can to stay safe."

"You could stick to decorating cakes."

"I could. But I'd never be rich."

"You're already rich, Malone, in every way that matters." There was such warmth in her eyes, it made my chest tighten. Part of me wanted to crack a joke, but she looked so serious, I couldn't do it.

"To be honest, I've never cared that much about how rich I am." I swept her hair off her face and over to the side, mainly because I loved running it through my fingers. "My daddy made good investments and had a big life insurance policy. Thanks to him, Momma and I never had to worry too much about money."

"He must have been a good dad."

"The best." I smiled. "He would have liked you."

She looked pleased. "Thanks. I hope so."

"What's not to like?"

"I used to want to be rich," she said. "I thought it would make me feel important."

"You're important," I told her, keeping her lovely eyes locked with mine. "Anytime you start to doubt it, just come talk to me. I'll set you straight."

Her smile was wide and beautiful, displaying her cute dimples to perfection. "You're one of a kind," she said. "Too sweet and caring for your own good."

"See." I kept my voice light with an effort. "I knew you liked me."

"Like you once told me, you have many excellent qualities. There's only one thing I'd change, and that's to make you more selfish. I'd take away some of that niceness, so you start protecting yourself better." With her hand on my bicep, she squeezed my arm against my chest as though giving me a lying-down hug. "This beautiful body of yours is a precious package. Please treat it with care."

"Yes, ma'am." I smiled at her, filled with tenderness.

I had an overwhelming urge to bake her more cookies. Hell, maybe I should spend the next decade becoming a medical researcher so I could find a cure for her illness. Suddenly, eight to ten years of study seemed like a small price to pay.

Carla had promised she'd never fall in love with me. She didn't have enough energy for a relationship and was focused on her health and her software. I got it; I really did.

Only I'd clearly been an ignorant fool because I should have been worrying about a more obvious and dangerous problem. A problem that chased away my smile and stirred the uneasy feeling in my gut back up.

What if I couldn't stop myself from falling in love with her?

CHAPTER 21

CARLA

- Three days to Valentine's Day -

Carla: Newsflash!
Magdalena: What's up, nerd?
Carla: I had sex with Noah.
Magdalena: Holy drought-breaker! How was it?
Carla: So good. But weird afterward. Instead of staying, he left. Maybe he had second thoughts?
Magdalena: Or he had to go to work early.
Carla: I like him, but I can't like him. It shouldn't matter that he left when this isn't a real relationship. But it does matter. UGH! Why am I twisting myself into knots?
Magdalena: And you're supposed to be the smart one?
Carla: Any advice, brat?
Magdalena: Don't be a nerd. Have more sex. Stay away from flannel.
Carla: Please stop giving me advice now.

*M*y mother was on the phone, and I wasn't enjoying our conversation. Mainly because it wasn't so much of a conversation as a monologue.

I sat on a stool in the kitchen with my hand cradling my forehead and my phone to my ear, listening patiently as my mother read out the latest magazine articles about my fabulous cousin. They were long and enthusiastic, full of words like *incandescent, vivacious,* and *brilliant.* And all I could think about was how awful I'd felt when I'd run out of the bakery, and how I'd let myself down.

"You still haven't seen Sienna?" Mom asked when she'd finished.

"I saw her," I admitted.

"You did?"

"Just for a moment. We didn't really talk."

"Are you going to see her again? She won't be in town for long. Why don't you invite her for lunch?"

"Mom, please stop."

Things couldn't go on this way. Noah was right. I'd gotten too caught up in comparing myself to her. I had to do something to turn it around.

"Stop what, Carlita? You need real people in your life, and not just on your computer all the time. You and Sienna used to be such good friends. Think how inspiring she'd be. Such a good influence. With her contacts, she could help you get back on your feet, and—"

"Mom," I interrupted. "I don't want to hear about Sienna anymore. Please stop talking about her."

"What? Why?"

"Because her success isn't going to rub off on me!" I took a breath, forcing myself to sound calm and reasonable. "Mom, I could spend a hundred years with Sienna, and never be anything like her. And I didn't ask to get sick, or to have to quit work, or spend all my time in bed, or change my entire life, or have to agree with Tomas that it'd be best for him if he left me. I have a real illness. And just because you can't see anything physically wrong with me, that doesn't mean I'm making it up."

"I know you're not making it up." Mom sounded shocked by the suggestion.

"Then how come you always act like you think I'm faking being sick?"

"I don't! But it's hard to see you lying around doing nothing when you're so smart and you have so much ability. Do you blame me? A mother wants her children to do well." Her tone was defensive.

"I'm sorry you're disappointed."

"Carlita, I only want the best for you."

"Then, please, don't talk about Sienna anymore."

"Fine. *Dios mío*! I won't mention her again if that's what you want." Mom was snippy, but she'd get over it.

"That's what I want. Thanks for understanding." Such a simple conversation, but I still felt relieved. I should have been that direct with her from the start.

"Anything else you don't like, Carlita?" Her tone still held an edge, but I could choose to ignore it.

"No, that's it. I love you, Mom."

She let out a sigh. "Well, I love you too."

When I hung up, I felt good about having finally told her how I felt.

A few minutes later there was a knock on the door.

Noah.

I took a breath, preparing myself to see him. Since he'd abruptly left after we'd had sex, I'd become more and more sure we'd made a mistake letting things get that far. As irresistible as Noah was, I should have resisted him.

Now I was feeling an impossible longing. Wanting a relationship I couldn't have. And it was my own fault.

Before opening the door, I gave myself a mini pep talk. We'd made a deal. I'd promised not to fall for him. I needed to keep that promise, for his sake and my own.

But Noah was as dazzling as ever. One look, and all the feelings I wasn't allowed to have flooded through me. I drank in the confident angle of his chin, his nonchalant smile, and the warmth of his eyes.

"Hey, Chuckles." He stepped forward as though to kiss me.

As desperately as I wanted his kisses, it would only make things worse.

I took a step back, registering the shadow that dropped over his eyes as I moved away from him.

"Let's go to the bakery," I said.

"Now?"

"Is Jennifer there today? I'd like to apologize to her while I'm feeling brave. Before I lose my nerve again."

He nodded, his easy smile returning. "Then let's go."

"You don't think Sienna won't be there, do you?" I asked a little later, when we were in his truck on our way to the bakery.

"You don't want to see her?"

"I do, but one thing at a time. Apologizing to Jennifer will be easier. I need to build up to seeing Sienna."

"Since starting work at the bakery, I've only seen Sienna once. The chances of her turning up again today are a million to one."

"I wonder what the statistical probability actually is," I said, trying to take my mind off where we were going.

He took one hand off the steering wheel to squeeze my knee for a moment. "I know you can do it, Chuckles. I believe in you."

"Thanks." Incredibly, I managed a real smile. Chuckles was such a silly name, but it had grown on me so much, it made me feel warm to hear it. When he called me that, I felt like I could do anything. He could ask me to scale Everest, and if he tacked on that nickname, I'd start climbing.

A little while later, I found myself at the door outside the bakery's kitchen. Noah held it open for me, waiting for me to walk inside. But even the open door was enough to trigger my pounding heart. The smells of baking and the hustle and bustle were just like they'd been the other day when Sienna had turned up unexpectedly, and I could only hope he was right about her not showing up again.

"Come on." He took my hand, linking our fingers together. "I'll be right beside you."

Drawing in a deep breath, I let him lead me inside. Jennifer was near the back of the kitchen, talking to a solidly built, bearded man who was wearing navy blue overalls. His beard was a little unruly, but when he turned to face me, I saw he had lovely blue eyes.

"Hey, Cletus." Noah gave the man a wave with the hand that wasn't holding mine. "Hey, Jennifer. You remember Carla?"

Jennifer shone her friendly smile at me, and Cletus gave me a nod.

Forcing a smile onto my own face, I said hello to them both. "I'm sorry for running out of here last time," I added, bracing myself to explain.

Jennifer waved a dismissive hand. "I often feel like doing the same thing. But I'm glad you're back because I wanted to ask if you ever use amaranth flour for baking?"

I'd been searching for the words to tell her why I'd panicked and run, so it took me a moment to find an answer to her question instead.

"Um. Not often," I said. "But I've used it to make flatbread."

Her eyes lit up. "Flatbread? How well did it hold together? Did it crumble?"

I blinked. Was she really going to make it so easy to ignore my last visit?

Pretending I was as casual about it as she seemed to be, I told her about my flatbread experiments. Pretty soon I was engrossed in an interesting discussion about the pros and cons of chia, amaranth, and quinoa flours.

In fact, I was relaxing entirely too much, because when I heard Noah ask Cletus if Sienna was still in town, I only stiffened a little. My mother had said that she was, so Cletus's nod didn't surprise me.

"Are she and Jethro in the homestead on Moth Run Road?" asked Noah.

"They are," Cletus replied.

"What's Sienna's favorite bakery treat? We're going to drop around to see her next, and we don't want to go empty-handed."

I swung to face him.

"Lemon cakes," said Cletus, as though he hadn't noticed my reaction.

"I'm sorry, but would you excuse me for a moment?" I said apologetically to Jennifer and Cletus as I dragged Noah to one side. "What are you doing?" I demanded.

"You said you wanted to visit Sienna."

"One thing at a time, remember?"

He put both hands on my upper arms, his expression serious. In the bright lights of the bakery, his green irises were scattered with tiny specks of gold dust.

"Why wait?" he asked.

Good question. I was too busy gazing into his beautiful eyes, panning for gold, to think of a single reason.

"Then it's decided," he said.

I swallowed. With an effort, I tore my gaze from his. Glancing around, I saw Jennifer and Cletus were smiling at each other and didn't seem disturbed by how rude I'd been dragging Noah away for a private chat. I'd been trying to seem less strange, and I wasn't doing myself any favors.

"I've met Sienna before," said Noah. "And believe me, if we turn up with a box of cakes, she'll be happy to see us both." Flashing me his irresistible grin, he leaned in close. "Come on, Chuckles. Say yes."

* * *

I couldn't believe I was doing it.

My hands were bathed in sweat, but I lifted one anyway, preparing to knock on Sienna's front door. Beside me, Noah was holding the box of lemon cakes. He gave me an encouraging nod.

Before I could knock, the door flew open, and a small boy and a dog came running out. The boy plowed into my legs and bounced off with a yelp. He scrambled to his feet, staring up at me before turning to yell back into the house. "Momma! Some folks are here!" Then he sprinted off after the dog, toward the expanse of grass at the back of the property.

A moment later, Sienna appeared in the doorway. She wore yoga pants and a stretchy top, and looked a little flustered. She had a splodge of something yellow on her top.

"Hello?" she said. Then her tiny frown turned into a delighted smile, and her eyes lit up. "Carla! How lovely to see you." She stepped forward as though to hug me, then glanced down with a laugh. "I was making lunch and dropped some mustard. I don't want to smear it on you."

I swallowed. My heart was kicking like a mule. What if I had another anxiety attack right here on her doorstep?

"Hi, Sienna," said Noah. "I'm Noah Malone. We met at the bakery yesterday. Also, I was a handyman on the set when you were filming in Cades Cove, but that was a long time ago."

"Nice to see you again, Noah."

He shifted the box of cakes to one hand and put the other on my lower back. His touch anchored me. I could do this.

"Um. I'm sorry for running out on you yesterday," I said, the words coming out in a tangled, nervous rush. "And for not calling you back."

"Oh, that doesn't matter. You're here now. Won't you come in?" Sienna's smile was dazzling. It held enough charisma to turn a pride of lions into pussy-cats, and her eyes sparkled so brightly, I could sunbathe in their glow.

The accolades from the articles Mom read out to me all flooded into my brain in a rush. When I opened my mouth to speak, the only words I could think of were *incandescent*, and *vivacious*, and *brilliant*.

"Um," I said, feeling tongue-tied. "We don't want to incandescent... I mean, inconvenience you." Dammit! I stopped to drag in a breath.

"We dropped by to say hello and bring you these." Noah held out the box. "They're lemon cakes from the bakery. Jennifer made them."

"My favorite! Thank you."

As she was taking hold of the box, the dog came bounding back, covered in mud. It dodged through our legs and tore into the house, spattering filth over Sienna's entrance rug. The small boy who'd bounced off my legs came thundering after it. He was coated with even more mud than the dog and went sliding on the rug, leaving a brown streak down the wall as he raced inside.

Sienna groaned, looking up to heaven as she shook her head. "That boy!" She shot me a look as though to say, *What can you do?* And it was exactly the look we used to share when we were kids and a sibling had done something to annoy us.

All at once, I found myself smiling back at her.

With a rush of relief, my chest loosened.

My cousin was still a mortal woman after all. Sure, she had a brilliantly successful career and a wonderful family. But maybe every single thing in her life wasn't actually perfect in every way. My mother had erected such a monument to her magnificence, I'd half-expected her to unfurl a pair of angel wings and fly away.

"You must come in," Sienna said, peeking into the box of cakes. "Share these with me. I insist!"

"I can't eat lemon cakes," I blurted.

"You can't?" Her eyes widened a little as though I'd announced something terrible, but she recovered almost instantly. "Well, come in for iced tea." She stepped back, opening the door wider in invitation. But I caught her shooting a quick glance at the splatters of mud that extended down the hallway. She had to be distracted by wanting to see to her son and dog, only she was far too nice to say so.

"We can't stay," I said. "I'm sorry."

"Are you sure?" Her expression fell and she seemed genuinely disappointed. She had mud on her floor and mustard on her shirt, yet those things didn't matter to her. They had nothing to do with who she was.

She wasn't just a movie star. She was also the girl I'd giggled with when we were young. When my parents used to visit hers, Sienna and I would take snacks into her room, play music, and talk about everything and anything. Our different personalities and experiences had only made us more interesting to each other. Back then, it hadn't even occurred to me to compare our achievements.

"I haven't been well," I said, acting on a sudden urge to get the worst part of our conversation over with. May as well rip off the band-aid. "I left my job, broke up with my fiancé, and for the past year I've been holed up like a hermit, trying to improve my health."

She nodded, her eyes softening. "Your mother told me. Are you okay?"

"Some days are good," I said. "Some aren't."

"The good days must be precious."

I nodded. "But even on my best days, I get fatigued easily, which means I need to conserve my energy. And today, I've already put enough stress on my system." I offered her an apologetic smile. "I'm a little shaky. Wouldn't want to overdo it."

"I understand." She said it sincerely, as though she really did understand. Then she stepped forward, tucking the box of lemon cakes into the crook of her elbow so she could put the other hand on my arm to give it a squeeze. Noah was on my other side, standing close. I could feel his unspoken support.

And amazingly, admitting my illness hadn't made me feel weak. The opposite. I felt strong, lifted up by my own burst of courage, as well as by the people who were willing to accept and care about me.

"Another time?" asked Sienna, her expression kind.

"Another time," I agreed, meaning it. "Definitely. I've missed you."

"Next time you see each other, ask Carla about the software she's been writing." Noah raised his eyebrows at Sienna. "And get ready to be impressed."

"I can't wait!" she exclaimed.

I gave an embarrassed laugh, reluctantly pleased by Noah's praise. "It's not nearly as impressive as the things you've been doing, Sienna."

"Oh, today is especially fabulous. I'm going to be cleaning mud off the floor, and not for the first time." She shook her head, but her eyes sparkled as though we were sharing a joke.

I'd forgotten how warm and caring she was. All those magazine articles had been stuffed with compliments, but none had mentioned the best thing about her: the size of her heart.

"Your boys are gorgeous," I said. "Next time, I'd love to meet them."

"Of course! Call me when you're having a good day."

"It'll be soon," I promised.

I hugged her, trying not to squash her box of cakes and not caring whether I got mustard on my top. Then, after exchanging goodbyes, Noah and I walked back to his truck. I slid in the passenger's side and when he got into the driver's seat, I couldn't help but grin at him.

"You did it," he said, grinning back.

"She's every bit as sweet as she used to be." I felt absurdly happy and relieved, as though I'd jumped out of a plane and survived. "Deep down, I knew she would be. But I was still dreading seeing her, thinking she was going to feel sorry for me. But even when I talked about my illness, she was cool."

"I'm proud of you."

"You know what? I'm proud of me too." I laughed for no reason, except that I felt like a weight had lifted. And even after he started the truck and pulled out onto the road, I kept breaking into an occasional snicker. "I don't even know why I'm still laughing," I said after a while, shaking my head at my own silliness.

"You can laugh all you want, Chuckles. I like hearing it."

I couldn't help another snicker, because it struck me as funny that he'd given me that nickname ironically, but I'd laughed more since meeting him than ever before.

When he gave me a lop-sided grin, his eyes shining like I was funny in a good way, I wanted him to stop driving so I could kiss the stuffing out of him. He was so sweet and thoughtful and handsome, it killed me. And I wanted more sex. A lot more sex. He'd made me realize that Tomas and the female orgasm hadn't been well acquainted. Now, to paraphrase the *Rocky Horror Picture Show*, I'd tasted bliss and I wanted more.

I loved him.

Dammit, I *really* loved him.

But our relationship wasn't real. It couldn't be real.

Spending any more time with him would be torture. I had to end it now before it got even harder.

Suddenly, I didn't want to laugh anymore.

The light, happy feeling inside me turned heavy. It felt like a storm cloud lowering. A black sky obliterating all traces of sunshine.

"I think we've done enough to ease my anxiety," I said.

He jerked his face to me, clearly startled by my sudden seriousness.

"What do you mean?"

I curled my hands into fists, moving my gaze to the road ahead instead of looking at him. "We can end our agreement. Thank you for helping me. Now I'll be able to go back to New York and release my software."

"But the spreadsheet isn't ticked off. We have dinner at Genie's tomorrow night, and a date on Valentine's Day."

I wanted to look at him, to read his expression. But if I turned my face to him, I might not be able to hide how much this was hurting me.

"Not necessary," I said. "We can cancel the rest of the spreadsheet."

He was silent a moment. Then he said, "We had a deal."

"You're going to Arizona soon. It's too late for your mother to set you up on any dates."

"She's got a thing about Valentine's Day. If I tell her we're not going out again, who knows what she might do?"

When I glanced at him, his beautiful eyes were shielded. His hands had tightened on the steering wheel, his knuckles whitening.

He was clearly unhappy about the idea of not finishing the tasks on my spreadsheet.

Was it because of his mother? Or because we'd slept together?

I swallowed, hating the thought of not seeing him anymore. He'd brought so much joy into my life. But as seductive as the dream of us dating for real might be, there was no way it could happen. The lesson I'd learned from Tomas had been too hard-won. It had been too difficult a road that had led to accepting my need to be alone. Losing Noah was going to be painful enough now, but it would only get worse.

"You said your ex left because you couldn't go out to dinner," Noah said. Despite his shielded gaze, his tone was casual. "You need to prove to yourself you can. And I already have a table booked at Genie's."

Saying that Tomas left me because I couldn't go out for a meal with him was a dramatic oversimplification.

But before I could argue, Noah shot me a sideways look. "Come on, Chuckles," he coaxed. "Don't let me down. You can't quit on our deal."

I dragged in a breath as my resolve wavered.

One last dinner with Noah.

Something to remember and hold onto when I felt lonely or sad.

One last chance to laugh together and enjoy being with him.

I rubbed my chest where it ached and gave Noah a nod. "Dinner," I said. "Okay."

When he pulled up to my house, I rushed out of his truck before he could open my door for me. Then I went as quickly as I could up the steps to my porch. If he tried to tempt me into a goodbye kiss, he'd be impossible to resist. So I gave him a quick wave and hurried to get inside before he could follow.

"See you tomorrow," I called.

As I shut the door behind me, I sagged against it, cursing my own foolishness. Falling for Noah was the worst thing I could have done. When we stopped seeing each other, it would hurt like hell. What if I crashed and didn't recover?

What if I was left with nothing?

A few minutes after I heard his truck pull away, my phone rang.

It was Noah's mother.

My heart sank as I stared at her name on my phone's screen, wondering why she could be calling. Whatever the reason, I was dreading being dragged even deeper into emotional quicksand.

I answered the call reluctantly. My heart plummeted even lower when I heard the excitement in her voice.

"I've found you the perfect office," she exclaimed. "It's right here in town. You're going to love it!"

CHAPTER 22

NOAH

- Two days to Valentine's Day -

"I can't remember the last time I went out after dark," said Carla as we walked into Genie's together, her hand wrapped around my arm. "I'm usually in bed by eight." I could tell she was nervous by the way her fingers were digging into my bicep. But she shot me a shaky smile anyway. "Freud gets upset if I go to bed any later. He may not say anything, but he has a way of twitching his ears that gets his point across."

I grinned back at her. "Well, I think you'll find Genie's Country Western Bar is worth it."

Her chin was high, and her lips fixed into a determined line. Her hair was loose over her shoulders, and she was wearing a wrap-around black dress that would make any man fall to his knees.

She was awe-inspiring. And not just because of the way she looked. Knowing how much she'd been through made every step feel like a triumph. I was proud of her just for walking into Genie's, let alone being able to joke while she did it.

"It's busier than I expected," she said, looking around.

"I've reserved a booth for us. It's over there." I'd stopped in earlier to figure out which booth was farthest from the speakers and likely to be the quietest. They didn't usually reserve tables here, but the waitress on duty happened to be Willa, someone I knew from years back. She'd been happy to do me a favor.

When we sat down, Carla took one side of the booth, and I sat on the other. She straightened her knife and fork, adjusted her napkin, and picked up the menu. After running her eyes over it, she put it back down, then dropped her hands into her lap. Her eyes darted nervously around the bar, and she shifted around as though she couldn't sit still. I could tell she hadn't read any of the menu.

"Try imagining everyone's in their underwear," I suggested, trying to help her relax.

"Am I in my underwear?"

"No, you're fully dressed."

"So everyone's in their underwear but me? They all got the memo and I'm the uncool one who was left out?" She was trying her best to joke around as though she wasn't nervous, and I laughed to encourage her.

"Okay, imagine I'm the only one in my underwear." I slid my arm across the top of the booth and leaned back to emphasize how comfortable I was, hoping that would help.

"Why would you be here in your underwear? Is it something you do often?"

"It could be my costume for a movie."

"An X-rated movie?"

"Good idea. I haven't been in any of *those* movies yet. If I was, I'd have the starring role, for sure."

The silliness of our conversation seemed to be having an effect because she picked up the menu again, but this time she actually focused on it.

"Is there anything on there you can eat?" I asked.

Before she could answer, Willa came over.

"Hi, Noah." She spoke loudly over the music, and I answered just as loudly.

"Hi, Willa. This is Carla."

Carla gave her a smile and a hello, and Willa returned the greeting.

"Are y'all ready to order?" Willa tugged out her notepad.

"I'll have fish and salad with a glass of white wine, please," said Carla.

"A burger and a light beer for me."

"Coming right up." Willa headed back to the bar.

"You're having a light beer?" asked Carla. "Less alcohol, right?"

I nodded. "Seeing as I'm driving, I'll have that, then switch to water."

"My glass of wine will be the first alcohol I've had in years. It'll spike my insulin, but it'll help me relax. Tonight, I'm willing to take the trade-off."

"You don't drink?"

"I used to like wine, only it has a lot of sugar." She shrugged. "What the hell, right?"

There was something different about her tonight. A fragile edge to her voice that I couldn't quite read. Maybe it was just nerves, but I couldn't be sure. Especially after she'd tried to call off our deal.

Willa came back with our drinks.

"Cheers," I said.

Carla clinked her glass against mine and took a sip. "Mmm."

"It's good?" I asked.

"I'd forgotten how much I like wine." She took a second sip. "It's probably my imagination, but I can feel it relaxing me already. I should have added it to my spreadsheet."

"Have you always been so organized?" I asked. "Spreadsheets for everything?"

"I like being organized. And I love spreadsheets. Especially when I get to make charts and graphs from the data and use them to visualize progress."

"Yeah, that sounds super fun."

She laughed along with me. "You sound like my sister. She's always giving me a hard time about being a nerd."

"You think any of your family will come and visit you? I'd like to meet them." As soon as I suggested it, I wondered why. I wasn't going to be here long enough to meet her family, not unless they turned up in the next few days.

Carla shook her head. "My father's a sales rep, and he travels a lot for work. And my sisters are busy with their own stuff."

"Do you talk to them often?"

"More than I used to when I was working long hours, but not as much as I'd like to. Sometimes I don't have the energy."

"What about your friends?"

She shrugged. "I spend time in chat rooms, talking to other people with ME. Some are really isolated, and the chat rooms are their only connection to the outside world."

"And your real-life friends?"

Her expression fell. "I haven't been so good at keeping in touch. I've been too focused on my health and my software."

"I'm sure they understand."

"I hope so."

"Tell me something I don't know about you," I suggested, wanting to change the subject.

"Like what?"

"Anything. Everything." There were so many things I wanted to know, I randomly picked one from my very long list. "How long did you live in New York?"

"We moved there when I was a teenager. Before that, we were in LA. But my first language was actually Spanish. My mom is from Chile. We lived there until I was three."

"Your accent is more New York than Spanish."

"That's because I never speak Spanish these days, and I'm so bad at it now, it's embarrassing." Her smile was brief but brilliant. "When I go to Chile, I stumble over my words, and everyone laughs at me."

"How often do you go to Chile?"

"I used to go every three or four years. But the last time was six years ago, for my grandfather's funeral."

"I'm sorry."

She toyed with the stem of her wine glass. "It was a nice funeral. As good as they get, anyway. My grandfather always seemed happy. He was *simpatico*, always laughing, even though he was poor for most of his life. Have you been to Chile?"

I shook my head.

"It's a beautiful country. But Mom had to drop out of school, and she was working as a maid when she met my dad. Her family lived in a house with a dirt floor and outdoor plumbing, but her father was ninety-seven and still dancing the cueca the week before he died. Whether rich or poor, you can't be too sad when someone's had such a long and healthy life, can you?"

Maybe I imagined it, but I thought she sounded wistful when she said 'healthy'.

"I can speak Spanish," I said, wanting to make her smile again.

"You can?"

"*Una cervesa por favor, señorita bonita.*" My accent was terrible, and I hammed it up, making it even worse.

Just as I'd hoped, she let out a belly laugh, and I grinned back.

"See?" I said. "I'm practically fluent."

She was still giggling a little, presumably at my accent. "All you know is how to ask for a beer?"

I pretended to be offended. "Hey, I ordered a beer *and* complimented the waitress. That takes talent."

"Now I don't feel so bad about how bad my Spanish is."

"I've never seen your dimples that deep before."

She tried to make her expression serious and didn't succeed. "What are you talking about? I keep telling you, I don't have dimples."

"They might be small, but they're definitely there, as cute as two very shallow buttons." I did what I'd been wanting to do and fit a fingertip into one of the depressions.

Laughing, she pulled back. "You're just pushing a hole into my cheek."

"I swear, you have dimples. Haven't you ever seen yourself laugh?"

"You think I laugh in front of mirrors?"

"Well, that last laugh rated a ten on your dimple-o-meter. They were at least the depth of a penny that time."

"Here's your food, Noah."

I'd been so engrossed in Carla, I hadn't noticed Willa come back. She gave us our meals and we dug into them, talking about the music and books we liked as we ate.

Finally, Carla put down her knife and fork. "We've been talking about me too much," she said. "Let's talk about you. It's your turn to tell me something I don't know."

I ate my last bite of burger, then pushed my plate away to focus my attention on her. Her hair was tucked behind one ear, and the soft light of the bar highlighted her cheekbones. The front of her dress dipped low enough that I could admire her cleavage. And the shine of the necklace she was wearing was nothing compared to the sparkle of humor in her eyes.

Did she have any idea how gorgeous she was, or how badly I wanted to kiss her?

"Well, what do you want to know?" I asked, ready to tell her anything. Hell, if she suggested I strip to my underwear and take to the dance floor, I'd probably do it just to get another glimpse of her dimples.

She leaned closer. "Tell me about the car accident when your friend died."

My heart lurched. "Why?"

"You couldn't feel anything after that. You were numb, and instead of getting therapy, you started rolling cars for a living. I think that's interesting."

I picked up my beer and took a sip, rolling it around in my mouth before swallowing.

"Liam should never have been behind the wheel," I said finally. "He was drunk. But he was upset and—"

"Wait! Tell me everything, from the beginning. Why was he upset?"

I drained my beer. Shame it didn't have more alcohol in it. To get this story out, I'd need all the help I could get.

"Liam was dating a woman called Lorelei," I said. "Not just dating her, he was crazy in love with her. The kind of mad, passionate, intense love maybe only twenty-one-year-olds can feel."

She nodded as though she knew what I was talking about, and I was stabbed by a jealous pang. Had she been in love like that? I hadn't fallen in love when I was twenty-one. In fact, I hadn't ever loved anyone like that.

Not until now.

I pushed the thought away.

"Anyway," I said. "Liam thought Lorelei felt the same way about him."

"But she didn't?"

I shook my head. "That night was the wrap party for the film we'd been working on, up in Cades Cove. I told you I had a job as a handyman on the set. There was a bar set up for the party, and the bartender was a friend. He kept slipping us free drinks."

"So you got drunk?"

"Liam was falling-down drunk, but Lorelei and I weren't far behind. She and I were friendly. Too friendly, probably. I don't know." I scratched my beard. "I've thought about it a thousand times, how I shouldn't have joked around so much with her. How I should have made it clear I wasn't interested in her that way."

Carla slid her hand across the table to mine, and I linked our fingers together, grateful for the gesture.

"When Liam went to get another drink, Lorelei told me she was in love with me. Then she tried to kiss me."

"And Liam saw it happen?"

I nodded. "She wasn't exactly subtle."

"That's when he got in the car?"

"He yelled at us first. Then he ran over to it. I didn't realize he was going to drive off until he'd jumped in. I ran over and managed to pull myself into the passenger seat. I was trying to talk some sense into him."

"Then what happened?"

"He drove off a cliff." I needed something else to focus on, so with my free hand, I straightened my knife and fork on my empty plate.

"That's awful."

"He looked me right in the eye as we went over. I still don't know if it was an accident, or if he was trying to kill me and didn't care if he died too."

I couldn't believe the admission was coming out of my mouth so easily. But the one thing I couldn't describe was the pain on Liam's face. The look of accusation… and hate.

We'd been like brothers, but in the moments before he died, he'd hated me.

Carla squeezed my hand. "No wonder you're messed up." She said it exactly the way I would have if I was trying to make her laugh.

And amazingly enough, I managed to make a sound that with a little imagination could almost have been laughter. "Thanks for noticing."

"Makes my issues seem trivial." She seemed a little tipsy, but I liked how relaxed she was. Maybe that's why I'd never been able to talk about Liam's death. All I'd needed was a gorgeous woman asking me about it in a bar.

"Yeah, I win." I pretended to grimace.

"That's the reason you keep your distance with women."

"Like I told you, they keep falling in love with me."

"And it's why you don't flirt."

I nodded, thinking of Lorelei. We'd hung out together all the time, the three of us. She was pretty, and she'd been good to talk to. I'd liked joking around with her.

"I probably flirted with Lorelei," I admitted. "Not even thinking about it."

"You were twenty-one. Of course you didn't think about it. You probably flirted with everyone."

"But she was my best friend's girlfriend."

"There are no perfect twenty-one-year-olds. Or any perfect thirty-one or forty-one-year-olds, for that matter. Everyone's done stuff they're not proud of. Liam didn't have to do what he did, and you don't have to take responsibility for it. He could have walked off. He could have stuck around and shouted. He could have done *anything*."

She tipped down her chin to look seriously at me over an imaginary pair of spectacles and despite the topic of conversation, I felt a smile tug at my lips. She was insanely cute when she thought she was being wise. And the fact that she was *actually* wise? Hell, I wanted to kiss her more than ever.

I took my hand out of hers so I could run my thumb up the inside of her arm. The skin there was incredibly soft. "Do you have any idea how sexy you are?" I murmured.

Her cheeks flushed. "Are you flirting with me?"

"Am I getting better at it?"

"I love spending time with you, Noah. It's been amazing. But you know it can't go anywhere, right?"

"Can it go back to bed?" I raised my hand to lift her hair off her shoulder. Her neck looked long and elegant in that dress and I badly wanted to kiss it.

"That would be a bad idea." But her eyes focused on my mouth, growing hazy as though she was picturing us making love.

"Didn't you have a good time?" I ran my finger slowly down the curve of her neck, enjoying the slight shiver of her skin under my touch.

"That's not the point." Her cheeks were growing pink. She bit her lower lip, and I burned to lick the place she was biting.

"Tell me you didn't enjoy it," I challenged.

"You know I did. But we had an agreement, and we can't break it."

I tugged on one of her silky locks, enjoying how it slipped through my fingers. I could imagine winding it around my hand and using it to tug her head back, angling her face so I could kiss her.

Carla seemed able to read my thoughts. Her expression of naked desire mirrored my own.

"Hi, Noah." A woman's voice interrupted my erotic daydream.

I was so focused on Carla, it took me a moment or two to drag my attention away from her. When I finally turned, Mandy was standing beside our table. She was dressed up in a silky pink dress and heels.

"Hey, Mandy," I said, surprised to see her.

She turned to Carla with a tentative smile. "You must be Carla."

I blinked. How did she know Carla's name? They hadn't met at the Piggly Wiggly.

"Nice to meet you, Mandy." Carla slid out of the booth, her cheeks red and her eyes bright. "I'm sorry to run out on you, but I need to go to the restroom. Talk to Noah while I'm gone." Without waiting for a response, she headed away.

I watched her go, admiring how her dress clung to her curves, and the way her hips swayed as she walked. When I looked back, Mandy was seating herself in the booth, taking Carla's place.

"Now you and I can catch up," Mandy said, adjusting her position until she was sitting uncomfortably close to me. "I want to hear all about what you've been doing."

"Who are you here with?" I leaned back and glanced around the bar. It was full, but I didn't see many people I recognized.

"I just stopped in by myself."

"Would you like a drink?" I started moving out of the booth to go to the bar, but she stopped me with a hand on my arm.

"No, thanks. Will you talk to me instead, Noah?" She left her hand on me, but I didn't want Carla to see her touching me and get the wrong idea. I moved my arm to shake off her fingers.

"What do you want to talk about?" I asked.

"Anything."

I waited for her to elaborate, but she just gazed at me through her long lashes, seemingly waiting for me to start speaking.

"What do you do?" I asked. "Do you have a job?"

She nodded, toying with her blonde hair. "It's just office work."

"Do you like it?"

"It's okay."

Sitting back, I searched for another question. I hadn't seen her since we'd graduated high school, and that was a long time ago. There should be plenty of things to ask her about, but my mind was blank.

"Tell me about your job," she suggested after the silence had stretched a little too long. "It sounds exciting! Have you met any movie stars?"

"A few."

"Who?"

I rattled off a few names and she oohed and aahed over each one, though some of them weren't well known.

"I *love* his movies," she exclaimed when I mentioned the star who'd given me the Lamborghini.

"You do?" I couldn't keep the surprise out of my voice, seeing as he'd played a psychopath in a series of bloodthirsty slasher flicks. "Which ones have you seen?"

"I'm not sure. What was the name of the one you did stunts for?"

"I've doubled for him in all his movies."

"Then they're all great."

She couldn't possibly have seen them. Some had been terrible. One had been so bad, the studio hadn't released it.

"What about *Cheer Squad Sacrifice Five: The Death Cheer*?" I asked, giving her a smile to let her know I was teasing.

"That was my favorite."

She didn't say it the way Carla would have. There was no humor in her tone, no sparkle in her eyes, no smile to answer mine. Mandy seemed serious.

Where was Carla? She should be on her way back by now, but there was no sign of her.

"Are you back in Green Valley for good?" asked Mandy.

I shook my head. "I'm leaving on the seventeenth. I have a contract for some work in Arizona."

"Oh." She sounded disappointed. "Isn't there anything I could do to convince you to stick around?" Lowering her lashes, she gazed at me from underneath them.

"I'm here with Carla," I said. "And I'm worried about how long she's been in the restroom." I turned to frown across the dance floor.

Mandy grabbed my sleeve. "Don't worry, Noah. It feels like she's been gone no time at all."

"I'm going to check on her." Pulling away from Mandy's hand, I slid out of the booth.

"Don't go. I'm sure she's fine."

"See you later, Mandy." I walked to the restroom and stopped a woman who was on her way in.

"Would you check if my girlfriend is in there?" I asked. "She has dark hair down to here." I indicated with my hand. "Black dress. Beautiful brown eyes. I want to make sure she's okay."

The woman nodded. "Sure, hon. I'll take a look."

She went in, and a few moments later, Carla emerged.

"Hey," Carla said. Her cheeks were flushed and she looked anxious. "What's up? Where's Mandy?"

"You were gone a while. I missed you."

"Did you think I'd fallen in?" She gave me a smile that seemed forced, like something was bugging her and she was trying to pretend she was fine. Was it Mandy's sudden appearance that had upset her? Or the fact we both so clearly wanted to tear each other's clothes off?

"I thought you'd escaped out the back way with Idris Elba," I said.

"Is Idris here?" She pretended to look around. "If he is, our agreement's off, Malone. You can't stand in the way of his epic lust for me."

The way she was craning her neck highlighted how smooth and tempting her skin was. All I could think about was how much I wanted to kiss her in the crease between her neck and shoulder.

Lowering my voice, I stepped closer. "What about my epic lust for you?" Putting a hand under her chin, I tilted her face up to mine.

Her eyes widened and darkened. Her lips parted a little, both with surprise and—I was sure—in a reflection of my own wanting. Her body swayed toward me as though she couldn't control it, and I let go of her chin to put my hand on her waist.

A slow song came over the speakers, and the people on the dance floor paired up and moved close.

"Dance with me," I demanded, my voice rough.

She dragged in a breath, her chest expanding in that fascinating way that made me burn to remove her clothes. "You're supposed to be talking to Mandy."

"Come on." I led her to the dance floor, then put my arms around her shoulders to pull her close. She felt like heaven. Her silky dress was wrapped tightly around her curves. Her perfume reminded me of the flowers that lined Momma's porch in spring.

Putting her arms around my waist, she rested her cheek against my neck. We swayed together slowly, and my heartbeat slowed as though it was beating in time with hers. This felt too good to end. She was just right for me. We were right for each other. We might only have been pretending to date when we started, but there wasn't anything false about what I felt for her.

"Carla," I murmured in her ear. "We're great together. This isn't make-believe."

She stiffened, then drew back from me, forcing me to let her go. Her expression was drawn, and her eyes had lost their sparkle. "Please don't say that, Malone. I've come to terms with being alone. It's the way it needs to be."

"Carla—"

She cut me off. "No, just think about it. Imagine if we tried to be together for real. You'd be stuck with a burden, not a girlfriend. What if I get sicker? Lots of people who have this illness get worse. What if I had to spend the next few years in bed? How would you like it then?"

"If that happens, I want to be there for you."

"No way. I'm a prisoner to my illness, and you're free. You're not going to lock yourself up with me. I won't let you."

"I don't care." I reached for her again, but she took another step back. Her eyes were sad, her mouth pulling down. The torment in her face tore at my heart.

"Malone, you don't get it. You said the thing your mother most wanted was grandchildren. Well, I can't have children. I don't have the energy. Do you really want to break your mother's heart by telling her she'll never have grandkids?"

I digested that in silence. She was right, I hadn't thought about that. I wasn't exactly pining for children. I'd only ever thought of them in a vague way, assuming they'd probably happen eventually. But Momma was so desperate for grandbabies, it would kill her if I didn't have any.

"See?" she exclaimed. "Whatever you're feeling for me, you need to stop."

"You think I can stop the way I feel?"

She clenched her hands by her sides and spoke in a rush. "This isn't like taking a job in the bakery because you want to help someone out, or crashing cars because that's how your friend died. In case you haven't noticed, you clearly have some kind of martyr complex. You're addicted to sacrificing yourself for others. And I'm sorry, but I'm not going to let you sacrifice your life for me."

"It's not a sacrifice—"

"Are you sure about that? I'll give you Tomas's number and let him tell you all about it."

I stiffened at the mention of her asshole ex. "I'm not Tomas." It came out as an angry growl. "I won't bail on you if things get tough."

"I *hated* watching Tomas get more and more unhappy. For months, he felt too guilty to leave. It made us both miserable." Her mouth twisted. "Better to be alone than have to go through that again."

"You don't have to be alone." My heart was breaking at the pain in her face.

Her chin lifted. "That's exactly what I have to be."

I took her arms, unable to stand the thought she might be ending things between us. I wanted to hold her against me. To tell her I'd never let her go. But she put both hands on my chest to push me away.

"If we stop now, it won't be so bad." Her voice was ragged. "We'll get over it."

"Your ex hurt you so badly you won't even give us a shot?"

"Mandy's right over there. She can give you all the things I can't."

I glanced over. Sure enough, Mandy was still sitting in the booth on her own, staring over at us. While I'd been dancing with Carla, she hadn't moved. Despite my own frustration and pain, I couldn't help but feel sorry for her.

"Dance with her," Carla ordered. "Take her to dinner on Valentine's Day. Make your mother happy."

"We're watching a movie on Valentine's Day. *Bridget Jones's Diary*."

"No, we're not." The resolve in Carla's eyes made me feel utterly helpless. "I can't see you again, Noah. I'm catching an Uber home."

"Don't. At least let me drive you." Maybe on the way, I'd be able to talk some sense into her.

"Dance with Mandy." She gave me another push as she moved away from me, heading to the door.

I was going after her when a hand wrapped around my arm.

"Noah?" Mandy tightened her grip, stopping me in my tracks. "Are you okay?"

Carla strode out the door without looking back.

"I'm sorry I showed up like that," said Mandy. "But Carla said you weren't here on a real date. She said you were only pretending."

Distracted from following Carla, I swung to face Mandy. "What?"

Mandy lowered her face, peeking at me from under her lashes. "I wasn't supposed to tell you."

I pulled my arm out of her grip, balling my hands into fists. "When did you talk to her?"

"I've let the cat out of the bag now, haven't I?" She grimaced. "Carla called me yesterday. She said she got my number from your momma."

I stared at her, my mind racing. Were Momma and Carla in cahoots, plotting together to set me up with Mandy? Did Momma know I'd been trying to fool her?

"Carla and I had an agreement," I growled. "Only she's called it off. She's afraid of getting hurt."

Mandy lifted her gaze to meet mine. Her lips curved down, and her eyes looked sad. "I can tell you're in love with her, Noah. I guess I was hoping you'd look that way at me, but after all these years I should know better."

"I'm not in love…" I stopped.

Truth was, I *had* fallen for Carla. There was no other explanation for the way my heart hurt. And she'd fallen for me, too. That was why she was pushing me away.

"See?" Mandy gave a humorless laugh. "It should be a relief. Maybe now we can finally be friends. That'll have to be enough."

I nodded, still a little stunned by the strength of my feelings for Carla. "Sure, Mandy. We can be friends."

"Will you sit down with me?" she asked. "As friends?"

"I should go."

"It's okay, Noah." She gave me a sad smile. "I only want to talk. Nothing more."

Hesitating, I glanced outside. Carla was long gone.

I needed some time to decide how to win Carla over.

What could I do to convince her to change her mind about us?

Gazing distractedly at Mandy, a thought occurred to me. If Carla wanted me to date her so badly, maybe I should call her bluff.

"Hey, Mandy," I said. "As my friend, would you consider doing me a favor?"

"Of course. You can ask me anything."

"It's about Valentine's Day," I said.

CHAPTER 23

NOAH

- Valentine's Day -

Valentine's Day was an exhausting last day at the bakery. I'd iced so many cupcakes, I was beat. I could have sworn we'd sold more cookies and cupcakes than there were people in the whole of Tennessee. And I'd been sad to have to say a final goodbye to Joy, Jennifer, and everyone else there. I was going to miss them.

When I walked tiredly through Momma's front door, she pounced on me right away. "How was your day?" she asked.

I eyed her warily. "Momma, were you waiting by the door for me to walk in?"

"I wanted to wish you a happy Valentine's Day." Her smile was wide and innocent. "Are you going to get ready for your date?"

"My date with whom?"

Her smile fell away. "What do you mean? You and Carla are going out tonight, aren't you?"

"Did you try to set me up with Mandy?"

She looked genuinely confused. "Why would I do that? Carla asked for Mandy's number when I called her. Did something happen?"

It was my turn to frown. "You called Carla? Why?"

"Well, she was thinking about going back to New York, but I found an office for her here instead. It's right in town, with a little reception desk and everything, so now there's no need for her to go anywhere. Y'all can stay right here."

"You called Carla to tell her you'd found her an office?" I repeated dumbly.

Carla must have freaked out. Maybe that's why she'd tried to set me up with Mandy.

Momma gave me a reassuring pat on the arm. "It's called problem solving, Noah. I'm simply arranging things how they should be."

"But Carla isn't only going back to New York for an office. She needs to find an investor and hire people. It's a lot more complicated than getting her a desk and chair."

"Can't she do those things over the phone?"

Shaking my head, I walked toward my bedroom.

"Did you talk to Jennifer today?" Momma asked, scooting along after me.

"About what?"

"About staying on at the bakery."

I stopped and turned to her. "Jennifer asked me to stay, but I had to turn down her offer." I softened my tone, finally understanding what was happening. "In two days, I'll be going to work in Arizona. I've signed a contract and I'm committed."

Her mouth set into a stubborn line. "But why would you leave a lovely woman like Carla? Now you have a girlfriend and a job here, it's time for you to give up that dangerous nonsense and move back to Green Valley."

The determination shining in her eyes broke my heart. I pulled her into a hug and kissed the top of her head. "I love you," I told her, squeezing her small frame. "But don't get your hopes up, okay? I promised I'd be on the movie set next week, and you know how much those things cost to shoot. They're expecting me to be there on time, ready to work. You wouldn't want me to let them down, would you?"

"Go ahead and let them down," she urged, hugging me back. I couldn't see her face, but there was a raw edge to her voice that made my chest ache. "Don't go back to that dangerous work. I miss you too much. And I can't bear to keep patching up all your wounds."

"I'm sorry, Momma, but I need to shower and dress for my date." I let her go and she turned her face away as though she didn't want me to see it. Maybe she'd teared up. But what could I do? I was committed to the movie set. I had to turn up to do the stunt I was scheduled for.

By the time I'd changed, Momma had gone out. She'd left me a note on the kitchen counter saying she was heading to a friend's place, and I figured she was trying to hide her disappointment.

It meant that I left the house feeling terrible. It had been hard enough turning Jennifer down when she'd approached me again to offer me a job at the bakery. And it wasn't like I didn't want to stay in Green Valley.

If Carla was willing to have a real relationship, I might consider breaking my contract. But she'd been very clear that wasn't what she wanted. She hadn't even agreed to a Valentine's date, and despite what Momma thought, she wasn't expecting me tonight.

Still, I stopped in town to pick up some food, then drove to the farmhouse and rapped on Carla's door.

When she opened it, she was wearing a long-sleeved top and the same sweatpants she'd been wearing on the day we'd met. And just like that day, she drew her back up when she saw me. But her eyes were a little puffy.

Had she been crying?

"What are you doing here, Malone?" she asked. "I told you I can't see you anymore."

"Mandy and I are about to go on our Valentine's date."

A little of the color drained from her face, but she lifted her chin and glared. "If you're going out with her tonight, why are you here?"

My phone rang.

It was in my hand, so I lifted it and looked at the screen. "It's Mandy calling." I put it close to my ear. "Hi, Mandy."

"Happy Valentine's Day, Noah," Mandy said. She spoke loudly, and I was pretty sure Carla would be able to hear her. "I'm looking forward to our date."

"So am I, Mandy."

I smiled at Carla.

She pressed her lips together. If looks could kill, I would have turned into a pile of ash.

"I'll see you later then," Mandy said. "Can't wait!"

"See you soon, Snookums."

Mandy let out a surprised laugh as I hung up.

"Snookums?" Carla's tone could cut through steel.

Had to admit, I was having some serious flashbacks to the day we'd met, when I'd been stunned by her good looks. The glare she'd given me back then had been almost as fiery as the one she was giving me now. I'd thought she was fierce and sexy then, but I hadn't known the half of it. Now I knew the world's tiniest dimples were hiding in her cheeks, waiting to peek out and delight me.

I kept my tone casual. "You're the one who decided I should date Mandy. But I suppose I *could* call her back to cancel our date. Admit you have feelings for me, and let's go inside. We can talk out how to make our relationship work, like two rational adults who don't try to set each other up with other people."

"But Mandy can give you everything I can't."

"I don't want the things Mandy can give me."

"We can't date, Noah!" She rubbed her chest as though it pained her. "I've explained why. Our deal was clear."

"Our deal was for a Valentine's date. You promised we'd watch a movie together."

"I'm sorry, but I can't." She started to close the door, and I put my hand out to stop it from shutting.

"Then I'll go out with Mandy, like you want," I said. "As long as you give me something first."

"What?"

"Condoms."

She flinched. "*What?*"

"We bought that big box of condoms. If I go out with Mandy, I might need them."

"I'm not giving you condoms, Malone!"

"Because the suggestion made you wildly jealous, and in your heart, you know that you and I belong together?"

"No!"

"Then I'll take those condoms."

"This is emotional blackmail."

"It's only emotional blackmail if you have feelings for me."

She ground her teeth. "Why are you doing this?"

I paused a moment, assessing her pale cheeks, shallow breaths, and the stiff way she was standing. Last thing I wanted was to get her so upset that it made her sick.

"Well," I said. "Ever since you said Bridget Jones wears enormous panties, I haven't been able to get it out of my head. It's something I have to see for myself, even if it makes me cry. We need to watch that movie tonight, and I can't take no for an answer."

Her frown grew deeper for a moment, then she puffed out a breath. "I can't win, can I?"

"Nope."

"You're more stubborn than your mother." She opened the door. "We'll watch the movie, then you'll go to Arizona."

I grinned at her. "I've got some supplies in my truck. Back in a moment."

When I came back from my truck with my arms laden with bags, she was standing in the hallway with her arms folded and her expression resigned. I gave her another grin as I went past, though what I really wanted was to put my arms around her and kiss the hell out of her. I wanted to tell her to stop being so damn obstinate and admit how great we were together. I wanted…

Well, it didn't matter what I wanted, because I did none of those things.

Instead, I piled the bags I'd bought with me on the kitchen counter, then handed her the gift box of cookies I'd bought from the bakery.

"Here," I said.

"What's this?"

"Heart cookies from the bakery. They're the same as the other ones I made for you, only this time I cut them into heart shapes and iced them with a custom-made, no-sugar frosting."

She opened the box and stared down at the cookies. I'd decorated each one with tiny hearts, just for her. "You did this for me?" She chewed her lip. Her eyes were shining, and I was suddenly afraid she might cry.

"Are you okay?" I softened my tone.

"Fine." She dragged in a breath and closed the box. "Thank you. They're beautiful. But nothing can change the fact that we can't date."

"We'll eat in the living room," I said. "We can watch the movie at the same time, so you're not up too late."

"There's no table in the living room."

"That's why I came prepared."

I grabbed the pile of blankets I'd bought with me and spread them out on the rug that was in front of the couch.

"What are you doing?" asked Carla.

"We're having a picnic."

"Don't you need to call Mandy?"

"Mandy knows I'm here with you."

She narrowed her eyes. "Your phone call was a setup?"

"Yup." I piled pillows onto the blankets, swiping other ones from Carla's bed to make extra sure she was going to be comfortable. Freud was on the bed, and he opened one eye to watch me take them but didn't look inclined to move.

Heading back to the kitchen, I put our food on plates and carried it out to the living room. "Sit down," I told Carla, motioning to the rugs.

"What's that?" She stared at the plates as I put them down. "It smells amazing."

"I picked up dinner for us." I'd stopped off at the Front Porch on the way to Carla's. It was Green Valley's best restaurant, and Hannah Townsen worked there. She'd arranged for some takeout that suited Carla's dietary requirements.

I turned on the TV and killed the lights, except a small lamp in the corner which I left on. Carla sat next to me and picked up a plate.

"I can't believe you did this," she said.

The lamplight highlighted the shape of her face, making her even more stunning. Her expression was soft and heartbreakingly sad.

"You're beautiful," I said impulsively. "I love you."

It was the first time I'd ever said those words to a woman who wasn't my momma, and something inside me seemed to fall into place as I heard them leave my mouth. The words were true. And important. I was in love with Carla. And if she didn't look so unhappy about hearing it, I might have said it again.

Her eyes grew even sadder, and she drew in a breath that sounded shaky. "Noah, I can't—"

"I know." I made myself smile, though I was filled with resolve. This was it. My only shot. If I couldn't convince her to give us a chance tonight, she never would.

I pulled up the streaming service on the TV and started the movie. *Bridget Jones's Diary*, just as she'd wanted. The food was as delicious as I'd hoped, and I was glad we were watching something light, funny, and romantic. It wasn't what I would have chosen, but I still enjoyed it. And when I pretended to cry during the scene with the enormous panties, Carla couldn't keep from laughing.

After we finished the meal, I made Carla stay where she was while I cleared the dishes, then I lay back down next to her, so close that our heads shared the same pillow. She didn't object. As we were watching one of the last scenes where Bridget runs out into the snow to chase down her man, I moved so my shoulder was against Carla's. Though I ached to put my arms around her, I didn't do it. Whatever happened next would be up to her. I couldn't force her to change her mind about us. All I could do was tip the scales in my favor.

The movie ended, and I switched the TV off so only the dim lamp illuminated the room. With the thick rug and several layers underneath us, our makeshift bed was comfortable.

Carla let out a little sigh. "Thank you for everything you've done for me. I'll never forget it."

"This shouldn't be goodbye. I know your energy is limited, but I'll take whatever you're willing to give."

She put a little distance between us, turning to face me as she lifted onto one elbow and shook her head.

"Noah, I want you to have all the things you deserve."

"I deserve you."

"But you don't deserve my illness."

"You are not your illness. It doesn't define you."

"You're right, it doesn't. But unfortunately, we come as a package deal, at least until there's a cure. It sucks, but there's nothing I can do about it."

"I'll take the package deal."

"You know your problem?" Her voice sharpened, a little anger seeping into it. "You're too nice. It's not healthy for anyone to be that nice, so just stop it, okay?"

I knew her well enough to recognize her anger for what it really was. A defense mechanism. Her anger meant she cared a lot more than she was willing to let on. It was a good sign.

"Fine. This is me not being nice." I'd ached to kiss her all night, and now I finally leaned in and brushed my lips against hers, allowing myself only the faintest taste of what I burned to devour.

When I tried to pull back, Carla grabbed me, holding me against her. She kissed me savagely. Furiously. Her lips were rough and hard, and I returned the kiss in kind.

I pulled her body tighter. Closer. She dug her fingers into my back, her hands as demanding as her mouth. But I didn't want just a physical response; I needed her to admit how she felt. So I dragged myself away from the warmth and passion of her lips and body, drawing back again so I could look into her eyes.

"Tell me you feel the way I do, Chuckles," I ground out. "Because all I want is to be with you. Whenever you walk away from me, I miss you. When you smile, I laugh. When you cry, I want to comfort you. And I want to make love to you so badly, I can't stand it."

She shook her head, her face twisted with anguish. "Stop it. Please stop talking."

"Touching you makes me hard. Can't you feel how badly I need you?"

Her eyes flashed. "Damn you, Malone!"

"You want me, too. I know you do."

"Even if I want you, I can't fall for you."

"Because you don't have the energy?"

"That's right."

"Then I'll give you my energy. As much as you need."

Her features were etched into a look of frustration. "You know it doesn't work like that. We have amazing physical chemistry. We do. But we can't let it turn into anything more than that. We agreed we wouldn't, right from the beginning."

"In the beginning, we didn't know each other. Now you're at least half-way in love with me. Why won't you admit it?"

"Stop!" She rolled away from me onto her other side, turning her back to me.

I put my arms around her and pulled her against me, spooning her from behind. She pressed her body hard against me, as though she was desperate for my touch and not looking at me was the only way she'd let herself have it.

To test my theory, I slipped my hand under her shirt at her waist. She made an encouraging noise that was almost a moan. Her bottom ground against my erection. When I stroked her body, she shifted to allow me to pull her shirt further up.

She wanted me, that was obvious, and I was so hard it hurt. But she had her eyes screwed shut as though that way she could pretend that this didn't matter. That it didn't mean what it so clearly did.

I drew back, leaving a cold gap between us that felt as wide as a chasm.

She turned back toward me, her eyes flicking open as she bit off a sound of protest.

"Tell me how you really feel," I said.

"Please, Noah, you're breaking me. Don't you understand why I can't?"

Her face was pale, her eyes beseeching. She was clearly in pain, and I had to harden my heart to keep going.

"Then tell me you don't want me to touch you," I demanded. "Tell me you don't want me to make love to you."

She let out a long sigh. "You don't play fair, Noah Malone," she whispered, her face drawn with anguish.

And at long, long last, she reached for me.

CHAPTER 24

CARLA

I knew I shouldn't do it.

Noah and I didn't have a future together and sleeping with him again would only make the end more painful for us both. But I couldn't be logical. My brain had given up on logic, overruled by my heart and my body.

I craved Noah more than I'd ever wanted anything. I needed his lips, his touch, his body against mine. I groaned with pleasure as he moved over me, kissing me with fevered urgency, as though he were claiming me as his. His lips felt so good, I was on fire for him.

He shoved my top up, and while I pulled it off, he unsnapped my bra. I pushed down my sweatpants, dragging my panties off with them, my body throbbing with need. I was desperate for his hands. For his touch.

He sat up to strip off his shirt, then lay back down next to me. "I love you." He stroked my body, raw hunger in his eyes.

Every time he spoke those words, my heart cracked even more. It was so fractured, it was barely holding together.

But I had to be strong.

"If we do this, it has to be for the last time," I told him, my voice hoarse with repressed need.

"No, it doesn't. And I'm going to use every trick I have to make you admit your feelings for me." He paused what he was doing to capture my eyes with his, staring so seriously at me that my chest ached with the pressure of keeping my feelings locked inside.

I swallowed, knowing it was a bad idea to ask, but unable to stop myself. "What kind of tricks?"

His grin was deliciously mischievous. "This kind." He moved down my body, parting my legs and kissing the inside of my thighs.

I groaned. Just the thought of feeling his lips on me made me feel like I was about to orgasm. And this time I knew better than to worry about not being able to come. It had never been easy with Tomas. Sometimes I'd even faked an orgasm, just to stop him from continually interrupting what we were doing to ask if I was close, or if I thought I'd be able to this time.

I'd always believed it was a problem with my body or mind. I'd even investigated orgasmic dysfunction to see if there were any links between that and ME.

Now I knew better.

Noah had full mastery of my body and was able to arouse me at will. If there was a grading system for sex, he'd have his black belt. He was a sexual sensei master.

I gasped, abandoning all thought as his warm breath blew over me. Then he lapped me. And despite how intense the sensation felt, I parted my legs wider. I trusted him to know exactly what I needed.

He licked me again and again, teasing me with his tongue, while the incredible sensation built up inside me. His fingers slid into me, and suddenly the pleasure was overwhelming. I cried out as my world shattered into ecstasy.

By the time Noah kissed his way back up my stomach and breasts, I was panting for breath and stunned into silence. He hovered over me, his weight resting on his hands and his gaze so softly cherishing, I couldn't look away.

"I love you," he whispered, his lips hitching up into a smile.

I made a whimpering sound, which was all my vocal cords were capable of.

He lowered himself so his lips softly grazed mine. "Don't worry, I have more tricks up my sleeve. I just need to grab a condom or two." Getting up, he disappeared into the bedroom while I lay back, trying not to dwell on the pain of knowing this was the last time we could be together. I closed my eyes, refusing to consider what a mistake this was, forcing myself to luxuriate in the feeling of post-orgasmic bliss.

When Noah came back, he dropped the entire box of condoms next to me. Then he shucked off his jeans while I admired his naked body. Every part of him was a feast for my eyes and I wished we had more time together so he could tell me the story of every one of the faded scars that were scattered over his body.

Physically, he was everything I could have dreamed of. But the most beautiful part was the way he looked at me. He made me feel like I could do anything.

He lowered himself over me. When he kissed me, he surprised me with his fresh breath.

"Minty?" I asked.

"I thought you might prefer that, so I used your mouthwash." Then he kissed me with such heat, the languor from my climax vanished, a new desperation for him surging to take its place.

I clawed at him, feeling wild for him. I couldn't wait, couldn't take it slowly. I didn't even want to take control.

Noah knew just what I needed, probably by the way I moaned his name and pressed my nails into his shoulders. He kissed me back with equal passion, and rolled a condom on so quickly, I barely had time to gasp a quick, "Hurry!"

Then he pushed my thigh up. As he slid into me, it was like a key entering the lock it was made for. As though he belonged inside me. As though only he could fill me.

If I'd thought I was wild before, it was nothing compared to how I felt when he rolled his hips into me, angling me for his pleasure and mine. I moaned and dug my fingers into his lower back, pulling him into me. I'd never felt pleasure that intense before, so powerful it was almost like pain. And Noah drove me relentlessly further and further into it, until I finally succumbed to it, losing myself so completely that nothing existed but the sensations shuddering through my body.

I barely heard Noah cry out with his own release as I was coming back to myself, regaining awareness. Then he let his weight rest on me, anchoring me to safe harbor once more.

Panting, he dropped his forehead against mine to gaze into my eyes.

Until now, I'd never looked at someone and known with absolute certainty they had no barriers up and weren't hiding a single thing. But Noah's eyes weren't just a lovely shade of green, but as clear as a mountain pool. Looking into them, I could see everything. His heart and soul. How beautiful he was, inside and out.

He trusted me, that was clear.

It was up to me to be worthy of that trust. To do the right thing and protect him from the thing that had hurt me the most. My illness had consumed my life. I wouldn't—couldn't—let it do the same to him.

"What are you thinking about?" He must have seen my expression change because his eyes clouded.

I shook my head, closing my eyes for a moment to hide the wave of unbearable sorrow and regret that threatened to engulf me. "That was amazing." I forced myself to sound light. "I think you broke me. I may never walk again."

"I love you." His voice was soft and serious. "And I know you have feelings for me. I can see it in your face."

My heart twisted. I loved him even more than he loved me, and I knew that was true because there was no way his longing for me could be as strong as mine for him. But I'd wished a million times to be healthy, I'd done everything humanly possible to get better, and I was a long way from cured. Wishing didn't make things come true, and wishing I could have Noah would only make it hurt more.

"Noah, I can't." My voice broke, and I cleared my throat, trying to hide it.

He rolled off me, turning his face away, and removed the condom. Then he got up in one fluid motion and padded away toward the bathroom. Not just to dispose of it, I assumed, but also to collect himself.

I lay on my back, staring up at the ceiling he'd repaired so well. It looked brand new. If only he could do the same to me. If only I could be fixed, my illness erased.

When Noah came back, he lay down next to me and pulled me close, cuddling me against him as though nothing was wrong.

"Comfortable?" he asked, kissing my neck.

"Mmm."

"Ready to admit you love me yet?"

I closed my eyes again. "Please stop. I can't bear it."

"Then go to sleep." His voice was a soft murmur. "When you wake up, it'll be the first thing you say. You'll say '*I love you, Noah*' before you're even fully awake. And you know what I'll say? I'll say, '*I told you so, Chuckles*'."

He snuggled me a little closer to him, and I let out a long, painful sigh. And I drifted slowly off to sleep with my hand against my mouth, just in case he was right.

I loved him too much to ever say the words he wanted to hear.

It was because I loved him so much that I had to let him go.

CHAPTER 25

CARLA

- Day after Valentine's Day -

Falling asleep on the floor, even in a nest of blankets and pillows, was a huge mistake. When I woke the next morning, I could barely move. My body was so stiff and sore, it felt like I'd spent the night being beaten, not loved. The sunlight streaming through the window made my eyes hurt and my head throb.

And my fatigue was worse. Much, much worse. I had to go to the toilet but could barely summon the strength to lift my head, let alone the rest of my body. For a long time, I'd had to ask Tomas to bring meals to me in bed, and I'd crawled to the toilet when I'd needed to go. Now I was terrified that instead of gradually getting my strength back after a crash, I'd keep getting worse. Some people needed catheters and IV drips, and permanent, full-time care. What if that happened to me?

Noah was next to me, still sleeping peacefully, unaware that I'd woken up with a body that had become a prison. My bones had turned into chains that felt locked to the floor. And looking at Noah, I felt a million times worse. How could I torture him this way? Why had I let him stay when I'd only hurt him more now that I had to kick him out for good?

Slowly I traced the lines of his face with my gaze. I treasured his shapes and angles, committing him to memory. The exhalation of his breath. The gentle curve of his eyelashes. The untroubled smoothness of his forehead. The hug of his short beard against his cheeks.

If only I could kiss his lips one more time. If only I could graze my finger down the nakedness of his neck or rest my nose against his. But that would be fatal. I was too far gone, too deeply, irrevocably in love with him. And any touch, any slight relaxation of my iron will, would give me away.

As if he could feel the intensity of my gaze, he stirred and opened his eyes.

"Morning, Chuckles." His smile was stunning. It was so warm it made his eyes glow. "Ready to admit you love me yet?"

Hardening myself, I swallowed the lump in my throat. Letting him see how I was dying inside would be a terrible mistake. On the outside, I would—I *must*—look the same as I always did. And if I'd survived our lovemaking without breaking down, I could survive this too. I had to.

I armored my face and my voice.

Cold, hard steel, inside and out.

"You need to go," I said, my voice curt.

He put a hand behind his head, his smile vanishing. "I've finished work. I have nothing else to do today but hang out with you."

"Not going to happen. I don't feel well." I turned my face away from him so he didn't see me wince as arrows of pain lanced up my spine. Though I *really* needed to use the bathroom, I couldn't stand up. If I tried, he'd see how much pain I was in. He had to leave so I could struggle there on my own.

"Then I'll stick around so I can make your meals," he said.

"You don't get it." Still facing away from him, I turned my pain into anger. "I can't talk to you. I'm not well enough." Even snapping at him was exhausting. Finding words. Hiding how breathless I was. It took so much work, I was faint with the effort.

"You don't have to talk to me." His voice was so gentle, it sliced through me like a knife. "I just want to help."

"You can't help. Nobody can. There's no happy ending for us, Noah. Why can't you understand?"

"Just because you have to stay in bed sometimes? Hell, sometimes all I want to do is lie around."

Turning my face to his was a mistake. I was swallowed whole by the impossibly soft beauty of his eyes. But when I pulled in a breath, it burned. As awful as this was, by making light of my condition, he'd just confirmed I was right. He had no idea what he'd be getting into.

"Go," I said. "Please."

"No."

"You're making things worse."

"I don't care. I love you. Deal with it." He frowned. "Can you get up? You're not moving."

"I can," I lied. "I just don't want to."

He got off the blanket and pulled on his jeans. "What do you need? A glass of water? Painkillers? Breakfast?"

I closed my eyes against a wave of regret so strong, it all but drowned me. He'd jumped up easily, so full of energy he was practically bouncing. I was an anchor. A dead weight who'd only drag him down.

"Just go," I whispered. "Please, Noah. Don't make me argue with you."

His jaw set into a stubborn line. "This isn't goodbye."

"It is." I sighed. "I'm leaving Green Valley."

"You're running from what we have?"

"I already told you, I have an office waiting for me in New York."

That was a lie. Yesterday, I'd called my friend and told her to give the office to someone else. My health was too uncertain. I couldn't commit to an office I'd only be able to use on the days I felt well enough.

Though I could face the reality of my illness, the fact I had to lie to Noah about it sucked. I didn't want to lie to him. I wanted to tell him the truth, that I wanted so badly to get to wake up next to him every morning, I'd be willing to sacrifice every other thing in my life, even my software.

The only thing I couldn't bear to sacrifice was his future.

"That's not why you're leaving," he said. "You're scared because your ex couldn't handle your illness, and you think I can't either."

I swallowed. Now his eyes were blazing.

He shook his head. "Never thought I'd hear you give up on me like that. And I didn't pick you for the running away type."

"I'm not going to chain you to me." My voice was thick.

"I told you, being with you isn't any kind of hardship."

"If it's not now, it soon will be."

"Carla, stop." He let out a frustrated huff of breath. Stalking away from me, he shook his head at the far wall.

I let anger fill me.

A surge of adrenaline would allow me a small burst of energy to overcome my exhaustion for a minute or two. I'd feel even worse afterward, but by then he'd be gone.

"I'm not a charity case, Noah." I managed to push myself up onto one elbow. "And I'm not your redemption. You can't be with me just because it makes you feel better about yourself."

"What are you talking about?" Running his hand over his beard, he stalked back toward me. He was still shirtless, and his muscles flexed as he lifted his arm. His raw, powerful beauty struck me so hard, it almost robbed me of the small amount of breath I had left. He was a gorgeous, perfect man in the prime of his life, in glorious, wonderful health.

"Why do you crash cars for a living?"

He frowned, dropping his hand to his side. "What's that got to do with anything?"

"You don't even seem to like stunt work. You have some deep-rooted guilt you clearly need therapy for, but instead of getting help, you're on a mission to punish yourself by breaking all your bones."

He was shaking his head before I'd finished. "You think I want to be with you to punish myself? No way! You know that's not true." He stabbed his finger at me. "You don't believe you deserve to be happy. Or maybe you're desperate to protect yourself. But just because your ex bailed on you, doesn't mean I will."

The energy surge was starting to ebb, and I was losing my strength. I fell back down on the pillows, biting back a gasp of pain. "I'm not trapping you in my life," I ground out. "I won't do it."

He knelt next to me, his face filling with anguish. "Just spending time with you is all I want. I told you I never get afraid? Well, I'm finally afraid, Carla. I'm scared you're going to shut me out and we'll lose this. In the last twelve years, the only thing I've ever been terrified of is losing you."

"Noah, stop."

"Just because we'll be dating for real, doesn't mean I'll expect you to do things and go places if you're not feeling well. And I don't always need to sit home with you if you're sick, if that's what you're worried about. I can do things without you. We can make it work."

I let out a long breath. The energy surge was all but gone, and exhaustion was on its heels. Pain was licking up my spine. In a moment, I was going to crash badly, and if Noah was still here, he'd see how awful my illness could get. Maybe if he saw it for himself, he'd understand.

Only I couldn't bear for him to see me so drained that I had to drag myself along the floor to the toilet, or not make it to the bathroom at all. I couldn't bear for him to see me get so dizzy I threw up where I lay, or so breathless I couldn't form words. I couldn't let him watch me lie in bed, day after day, both of us helpless as my life wasted away.

It had been hard enough watching Tomas slowly tire of caring for a girlfriend who didn't have the strength to do anything. Letting Noah become my nursemaid would destroy us both.

"No." I said the word blankly. Flatly. "I don't want that. I don't want you."

He reeled back as though I'd hit him. The pain in his eyes tore me into pieces.

"Go!" I hissed the word at him in desperation. "Get out! Leave me alone."

And thank goodness—thank *goodness*—he scooped up his shirt and shoes, and did what I asked. Because the front door had barely closed behind him before my last scraps of my dignity were gone.

CHAPTER 26

NOAH

- Six days after Valentine's Day -

I was in Arizona, standing on the old, unused bridge we were going to use for filming. It was a ramshackle, picturesque bridge that went over a river, and despite the noise and frenetic energy of the film crew who were scurrying all over it, the bridge somehow still managed to retain an air of tranquility. Trees grew along the riverbank below, and the bare ones were already sprouting new leaves, getting ready for spring. The regular changing of seasons was probably the most excitement the bridge had seen for many years, until the film crew had arrived a few days ago.

With the blue expanse of sky overhead, and the sparkling water below, it was a pretty setting. It seemed a real shame the bridge was about to be destroyed.

But I had bigger issues on my mind.

I'd spent the last hour going over the car I was about to use for the stunt, double-checking its safety measures and the explosives wired underneath it. Unfortunately, there was only so much I could check. I just had to trust the engineer and explosives team had done their job correctly.

Brash was leaning on one of the only still-intact pieces of the bridge's handrail, staring down at the water. When I'd arrived in Arizona, he hadn't been happy to see me. After having been thrown out of Carla's house, his unfriendly face had felt like a fresh blow.

The thought of Carla made my chest feel hollow, like every bit of joy had been carved out of it, but I pushed her out of my mind for the thousandth time since I'd left Green Valley. I couldn't afford to be distracted. Not today.

Walking over to Brash, I leaned my elbows on the rail next to him. I didn't say anything, just let the silence sit heavily between us for a while. Finally, Brash let out a sigh.

"I wanted to do the stunt myself." He frowned at the water. "I messed up and spent too much on some stupid shit, so I could really use a sweet payday."

The money *was* good. The pay went up on a sliding scale according to how dangerous the stunt was, and I'd negotiated an outrageous rate for this one. But there was no way I'd let Brash do it, and I refused to ask how much money he needed. I wasn't going to fix his problems for him.

See, I didn't have a martyr complex.

Or if I did, I was getting over it.

"There'll be plenty more jobs," I said.

"Will there? Old timers like you get all the high-paying ones."

"Will you quit calling me old? There's barely ten years between us."

He gave me a reluctant sideways grin, and I figured I was forgiven for coming back to work. "Just don't mess it up today, Grandpa. Your reflexes aren't what they used to be."

I rolled my eyes and gave in. "Watch and learn, sonny."

Despite my light tone, the stunt made me nervous. Too many things had to work in perfect time with each other, which meant the number of things that could go wrong was a lot higher than I'd like.

Carla would be horrified if she knew how risky this stunt was. She'd hate that I was endangering my life, no matter how big the payday.

Maybe the things she'd accused me of were at least partly true, and my stunt work was driven by the guilt I'd carried after watching Liam die. Perhaps every stunt I did was a warped do-over, something inside me determined to change what had happened somehow, by reliving it over and over.

Whatever the reason, it didn't matter anymore.

I'd changed. If I'd been punishing myself, my need to do it had faded. Just like I couldn't save Carla from her illness—and that was something I'd had to struggle to accept—I couldn't save Brash from his reckless nature. He wasn't

Liam, and he wasn't my responsibility. I'd done all I could, given him all the help and warnings he'd accept, and now it was up to him.

Once I walked away from stunt work, I'd never look back.

Too late to walk away from this stunt, though. I was the one who'd trained for it, and changing drivers now would be too dangerous. But this would be my last stunt. Once I was done here, I was finished for good.

Decision made.

I felt lighter. As torn up as I was about the way Carla and I had left things between us, at least there was one thing in my life that would change for the better. If I'd been hanging onto the past, that was over now. The future was bright. At least, it would be, once I convinced Carla we were worth fighting for.

If she'd thought I'd give up on her that easily, she was wrong.

All I needed to do was prove to her I was in it for the long haul and wouldn't ditch her when things got tough, like her asshole ex had done. That her illness didn't need to come between us. And if we couldn't find a way to have a family, we'd have each other, and my heart would still be full. Momma had plenty of friends with babies she could play with. She'd come to accept it.

Now I'd decided to give up stunt work, I had time to spend with Carla, whether that was in Green Valley or New York. I'd make it clear there was nothing standing in our way.

I smiled to myself, picturing her face when I turned up and told her I was giving her another chance to tell me she loved me. She'd fix me with one of her killer glares. My challenge would be to coax her dimples out of hiding.

I couldn't wait.

"Looks like they're ready for you," said Brash, nodding to the car that was waiting for me.

"See you on the other side." I put on my helmet as I got in the car. It had my blood type scrawled on each side, just in case. A microphone and speaker were fitted inside.

Apart from the helmet, I was wearing the same clothes as the actor I was doubling for, who'd already been filmed driving over the bridge. Though my car looked like his on the outside, its frame had been reinforced, it had a roll cage, and the straps holding me to the seat had been padded. Two cameras were filming from behind me. They'd capture my hands on the steering wheel and the view through the front window. When the car got to exactly the right point at the top of the bridge, it would explode. As it launched into the air, that section of the bridge would crumble. The driver's seat had a release mechanism which would also take out the front window. I'd launch myself out and land on the bank at the far side.

Driving to the point I was going to start my run from, I was acutely aware of the explosives strapped under the car. Every bump in the road felt like it could set them off. Accidentally killing myself now would be monumentally stupid. If there was a chance Carla would admit she had feelings for me, I wasn't about to blow myself up before it could happen.

Getting to the starting line, I focused my attention on the bridge ahead of me.

"Ready," I said into my microphone.

"We'll count you down," said the director in my ear, his voice tinny through the speaker.

"Five… four… three… two… GO!"

I floored it, getting the car up to the right velocity for the stunt to work, and steering for exactly the right spot on the bridge. I hit the right speed at just the right moment, and braced for the explosion, ready to jettison myself from the seat.

Nothing happened.

What the hell?

I slammed on the brakes as the car careened down the opposite side of the bridge toward the water.

"Shit!" The director yelled into my ear. "The detonator failed."

It was a bad sign. I was sitting on a bomb. If the engineer couldn't get the detonator to work when it was supposed to, how could I trust it wouldn't go off at the wrong time?

"Okay," I said into my microphone. "I'll drive back to the start—"

There was a deafening bang, muffled by my helmet.

The car flew up with enough force to kick me back into my seat. The world spun through the windshield, and I was jolted violently as it tumbled over and over.

I tried to reach the button that would release the straps holding me into my seat, but the tumbling car smashed into something hard, and blinding pain stabbed through my legs.

Along with the pain came a moment of clarity, cutting through the terror.

I was going to die.

What a waste of my life. What a fool I'd been to throw it away.

Carla, I'm sorry.

Then cold water was surging around me, covering me. I was dragged into the river, still strapped into the car. I tried to grab a breath before the water closed over my head, but the pain was too great, I was gasping too hard.

Water rushed into my lungs and the pain was worse than anything.

Agony.

Fear.

Then nothing at all.

CHAPTER 27

CARLA

"You haven't heard from him at all?" Mags asked.

My sister was walking along the street, her phone held up in front of her. Behind her, New York looked cold and gray. Cars rumbled past and I could hear a siren in the distance. Mags was bundled up, her hair cascading over a thick scarf. She looked as lovely as ever, her cheeks flushed with either the excursion or the cold.

I could also see my own image in a tiny window in a corner of my phone's screen, and I looked terrible. I hadn't been sleeping, and my eyes were swollen from all the crying I'd been doing. Things had been rough since Noah had left. Though my energy had slowly been improving, I was still suffering from fatigue, headaches, and nausea. Not to mention an overwhelming sense of heartbreak and loss.

Shifting on my pillows, propped up against my bed's headboard, I rubbed my grainy eyes.

"I haven't heard a word," I said. "How is it even possible to miss him this much? I'm so much worse than I was with Tomas, and we'd been living together for three years. Noah and I were only pretend dating for a few weeks, and now he's gone, I feel like I'll never be happy again." I let out a heavy sigh. "Tell me how pathetic I am, Mags. I can take it."

She frowned. "You've tried calling him, right?"

I nodded. "It goes straight to voicemail every time, like his phone's always switched off. I've been lying awake at night because I'm so worried about him. What if something went wrong with his stunt? What if he's in a hospital bed somewhere? What if it's really serious?"

"Or he could have his phone off because he's working on a film set and can't take calls." Her tone was dry. "You don't need to jump straight to death and dismemberment. There are other options."

"But I've left a message and he hasn't called me back."

"Hmm." She tapped her finger against her chin as though she was thinking it through. "How confusing. You kicked him out of your house, telling him to go away and never come back. So why on earth wouldn't he call you? Does it mean he's in a coma?" She lifted her shoulders in an exaggerated shrug. "It's too hard for me to figure out, but I'm not the smart one in the family. Might need to check in with my genius older sister."

"Ugh." Closing my eyes, I covered them with my free hand. "I've ruined everything, haven't I?'

"That's enough." Her tone was so sharp, I jerked my hand away. She was glaring at me. "You're better than this, nerd. Cut the self-pity before I disown you."

I managed a smile. "This is why I need you, Mags. You're right. I'm wallowing and I need to stop."

"So what are you going to do? Keep feeling sorry for yourself?"

"I'm going to call his mother to check if he's okay. She would have been told if anything bad had happened to him, so she can put my mind at ease. Once I know he's not hurt, then at least I can stop worrying about him, and concentrate on getting over him."

"I suppose it's a start."

"Thanks for talking sense into me. I love you, brat."

She rolled her eyes. "Why are you still talking to me? Just go and do it already."

* * *

I was horribly nervous making the call. I had no idea how much Noah's mother knew about our breakup, and what she thought of me now that I'd hurt her son. But my sister was right, I couldn't keep moping.

If I had to make a spreadsheet laying out the steps I needed to take to heal my heart, I would. But the first step was making sure Noah was okay. Even if his mother yelled at me, or hung up on me, I had to know.

"Hello?" said Noah's mother.

"Mrs. Malone? It's Carla."

"Oh, Carla. Have you heard?" She sounded so upset, my stomach dived. "I can't talk for long. I need to concentrate on the road."

"You're driving somewhere?"

"To the airport in Knoxville. There's a flight leaving in an hour, and I think I can make it."

"Where are you flying to? What's happened?" I held my breath, praying I was jumping to the wrong conclusion.

"Noah's hurt. Whatever he was supposed to be doing, something went wrong. He's in the hospital in Arizona."

My heart stopped beating. "Is he okay?"

"I don't know anything. They only just called me. I'm going to find out." Despite the tremor in her voice, she sounded determined. A mother lioness, rushing to protect her cub.

Struggling out of bed, I headed to the closet to pull out my suitcase. "I'm going too," I said, then hesitated, realizing she might not want me there after what I'd done to Noah. "Is it okay if I fly to Arizona as well, so I can see him at the hospital?" With my hand on the closet handle, I held my breath. If she said no, I didn't know what I'd do. How could I stay here, not knowing if he was even alive?

But even if she agreed, Arizona was a long way. Could I make it that far? What if I crashed so badly, I couldn't sit upright on the plane? How would I get to the hospital if I got so breathless that I couldn't stand or talk?

"Yes, of course," she said. "But I have a head start on you, and I'm not sure I can wait."

Relief and resolve surged through me in equal measures. Nothing mattered but getting to Noah and making sure he was okay. I'd just have to tackle it step by step.

"Don't wait for me." Tearing open the closet, I grabbed my suitcase. "I won't make it in time to catch the same plane, but I'll be on the next one."

The adrenaline flooding my system was giving me a burst of energy, but it wouldn't last, and I'd feel worse once it ebbed. I couldn't drive all the way to

Knoxville. An Uber would be expensive, but it was my only choice. I could rest in the back seat. Once I got to the airport, I'd worry about how to make it onto the plane.

Freud lifted his head and blinked sleepily at me. I'd better call my neighbor to see if they'd mind feeding him and the chickens while I was away.

When I lifted the suitcase onto the bed, a sudden wave of dizziness hit me, and I sat down suddenly, flattened by the effort of picking it up.

Then I gathered my strength and stood.

Screw my illness. One way or another, I was going to get there, even if it took so much out of me, they had to wheel me inside and put me in the bed next to Noah's.

* * *

By the time I landed in Arizona, I knew for certain that there was nothing I wouldn't do for Noah.

Though I made it into the hospital without a wheelchair, it was a close call. When I got there, I was trembling, fatigued, dizzy, and desperate to lie down. But as soon as I dragged myself into Noah's hospital room, my illness faded into insignificance.

He was lying still, hooked up to a machine that let out regular beeps. His eyes were closed, and his skin looked gray. A bruise covered one side of his face, and that eye was swollen. His mother was sitting in the chair beside his bed, holding his hand. She looked almost as gray as he did, and her eyes were wide with fear.

"How is he?" I asked.

"He's just come out of surgery. His legs are broken, and his brain is swollen. They're keeping him unconscious until the swelling goes down."

What little strength I had drained out of my legs. I sagged, clutching at the end of the hospital bed to hold myself up.

"Are you okay?" She looked alarmed, starting to rise.

"Yes, I'm fine." There wasn't another chair in the small, sterile room, so I eased myself onto the edge of Noah's bed, hating to give her anything else to worry about. The hospital bed was hard enough that my weight didn't disturb him, or any of the tubes going into him, thank goodness.

"Will he be okay?" I asked, taking hold of his other hand. I was horrified to hear my voice break. The last thing I wanted was to make a scene or bother Noah's mother. I felt bad enough without that.

She met my gaze. "He isn't ready to go to heaven yet, and I can't lose him. So, yes. He's going to be okay."

Nodding, I squeezed his hand and leaned forward to talk to him. "Noah, I'm here with your mom. It's Carla."

His skin was too sallow. It was terrifyingly wrong. Noah was too vital, too *alive*, to be lying so still. He was always active. Always busy. He never had his eyes closed unless he was sleeping.

I should be the one in the bed, not him. He needed to open his sparkling eyes and shoot me his rakish grin. To saunter over rooftops and scale ladders. To stride around as though the world belonged to him. Because it did, dammit. It *did*.

"I'm going to find the doctor." Noah's mother got up. She came around the bed to squeeze my shoulder. "Thank you for coming."

I blinked at her, confused about why she'd thank me. "Of course I came. I had to come."

"Will you stay with him? I didn't want to leave him alone before, but I need to find the doctor. I have to know what's going on."

I nodded wordlessly, my hand tight around Noah's.

When she was gone, I leaned forward, a wave of dizziness almost making me topple too far. "Damn you, Noah," I whispered. "I love you, okay? I'm desperate for you. I didn't want to tell you, but you were right about everything. I was wrong, and I'm so sorry. Please, wake up so I can tell you how sorry I am and how much I love you." I drew in a shuddering breath, unable to bear seeing him so motionless.

Could he be dying? Wouldn't there be doctors around if he was dying?

I stared at the hospital bracelet around his wrist, a thin strip of plastic with his name printed on it. Then I looked back at his beautiful face, willing him to open his eyes.

"If you wake up, I'll tell you how much I love you every single day for the rest of my life. I promise I will. Twice a day, morning and night. And lunchtimes, too. More, if you don't get tired of me saying it." I felt a tear trickle down my cheek and quickly wiped it away. It would only make things worse for Noah's mom if she came back and saw me crying.

Noah didn't move. I couldn't even see him breathing. The sheets were pulled up under his arms, and he was wearing a hospital gown. I couldn't see if his chest was going up and down. There was no trace of his delicious scent, just the horrible antiseptic hospital smell. And only the soft beeping of the machine and the warmth of his hand reassured me he was still alive.

"Please," I whispered. "Please wake up. I'll do anything. Please just tell me, what can I do?" I lifted his hand to my face and held it against my cheek, wishing I could transfer my life force into him. His arm was heavy, sagging as though lifeless. But he was warm. That was something, wasn't it?

"The doctor was with another patient," said Noah's mom, coming back into the room. "She's coming to see Noah in a few minutes."

I gently rested his hand back down on the bed, keeping both of my hands around it. "Did she say anything?"

"Nothing." Noah's mom didn't go back to the chair but stood beside me and put her hand on my arm. "Move to the chair. You're swaying. You look like you're about to faint."

I gave the chair a longing glance. It was hard to sit unsupported, and I kept having to catch myself from falling off the bed.

Steeling myself, I shook my head. "No, I can't take your chair."

"Why not?"

Looking into her sweet, worried, puzzled face, I blurted, "Noah and I broke up. It was my fault. I hurt him and I'm so, so sorry."

She squeezed my shoulder, her expression still soft. "Take the chair."

I wanted to refuse. Would I be more trouble if I took her chair, or if I fell on the floor and gave her a fright?

Letting go of Noah's hand, I pushed myself up to standing with an effort. My head swam, but I walked the few steps to the chair and sank into it.

"I love him," I said, tears blurring my vision.

"Does he love you too?"

"He said he did, but I didn't want to be with him. Because of my illness."

"I don't understand."

I blinked hard, trying to gather enough strength to explain. "There's no cure for what I have," I said, dragging in a breath. "There aren't even any recognized treatments. I find it hard to do things. Even leaving the house is a challenge. And I don't know what's going to happen, whether I'll get worse. If I do, I could be bedridden. Maybe for years. Or forever. I just don't know."

She sat in the place I'd vacated on the bed and picked up Noah's hand, rubbing her thumb over the back of it. "Nobody knows what's going to happen to them in the future," she said in a tone that seemed far too reasonable. "Look at Noah. Sickness and accidents can happen to any of us at any time. It's no reason not to love each other."

"I don't think I can have children," I blurted. "I wouldn't be able to give you grandchildren."

She stared at me silently for a few moments, as though she needed time to take that in. Then she gave a little nod.

"All I care about is seeing my son safe and happy. I'm not going to lie, I'd love to have grandbabies. But Noah is everything to me. My sun rises and sets with his smile."

"Mine too," I whispered, my heart breaking as I wished I could give this kind, wonderful woman every single thing she wanted.

"If I can trust you to make him smile, then that's enough for me."

I swallowed back more tears, refusing to let them out.

"I'm scared," I said in a thick voice. "I'm afraid he'll have to sacrifice too much to be with me, and I'm afraid…" I hesitated. "I'm terrified that he'll regret it. That he'll decide I'm not worth it."

She frowned at me as though I were a puzzling mystery. "Whatever gave you the idea you wouldn't be worth it?"

I thought of how helpless I'd felt when I'd had to quit work, and how much worse it had been after Tomas had left me. I'd been bedridden for months in my parents' house, and every morning Mom would bustle into my bedroom, sweep my curtains open, and tell me what a beautiful day it was, and that I should get up so I could enjoy it.

"This illness is cruel," I said. "Noah should live a big life. I don't want him to make his life smaller to match mine."

She tutted, as though I'd said something foolish. "Take it from me, not being able to be with someone you love is what makes your life smaller. If I could have Noah's daddy back, I wouldn't need another thing. So you let Noah decide what he wants, you hear me?"

My tears came then, and I couldn't stop them.

Noah's mother passed me some tissues, and after a while, she asked, "Are you going to be okay, sweetheart?"

I nodded and blew my nose. "I just need him to wake up." My voice was hoarse, my throat raw.

"He will." She sounded sure of it. "He's strong and stubborn, like his momma."

"I know he is," I said, to comfort her. "Very strong and very stubborn."

I had to believe that would be enough.

CHAPTER 28

CARLA

- Eight days after Valentine's Day -

oah was stirring.

I stood at the end of his hospital bed, squeezing the metal foot rail to hold myself up. Noah shifted in bed, but I couldn't see his face because his mother was leaning over him, holding both his hands. She was crying and saying his name over and over, pleading with him to answer her.

All I wanted was to move closer so I could see him, to make sure he opened his eyes. To make sure he was okay.

But I was afraid. After the way I hurt him, Noah may not want to see me. What if my presence upset him so much, it actually damaged his recovery? I couldn't risk doing anything that might set him back. It was better for his mother to have time alone with him. If I heard him speak, that would have to be enough.

"Momma?" His voice was a weak croak, but I had to bite my lips together to keep from crying out with relief.

"Noah, honey. You're awake."

"Hi, Momma." He coughed a little, and when he spoke again his voice was stronger. "Hey, don't cry. It's okay, Momma."

I'd all but fused my fingers to the bed rail, and they were so stiff it hurt to unpeel them. I staggered outside as quietly as I could, collapsed onto a chair in the hallway, and lowered my head to my knees.

"Thank you," I murmured through my tears. "Thank you. Thank you. Thank you."

The doctor had said Noah was going to be okay, but I hadn't dared to believe her.

Just as I thought about the doctor, she came past with a nurse, headed into Noah's room. They were talking and didn't notice me, but they didn't seem to be in a hurry. That had to be a good sign, right?

I waited, watching the door to his room. They were in there for ages. So long, I started getting afraid all over again. I was about to get up and stagger in when the doctor and nurse came back out.

"Excuse me." I stood up on shaky legs. "Is Noah okay?"

The doctor's smile sent a rush of relief through me. "He'll recover over time. He's lucid now, and you can go in and see him, but don't tire him out."

"Thank you," I said. And then, because it didn't seem enough, I said it two more times before sinking back onto the chair.

After what seemed like a long time, Noah's mother came out of his room. She spotted me and strode over. Her eyes were red and puffy, but she was smiling. "He's asking for you," she said. "Will you go in and see him?"

I stared at her wordlessly for a moment. Then I nodded. My heart was beating too hard, and my throat was too dry to speak. My legs were so weak, I had to force them to move toward Noah's room, and I paused for a moment, clutching the door frame, to glance back. Noah's mother wasn't following. She gave me an encouraging nod, then turned and walked down the hallway in the other direction.

When I went into the room, Noah's eyes were closed. He looked like hell. His skin had no color apart from the bruise on his face which was turning a nasty shade of purple. At least the swelling around his eye had gone down, but it still looked sore, and his beard was rough.

"Noah?" I whispered.

He opened his eyes and smiled at me. One of his eyes was bloodshot, but he gave me the best, most beautiful smile I'd ever seen.

"Hi, Chuckles," he said. "Don't cry."

"I'm not crying." I didn't have a tissue, so I wiped my eyes with the heels of my hands as I sat on his bed. It wasn't entirely a lie, because I was so damn happy to see him awake, it felt more like laughing than crying.

"Come here." He opened his arms for a hug.

"I don't want to hurt you."

"You won't."

Being as gentle as I could, I lowered my face onto his chest. He wrapped his arms around me, and he felt so good, I couldn't stop more sobs from forcing their way out. Being in his arms was my favorite place in the world, and I'd been terrified I'd never get to be there again.

"I'm sorry," I mumbled into his chest. "I'm so sorry."

"Shh. It's okay. Don't cry. It's okay."

I felt him kiss my hair and that only made things worse. It took an embarrassingly long time before I could regain some control.

"I'm not hurting you, am I?" I asked finally. "I'll sit up."

He loosened his grip on me and I pushed myself up to sitting.

"How do you feel?" I asked.

His mouth twisted ruefully. "I'm a little sore," he admitted. "And I'm tired. The medication's making me sleepy."

"You should sleep. I should let you rest." I moved to stand up, but he grabbed my hand, stopping me.

"Stay," he said with another small smile. "I want to look at you some more."

"You were right about everything," I blurted. "I love you. I'm in love with you. I'm just afraid that being together will hold you back from living the life you deserve. I'm afraid it wouldn't be fair to you."

He nodded, his expression serious. "You're right. It wouldn't."

A heavy ache swallowed my chest. "Okay," I said, trying not to show him that my heart was breaking all over again. After the way I treated him, I shouldn't have gotten my hopes up. I had no right to ask for anything.

"Apparently, I have two broken legs," he said. "One's pretty messed up. I'm not going to be able to walk for a while."

I squeezed his hand. "The doctor told me. I'm so sorry."

"I won't be able to do things." He frowned. "Might not be able to go out to dinner for a long time."

"Out to dinner?" It was a strange thing to mention.

"And if I can't go out to dinner, that rules out a relationship. Doesn't it, Chuckles?"

I narrowed my eyes at him, suddenly suspicious. "Are you making fun of me?"

He shrugged. "I'm just telling you how it is. We can't date if I can't leave the house. And I'm going to be busy putting together a spreadsheet to figure out how I'll get to walk again, so that's where my focus will be. Won't be any time left for love."

"Your broken legs are nothing like my illness. You'll be in a wheelchair for a while, that's all."

"No, you can't convince me otherwise." He shook his head. "Being with a guy with broken legs won't be any fun, and I don't want you to be held back. So we can't date, and you don't get a choice in that."

I huffed, pulling my hand out of his. "You stop that right now, Noah Malone. It's not funny."

His lips drew up. "It kind of is."

"Is not!"

With his smile widening, he recaptured my hand. "Okay, it's not. We're officially dating for real now, and we're stuck with each other, good and bad, sickness and health."

"We'd better be." I was so grateful to see his eyes sparkling with life, I could barely pretend to be mad at his antics.

"We are." He tugged on my hand. "You'd better kiss me now, so we can seal the deal."

"Did you say *kiss* or *kill*?'

With a laugh, he pulled me toward him. For a moment I just stared into his eyes, dumbstruck by the love I saw shining there. He looked at me as though I was the best thing he'd ever seen. Nobody had ever looked at me that way, and my heart expanded with wonder.

My lips found his, and I sighed into him. He felt so good, so *right*. I was dizzy and fatigued, and my head throbbed, but those feelings faded into the background. The only thing that mattered were his amazing lips, and the comforting, wonderful weight of his arms around me, holding me close and loving me more than I'd ever been loved before.

"I love you," I murmured after a long, perfect kiss. "In sickness and health. No matter what."

He pulled back to look at me again, his hands on my face, and his gaze so cherishing I could barely breathe.

"I told you so, Chuckles," he said.

EPILOGUE

NOAH

- One year later -

When I let myself into the farmhouse, I was humming a tune. I found myself doing that a lot these days. I never used to be a hummer, but it seemed to be something that happened when I was happy, so I was going with it.

My leg was aching a little because I'd been standing all morning. I'd spent most of the morning in my workshop working on a custom car restoration for a client, then stopped at the bakery to pick up a special treat for Carla. But as I never took being able to walk for granted these days, I didn't mind the ache. Sore or not, I appreciated every step I took. Especially when I earned that ache by painting a unique design on a beautiful car. My new business was turning out to be the best fun I'd ever had.

"I'm home," I called out, hanging my coat up by the door.

"Hi, honey." Carla came out of her office, a big smile on her beautiful face. She wore yoga pants and a top that accentuated her miraculous curves. I loved the way she looked in that top. But then, I loved the way she looked in pretty much everything. And I loved it even more when she wore nothing at all.

"Happy Valentine's Day again," I said. The 'again' part was because we'd already celebrated the occasion this morning. Twice.

"Are you looking forward to watching the sequel to *Bridget Jones* tonight?" she asked.

"Absolutely. And I got you something."

"But you already gave me that beautiful necklace!"

"It wouldn't be Valentine's Day without something sweet." I handed her a box tied up with a ribbon, then leaned in for a kiss. She tasted good, my woman. And when I put my hands on her waist to draw her close, I loved how she melted against me.

"Wait!" She laughed against my lips. "We're going to squash the box."

Reluctantly, I let her go. "Are you hungry?" I asked.

"Always. Oh, wait, do you mean for food?" Her dimples appeared, as cute as ever. I loved how they only appeared when her smile was wide. They were like a secret she only shared with me.

"Jennifer made you strawberry donuts," I said.

"She didn't!"

"Gluten free and sugar free, with some nut flour to give it some protein and strawberries to give it sweetness. It probably doesn't have *enough* protein to fit with your regular diet, but I figured you wouldn't mind—"

"Ohmigod! Stop!" Hurrying into the kitchen, Carla put the box on the counter so she could tear off the ribbon and pull out a donut. "How did she get it so fluffy? It even feels like a real donut." Her eyes were wide. "What kind of sorcery is this?"

"Jennifer's a genius. And so am I, seeing as the strawberries were my idea."

Carla's smile was *everything*. "Did I tell you how much I love you? I'm nominating you for a Best Boyfriend award. Is that a thing? If not, I'll create it. I'll start a campaign."

I grinned back at her. Hopefully she'd soon be nominating me for a Best Fiancé award, seeing as I'd started to plan a romantic proposal.

"Are you going to taste that donut or waste time talking?" I asked.

She lifted it reverently, as though I'd given her something precious. Then she took a huge bite and closed her eyes, moaning in a way that made me consider how I could maneuver her toward our bedroom and convince her she didn't need to do any more work for the rest of the day.

"It's incredible," she mumbled with her mouth full. "It tastes even better than the donuts I used to eat before I got sick."

I waited until she was done, then said, "You have a little strawberry on your lips. Let me help you with that." Putting my hands on her hips, I pulled her close and kissed her.

When she kissed me back, she tasted like strawberry donut. And like home, and love, and laughter, and happiness, and all the things she'd come to mean to me.

"Has your day been busy?" I asked eventually. It was the opening gambit in my campaign to talk her into spending the afternoon in bed.

"My mother called."

"How is she?"

"Like a stuck record." Carla wrinkled her nose at me. "All she could talk about was you, and how wonderful you are."

"Your mother is a perceptive woman," I said. Her family had recently visited, and I'd enjoyed getting to know them.

"I thought she'd want to hear about the spa day I had with Sienna. But no. It was Noah this and Noah that. You're her new obsession."

"To be fair, I am wonderful."

"Best Boyfriend award winner."

"And skilled with my hands."

"I've heard the rumor." She grinned with her mouth full of donut.

"How's work going? Almost finished for the day?"

Her eyes brightened with excitement. "It was a great morning. I'm gathering a ton of data, you have no idea. You should see the graphs I've generated!"

I bit back a smile. She was so excited by how well her software was doing, she was oblivious to my ulterior motives. But I couldn't blame her. She'd found an investor and had a remote team of programmers working with her from their own homes. Not only did most of her programmers have illnesses like hers, but the number of people using her software was growing rapidly. She was helping folks, and that meant a lot to her.

"So, no time off for you today?" I kept my tone casual.

I tried to be respectful of the hours she worked, especially seeing how important it was to her to make the most of the days when she had enough energy to spend time at her computer. And when I came home to find her in bed resting, I'd crawl in with her and hold her. Freud didn't seem to mind sharing.

"I want to spend the rest of the day eating donuts," she said. "You're spoiling me with all the delicious treats you keep bringing home. I'm officially ruined."

I leaned in again, drawing her hair aside so I could kiss her neck. "Good," I murmured against her skin. "I like you ruined."

"And I like you just the way you are."

"That's a quote from *Bridget Jones's Diary*."

"Is it?" There was a smile in her voice. "Maybe I'm trying to get you even more excited about tonight's movie date."

"Oh, I'm plenty excited already." I pulled her against me to prove it, and she shivered a little as my lips grazed the crease where her neck met her shoulder.

"Mmm, that's nice." Her voice had gone breathy.

"Have you decided to take the rest of the day off yet?" I used an innocent tone, even while I slipped a hand under her top.

She laughed. "Noah Malone, you're a bad man."

"And you're an incredible woman," I said with complete sincerity, running my hands over the curves I loved even more every day.

She let out a groan of pleasure, then shook her head. "Are you trying to make me forget about today's spreadsheet?"

"We could make a new spreadsheet."

"You silver-tongued devil." There was a smile in her voice.

"It could have charts. And graphs."

She let out a pretend moan. "Could we implement a project timeline?"

"Sure. And we can color the squares before we tick them off." When she pretended to moan again, I grinned. "There might be a presentation. With a handout."

Taking my hand, she linked her fingers in mine and led me toward the bedroom. "Stop. You had me at *spreadsheet*."

"That was almost another movie quote," I said, thinking of *Jerry Maguire*. "I must be rubbing off on you."

"You can rub off on me anytime you like." She wagged her eyebrows at me, her grin wicked. And as she tugged me through the bedroom door, the lightness of her laughter made its way straight into my heart as usual, filling it up just a little bit more. I'd thought I couldn't feel any happier, and that by now, it wouldn't have any more room to expand.

But somehow, it always did.

AUTHOR'S NOTE

I met my husband in 1997. He was a programmer, and I was the technical writer he hired to write the user manuals for his software. We bonded over our love of science-fiction movies and video games, and our true-life nerdy love story was born.

In 2009, after contracting a flu-like virus, my husband started experiencing fatigue. Despite his health declining until he became too sick to work, he was described as having an undiagnosed chronic illness until 2020, when he was finally diagnosed with myalgic encephalomyelitis/chronic fatigue syndrome (ME/CFS).

It's estimated up to 30 million people suffer from this disease worldwide. It's a complex, multi-system illness, and sufferers can experience a wide range of symptoms, not all of which are portrayed in this book. The illness largely affects women (around 75% of sufferers are female) and it has a history of being called 'hysteria', and dismissed by many medical professionals as being imaginary, or purely psychological.

Recently, the striking similarities between ME/CFS and Long Covid (when Covid-19 symptoms linger for longer than three months) have put the illness into the spotlight. New medical studies have been funded and awareness is spreading. If ever a terrible virus had a silver lining, it's the fresh hope the Covid-19 pandemic has given to ME/CFS sufferers all over the world. With exciting new research being done, my husband and I are looking forward to the day there's a cure.

If you'd like to know more about ME/CFS, I recommend Jennifer Brea's award-winning documentary, *Unrest*, which is available to watch at www.unrest.film and on Netflix.

ACKNOWLEDGMENTS

From the opening scene of Truth or Beard I've been hooked on all things Penny Reid… sexy Gandalf for the win! Thank you, Penny, not only for writing my favorite books, but for allowing me to imagine my characters living in Green Valley. Thank you also for being so generous and kind, and for not taking out a restraining order after that embarrassing Zoom call when I blurted incomprehensible fan-girl babble at you.

Thank you to Fiona and Brooke for all your help and support, and your skillful author-wrangling. And thanks to all the fabulous Smartypants authors for welcoming me.

A big reason I wanted to portray a heroine with a chronic illness was because so many readers I've spoken to are also struggling with their own health challenges. Thank you to all of you for taking this journey with me.

ALSO BY TALIA HUNTER

Upcoming Release!

The Billionaire and the Burglar (A Grumpy/Sunshine Romantic Comedy)

The Lennox Brothers Romantic Comedy Series

No Funny Business

No Laughing Matter

No Fooling Around

The Lantana Island Series Contemporary Romance Series

Boss With Benefits

The Engagement Game

The Devil She Knew

ALSO BY SMARTYPANTS ROMANCE

Green Valley Chronicles
The Love at First Sight Series
Baking Me Crazy by Karla Sorensen (#1)
Batter of Wits by Karla Sorensen (#2)
Steal My Magnolia by Karla Sorensen (#3)
Worth the Wait by Karla Sorensen (#4)

Fighting For Love Series
Stud Muffin by Jiffy Kate (#1)
Beef Cake by Jiffy Kate (#2)
Eye Candy by Jiffy Kate (#3)
Knock Out by Jiffy Kate (#4)

The Donner Bakery Series
No Whisk, No Reward by Ellie Kay (#1)
Dough You Love Me? By Stacy Travis (#2)
Tough Cookie by Talia Hunter (#3)

The Green Valley Library Series
Love in Due Time by L.B. Dunbar (#1)
Crime and Periodicals by Nora Everly (#2)
Prose Before Bros by Cathy Yardley (#3)
Shelf Awareness by Katie Ashley (#4)
Carpentry and Cocktails by Nora Everly (#5)
Love in Deed by L.B. Dunbar (#6)
Dewey Belong Together by Ann Whynot (#7)
Hotshot and Hospitality by Nora Everly (#8)
Love in a Pickle by L.B. Dunbar (#9)

Checking You Out by Ann Whynot (#10)
Architecture and Artistry by Nora Everly (#11)

<u>Scorned Women's Society Series</u>
<u>My Bare Lady by Piper Sheldon (#1)</u>
<u>The Treble with Men by Piper Sheldon (#2)</u>
<u>The One That I Want by Piper Sheldon (#3)</u>
<u>Hopelessly Devoted by Piper Sheldon (#3.5)</u>
<u>It Takes a Woman by Piper Sheldon (#4)</u>

<u>Park Ranger Series</u>
<u>Happy Trail by Daisy Prescott (#1)</u>
<u>Stranger Ranger by Daisy Prescott (#2)</u>

<u>The Leffersbee Series</u>
<u>Been There Done That by Hope Ellis (#1)</u>
<u>Before and After You by Hope Ellis (#2)</u>

<u>The Higher Learning Series</u>
<u>Upsy Daisy by Chelsie Edwards (#1)</u>

<u>Green Valley Heroes Series</u>
Forrest for the Trees by Kilby Blades (#1)
Parks and Provocation by Juliette Cross (#2)
Letter Late Than Never by Lauren Connolly (#3)

<u>Story of Us Collection</u>
My Story of Us: Zach by Chris Brinkley (#1)
My Story of Us: Thomas by Chris Brinkley (#2)

<u>Seduction in the City</u>
<u>Cipher Security Series</u>
<u>Code of Conduct by April White (#1)</u>
<u>Code of Honor by April White (#2)</u>

Code of Matrimony by April White (#2.5)

Code of Ethics by April White (#3)

Cipher Office Series

Weight Expectations by M.E. Carter (#1)

Sticking to the Script by Stella Weaver (#2)

Cutie and the Beast by M.E. Carter (#3)

Weights of Wrath by M.E. Carter (#4)

Common Threads Series

Mad About Ewe by Susannah Nix (#1)

Give Love a Chai by Nanxi Wen (#2)

Key Change by Heidi Hutchinson (#3)

Not Since Ewe by Susannah Nix (#4)

Lost Track by Heidi Hutchinson (#5)

Educated Romance

Work For It Series

Street Smart by Aly Stiles (#1)

Heart Smart by Emma Lee Jayne (#2)

Book Smart by Amanda Pennington (#3)

Smart Mouth by Emma Lee Jayne (#4)

Play Smart by Aly Stiles (#5)

Look Smart by Aly Stiles (#6)

Smart Move by Amanda Pennington (#7)

Lessons Learned Series

Under Pressure by Allie Winters (#1)

Not Fooling Anyone by Allie Winters (#2)

Can't Fight It by Allie Winters (#3)

The Vinyl Frontier by Lola West (#4)

Out of this World

London Ladies Embroidery Series

Neanderthal Seeks Duchess by Laney Hatcher (#1)

Well Acquainted by Laney Hatcher (#2)

www.ingramcontent.com/pod-product-compliance
Lightning Source LLC
Chambersburg PA
CBHW060519220726
48290CB00015B/2051